About the Author

Jill Yielder is a Jungian analyst and psychotherapist working in private practice. Her first novel, in the Anam Cara Trilogy, 'Through the Labyrinth', was published in November 2021. She has also published a wide range of non-fiction articles relating to higher education, psychology, health and wellbeing, having previously worked in academic roles. She lives in Auckland, New Zealand.

Return to Greyvyn

Jill Yielder

Return to Greyvyn

Olympia Publishers
London

www.olympiapublishers.com
OLYMPIA PAPERBACK EDITION

Copyright © Jill Yielder 2023

The right of Jill Yielder to be identified as author of this work has been asserted in accordance with sections 77 and 78 of the Copyright, Designs and Patents Act 1988.

All Rights Reserved

No reproduction, copy or transmission of this publication may be made without written permission.
No paragraph of this publication may be reproduced, copied or transmitted save with the written permission of the publisher, or in accordance with the provisions of the Copyright Act 1956 (as amended).

Any person who commits any unauthorised act in relation to this publication may be liable to criminal prosecution and civil claims for damage.

A CIP catalogue record for this title is available from the British Library.

ISBN: 978-1-80439-134-1

This is a work of fiction.
Names, characters, places and incidents originate from the writer's imagination. Any resemblance to actual persons, living or dead, is purely coincidental.

First Published in 2023

Olympia Publishers
Tallis House
2 Tallis Street
London
EC4Y 0AB

Printed in Great Britain

Acknowledgements

Special thanks to Andrew, Rachael, Christine and Glenda for their support, advice and editing. I'm also very grateful to Juliet Sharman-Burke and Liz Greene for their generous support in giving me permission to quote and reference the book that accompanies their wonderful Tarot deck, The Mythic Tarot.

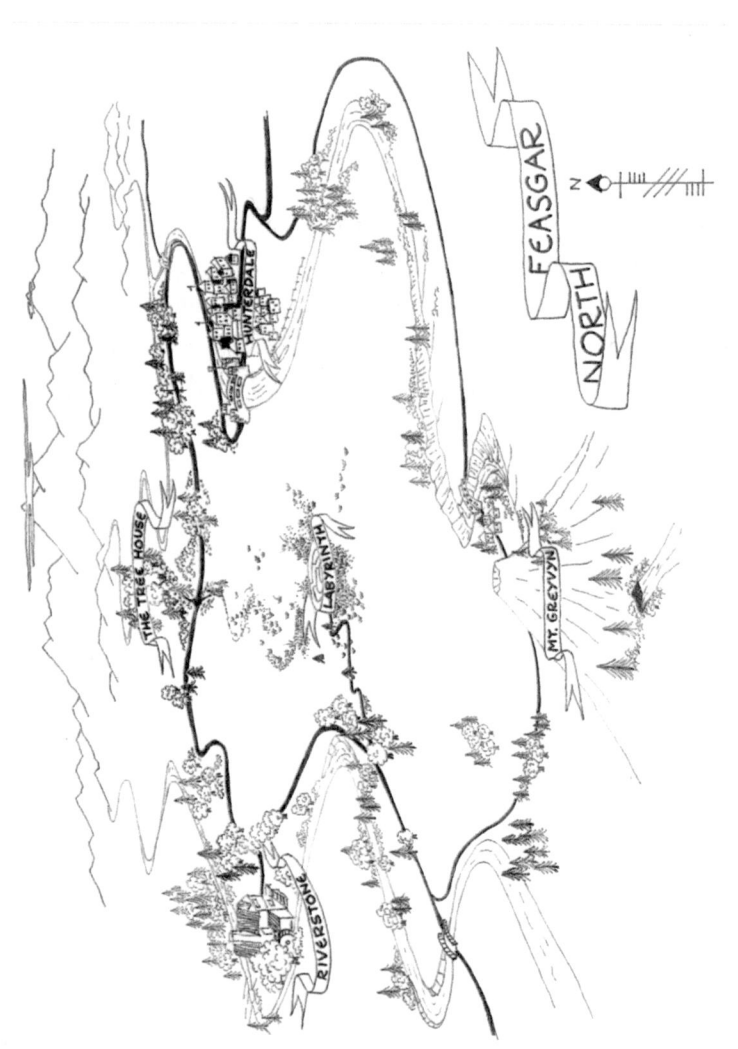

Preface

Stories bring people together. Through stories we can connect to experiences or feelings and explore them as if they were our own, finding a sense of connection from a 'safe' distance, allowing them to percolate in our psyche. We don't have to do anything other than read or listen, just absorb the story and grow our understanding through the effect the story has on us.

This is the second book about two teenagers, Tom and Sarah, who have found their way into a parallel world called North Feasgar. It picks up the threads a little more than two years after the conclusion of 'Through the Labyrinth'. This book too, can be read in two ways: either as an adventure story; or for older readers, as an allegory to illustrate the tasks that a person, male or female, may need to undertake psychologically in order to find a sense of wholeness. Because of this, a section called 'A Jungian perspective for the older reader' can be found at the end of the book.

The story so far…
    In 'Through the Labyrinth', Sarah and Tom, both thirteen, struggling with their home lives, found themselves in a parallel world after slipping through a rift. The land they arrived in is called North Feasgar. They were initially helped by a healer called Morwyn, but it quickly became apparent that Morwyn

had ulterior motives and kept Tom captive while sending Sarah on a quest to find an elixir that would prevent her from aging. During her travels Sarah rescued Mary and Arthur Birch from where they'd been kept captive by a man called Willard, and they became friends to both Tom and Sarah. They also met Hermione, a magical cat, and a hawk called Ryder, both of whom can communicate with them. In the climax of the story, Morwyn died and Sarah and Tom's new friends helped them to choose whether or not to return to their own world through a labyrinth at the resolution of their adventure. Sarah chose to go; Tom chose to stay with the Birches.

Chapter I

The High Priestess

The rock was rough under her hands and knees as she crawled through the narrow passage, a sense of menace filling the tunnel behind her, pushing her onwards. A rising feeling of panic overtook her and she scrambled faster, her palms and knees catching on sharp shards of rock as she moved, gasping for air, each inhalation as if it was to be her last. Her hair snagged on something, jerking her head painfully backwards. As she untangled it, she could feel the closeness of the air, and sweat and fear tingled her scalp. The walls of the passage closed in on her and she fought back a scream of terror in the dark, just as her fingers found an edge on the uneven ground. She slumped forwards from the tunnel, the front half of her body resting on the floor of a cavern, head on her hands, body heaving as she gulped for air, shaking and drenched in perspiration. A voice filled her mind...

"*Sarah, come on, just a little further. It's time. We need you.*" *It was Hermione's voice.*

"Sarah... Sarah!"

Sarah woke up to find her friend Jas shaking her shoulder.

"Come on Sarah, wake up, we're late." She was lying on her stomach in the shade of an oak tree in the school grounds. It was a hot summer's day and as she sat up she could see the front of her uniform, crumpled and damp where she'd been perspiring against the grass. She ran a shaking hand through rumpled hair, unpeeling it where it stuck to her face, her hair and the grass leaving an imprint on her skin. She shook her head to clear it from the vivid dream.

"It's okay, you go ahead Jas. I need a moment to wake up properly. Could you tell Miss McAulay that I'm not feeling well? I'll get a note from the nurse."

"Are you sure you're okay? You're looking a bit... spooked?"

"I just need a bit of time, don't worry, I'll be there for next period."

Jas got up, smoothing down the skirt of her uniform and, with a worried look at Sarah, hurried off over the grass to the school buildings, where a few other late stragglers were scurrying to get to class before the final bell. Sarah watched her as she walked away, her long brown hair swinging down her back. She was so lucky she'd met her and her other friend Lara—it was going to be hard not seeing them over the summer break.

Sitting cross-legged in the shade of the tree, Sarah tried to pick through her complicated feelings. She partly felt weird because of the approaching break from school and the family stuff coming up because of that, but mostly she felt really disconcerted about her dream. It's not as if she'd forgotten Hermione, but over the past two years she'd kind of faded into a more distant memory. Now she was suddenly present again, pushing herself into the front of her consciousness, bringing with her a flood of other memories about her time in North

Feasgar. Tom, Ryder, Mary and Arthur... she wondered how they were, what they were doing now, whether they missed her, as she had a thousand times before. She'd always known she'd have to go back, but how would she know when? What if they needed her now? What if Hermione was trying to tell her through her dream? And she was still feeling shaken by how scary it had been. It reminded her a bit of the one she'd had when she'd been in North Feasgar before—when she'd fallen down a hole into an underground cavern. Quite often her dreams seemed to actually happen—not always literally, but in a metaphorical sort of a way... Like the time she'd dreamed that she'd lost her parents. She'd looked everywhere for them but no one knew where they were—they'd just disappeared. She'd woken up with a sick, anxious feeling and that was the day they'd told her that her dad had been offered a really good job in Singapore and they'd decided to go. She'd been really upset with them and they'd given her the choice of going with them or going to boarding school in England. This dream had the same kind of 'real' feeling. The last thing she'd want would be to be stuck underground—she got claustrophobic and panicky even in a small lift if she imagined it getting stuck between floors! What else could it mean? The most insistent part she was left with was Hermione calling her...

When she'd first come back from North Feasgar her parents were so happy she was alive and well that they'd tried really hard to communicate better, both with her and each other. She'd gone back to school and that felt really different too. It was like she'd switched some sort of message stuck on her forehead from 'I'm a loner' to 'don't mess with me!' It was amazing how much feeling differently about herself changed things on the outside. Suddenly she was included when she wanted to be and yet totally happy to have time on her own when she wanted it, without feeling like a loner. She and Hannah stayed best friends and were looking forward to the summer break and starting back at school together. Her parents then dropped their bombshell. On the one hand she could see how important it was for them to prioritise their relationship and have a new start, but they hadn't even talked to her about it before they made their decision! That really hurt! All her feelings of being unwanted and not belonging had come up again. If she hadn't learnt so much in North Feasgar she didn't think she could have coped. As it was, she'd angrily decided not to go with them, partly, she had to admit, to try to teach them a lesson. Her parents seemed to have packed up the house, rented it out and bundled her off to High Grange, about an hour by train from their village, in a heartbeat. Actually though, the school had worked out well for her. It was a bit old-fashioned, with rules they all had to follow, but somehow, she quite liked knowing what she had to do and when to do it—it made having her own time outside of that even better. And the staff seemed to genuinely care about them; they weren't horrible, like she'd imagined they might be in a boarding school. Some of the girls were bitchy and self-centred, but that was pretty much like her old school, though not having boys there meant some of them never stopped going on about them and how they wanted to sneak off to the village and 'hang out'. That was just so boring! She and Jas and Lara had fun thinking about clothes and make-up and boys, but they had plenty of other things they liked to talk about as well. Like she'd been checking out the Anam Cara symbol that she'd found in Morwyn's book in North Feasgar and found that it was written in an ancient language called Ogham and the three of them had started writing notes to each other using the Ogham alphabet—it drove the other girls wild that they couldn't understand them!

The worst bit about school though, was not having a 'home' to go back to, nowhere she belonged. The first year she'd spent her school breaks with her grandparents, but then they'd decided their house and property were too much for them and downsized to a small cottage in a retirement village, so since then she'd either stayed with Hannah or had been one of a small group of girls who stayed at school for the shorter breaks. The loss of her safe place with her grandparents had been almost harder than her parents going away, but at least she knew she could still talk to them whenever she wanted to—she never doubted them being there for her in the way she doubted her parents.

Last summer holidays her parents had persuaded her to spend time with them in Singapore. That had been really confusing! They'd been so pleased to see her, yet they had a whole life there that she wasn't part of. Thinking about it now she found herself tearing tufts of grass up from the ground and shredding them, feeling really agitated. She was still *so angry* with them and the way they always put themselves first!

Singapore itself had mostly been fun. She loved the heat and the differences, like wandering around Little India and the small streets of the Arab Quarter, looking at colourful materials stacked in bolts or hanging in doorways alongside lanterns, enticing people in with the promise of the riches of an Aladdin's cave. Smelling perfumes from tiny glass bottles; walking past outdoor cafes selling such a variety of unusual foods that she hadn't experienced in England; people sitting around drinking coffee out of small glasses as if they had all the time in the world; hearing people speaking in a multitude of different languages, selling their wares from carts and stalls. Her mother wasn't great with any of that though—too hot, too dirty, too everything really! She just wanted to take her shopping in the air-conditioned malls, with their glitz and marble and sameness! It had shown her how different they really were, even though she'd thought they shared a lot on an intuitive level. Maybe that was all about how she'd shared her mother's anxiety, only now it felt as if she was the one who had grown up and her mother hadn't!

Her father had hardly been present during her time there—he was so absorbed in his new job. They wanted her to go to Singapore again this summer and she felt really conflicted. Part of her would love to explore more of the island, but her mum had a job now too, so there was no point fooling herself that she would be going to spend time with them. Sarah had told her mother she'd think about it if she would take a couple of weeks off work to be with her while she was there, but she hadn't given her an answer yet.

Looking up at the trees above her, she noticed how incredibly bright green the leaves were, standing out against the sky. Summer had started with a determined rush, though who knew whether it would last long… a slight breeze was ruffling the leaves and taking the edge off the hot sun. There was a distant sound of the gardener mowing the grass with the ride-on mower, accompanied by the slight scent of cut and bruised grass, but everything else was quiet with all the other girls in class. She just needed a bit of time to think things through without the constant interruptions that went on at school, but she needed to be back in time for biology, next period. The use of herbs and plants as medicines still drew her interest and bio was the closest subject she'd come across so far that helped her learn a bit around the edges of what might help her in the future. Her parents thought that meant she'd study medicine or pharmacy, but she also thought about naturopathy, which her dad said was flakey! None of them seemed quite right—medicine and pharmacy were too scientific and not very natural, not allowing for much intuition, but she guessed he might be right in thinking that naturopathy didn't generally get much respect. She'd seen a place in the town near her home that advertised itself as 'GP-led holistic health care'—maybe something like that would be a good combination? She was still really drawn to the notion of an old-fashioned apothecary, but maybe that was just a dream!

As Sarah sat musing, she suddenly felt a sprinkle of cold prickling her legs. She jumped up – the lawn sprinklers had come on – time to go! She brushed dust off her skirt and bent to pick up her library book from where she'd left it open beside her. She shook it a little to remove the bits of shredded grass that had fallen on it and something fell out of the back of the book onto the ground. It was a dark-blue piece of card with a gold border and a symbol in the middle. Picking it up and turning it over, she saw that it had an image on the other side of a woman with long dark hair and pale skin. She was standing between two old, Greek-looking pillars, and had a crown on her head and something in her hand. There was a title at the top of the card—The High Priestess. How odd—she'd been reading the book for the past few days and hadn't noticed it before. She thought it might be a tarot card, but she didn't really know much about them. She felt tingly—that sense of recognition she felt when something important had just happened that she needed to take notice of. Like when she first spotted the Anam Cara symbol on Morwyn's book. North Feasgar again – she wasn't going to be able to forget it – something was tugging at her, pulling her back towards her destiny maybe… There was nothing identifying the card other than small writing at the bottom of the blue side saying 'copyright© Tricia Newell 1986'. Maybe she'd google it when she was back in her room and see what she could find out. Meantime she moved out of the range of the sprinklers and slowly walked towards the cluster of school buildings—she'd need to go to class via the nurse and get a sick note to excuse her from the class she'd just missed.

***

At the end of the day, back in her room, she looked up Tricia Newell 1986 on the internet and came up with an entry for 'The Mythic Tarot Cards' on eBay. It looked as if she was the illustrator for a set of tarot cards. They were quite old, though supposedly in good condition. After searching on The Mythic Tarot she could see that a newer version was available, but that it had a different illustrator, so she went back to the original and impulsively ordered it before she could change her mind. She hoped the set would arrive before the end of term, because she was really curious about the way it had appeared at a time that she needed some sense of direction. Googling 'tarot cards' gave her some background about how originally, in the fifteenth century, they were used as a card game, then later for divination; and the way a pack is divided into four suites of cards, and organised into Major and Minor Arcana, or greater and lesser secrets. She imagined she'd find out more about the mythical version when she got the book.

She lay back in bed taking in the large Anam Cara symbol she'd drawn and pinned against the side of her mirror. She'd also been having a go at drawing some of her favourite herbs, in black ink, from a botanical book she'd found in the library and had stuck them on the walls. She liked her room—it gave her a sense of home, quite different to a lot of the other girls, who used it just as a place to sleep because they were so busy playing sport or doing things together most of the time. Some of them did personalise their rooms by plastering the walls with posters, or even worse, some of them put up cut-outs of words like *love* or *friends forever*—as if they had to have reminders on the outside to make them feel okay. For her, it was books and creative things that were beginning to define how she wanted to be in the world. She stroked the deep burgundy velvet cushions on either side of her on the bed, a present from Hannah when she'd left, feeling the soft pile against her fingers, reminding her of Hermione with a sharp intake of breath and a pang of longing. She distracted herself by picking up her phone.

She checked the *New Zealand Herald App* as she did regularly out of habit. She hadn't seen any reference to Tom's disappearance for quite some time. She'd downloaded the app when she first got back and for several weeks there had been a flurry of articles about the search for Tom, after a time becoming a search for his body. Three months later the police arrested his stepfather, Gerald, with his sister and grandparents attesting to his abuse of Tom. He was charged with murder, but by the time it finally went to trial last year he was acquitted due to lack of conclusive evidence. There had been pictures in the paper of a grim looking man beside a small woman who looked cowed and sad, who must have been his mother. She'd also followed Leah on Instagram and Facebook and knew that she'd left school and home and was now living in Australia, working in a cafe in Byron Bay, and going out with someone called Aaron. Her phone pinged—her mother wanting to know if now was a good time to Skype her…

"We need to book your tickets right away while Singapore Airlines has a sale. Your school website says the school is closed from the 22nd of July to the 30th of August, so your dad says you can get the train to London on Saturday the 21st and he'll book a plane out that night so you don't have to find somewhere to stay overnight."

"But I was going to see Gran and Grandad and Hannah at the beginning of the holidays…"

"Well we want you to come straight here. We haven't seen you since we came to England at Christmas and we'd…"

The screen went pixely and her mother froze for a few seconds, unattractively with her mouth open.

Sarah realised that she was feeling really negatively about their conversation, and when she came back online, she jumped straight in saying, "So have you managed to get some time off while I'm there then?"

"Well, no, sweetie, I can't. Your dad and I need to save some leave for a trip to a retreat in Thailand in September.

We've found a place that does really good relaxation and healthy eating programmes, and we think it could be just what we need so that I can have another go at getting pregnant."

"I don't know why you're bothering when you don't even notice the living and breathing child you already have!"

"Don't be like that, Sarah!"

"Don't be like what? The kid you left so you could put yourselves first? I wonder why I'd be upset by that? And anyway, if I feel angry and abandoned, that's how I feel—you can't tell me not to feel that way!" Her voice was getting loud and quavery—she hated it when she did that, but she wasn't going to back down. They'd been really good when she'd first come back from North Feasgar, when they'd thought she was going to die—that had made them appreciate her, but it hadn't taken long before they decided to do what suited them best. She knew her mum had had a difficult time, trying so hard for a child, then miscarrying—she'd evidently been depressed all that time before she went away, but why hadn't they talked to her about it? How come everything was either 'nice' and on the surface, or else had to be buried and not talked about? She'd learnt so much while she was away that she couldn't just suck it up any more. She realised that she was feeling really furious, so when her mother changed the subject and said that they'd be booking the tickets anyway, she told her that if they did, they'd be wasting their money because she'd be staying with Hannah. Her mum started arguing with her, so she put her finger on the red hang-up button. She'd be wild with her, but she couldn't be bothered talking about it any more. They couldn't *make* her get on the plane unless they came to England to get her and that wasn't going to happen—that would take far too much effort!

***

After a couple of days with no contact, feeling bad, Sarah sent a peace-making text, asking how they were. No reply. The silence extended on for the rest of the week. Not for the first time, she wondered, *who are the adults here?* But then she started to doubt herself. Was it somehow her fault? She didn't think she'd been mean or disrespectful, but she'd said what she thought, maybe quite directly. That seemed to be the main problem she'd had over the last two years—growing up and trying to be herself didn't seem to agree with them! She wondered again why on earth they wanted another child when they couldn't deal with the one they had.

Wandering down to the dining halls for breakfast, she was immersed in going over and over it, wondering what to do next without doing what they obviously wanted—giving in and sucking up!

"Hey, what's up? You look like someone just ran over your cat!" Jas ran up to her, punching her lightly on her arm.

"Don't say that! That's awful!" responded Sarah crossly.

"But you don't have a cat, do you?"

"Well kind of…" How could she explain about Hermione? As if she would ever believe that she could talk to a cat?

"You've never…"

"Later!" Sarah said, cutting across her.

"So, something's up. Want to talk about it?"

Sarah found herself spilling out all her angst about her parents and the holidays.

Jas was a good listener—at the end, while they were eating breakfast, she just said, "Why do you try so hard to make things right? I know you're good at it, but maybe your parents need to work a bit harder at it too. Do you have somewhere else you can be if you don't go to Singapore?"

"Well I wanted to see Hannah and my grandparents at the beginning of the holidays, but I don't really have anywhere to be for the whole six weeks."

"I'm going away for the first three weeks, but you could come to our place after that. I'm sure my parents would be happy to have you with us—we could go camping. But if you don't think your parents are able to break their silly silence, you could try a compromise and ask them to book your flights for the last couple of weeks. I bet there's heaps you could do in Singapore for a while even if your mum's working. And that way you get to feel good about yourself rather than seething and beating yourself up."

"Yeah. I did some research last time and only got to half the places I wanted to because she wasn't interested. It's a really safe place to wander on your own too… Thanks Jas!" Her eyes filled with tears. She was so fortunate to have good friends like her and Lara.

On her way back to her room, before she could change her mind, she sent her mum a text saying, 'Hey Mum, want to Skype sometime?' She then dropped into reception to check her pigeonhole—there was a brown paper package waiting for her that she picked up and quickly took upstairs with her. She didn't have long before first period and she wanted to see if it was the tarot book. Pulling off the paper, she found a small dark-blue book, a piece of black cloth and a deck of cards, exactly the same as the one she had found in her book. She rifled quickly through the book, and found the explanation for The High

Priestess.

Her phone pinged and she tore her eyes away from the book and picked up a text from her mother.

'OK. We'll be home tonight from 5.30.'

She replied, 'Will have to be in my dinner break. You'll be in bed by the time I finish last period. OK to Skype you 12.30 my time?'

'Yes.'

Sarah suddenly felt wild and had the urge to throw her phone at the wall. Why was her mum carrying on with this shitty, uncaring game? Her phone pinged again. When she picked it up this time, it said: 'Sorry x'.

She felt so relieved. All her angst evaporated and she was left feeling worn out and teary. She realised just how uptight she'd been over their impasse. It was horrible to be so affected by her parents—it took such a small gesture for the dynamic to change. Was that normal in families? Most of her friends didn't take everything so seriously and didn't worry like she did. But then, maybe they felt more relaxed with their families. She still had to fight with the idea that somehow, she wasn't good enough, which Jas and Lara said was a stupid thing to think. She had thirty minutes before her first class. To distract herself she picked up the book again…

She read about how Persephone ruled over the underworld with her husband, Hades, for three months of the year, then spent the remaining nine months in the daylight world with her mother, Demeter.

She was so fascinated with the description that she read out loud: "Persephone, the High Priestess, is an image of that natural law at work within the depths of the soul which governs the unfoldment of destiny from an invisible source, and which is revealed only through feeling, intuition and the night world of dreams." Wow, that really spoke to how she'd been feeling since going to North Feasgar. 'On a divinatory level, the appearance of the High Priestess in a spread augurs the heightening of the powers of intuition, and implies there will be an encounter of some sort with the hidden inner world which Persephone rules... through the effects of a powerful dream or the uncanny sense that 'something' is at work in one's life... Thus The Fool now enters the night-world, and comes, often with confusion and bewilderment, to the womb of the unconscious in which the secret of his real purpose and the pattern of his destiny are contained.' [1 p.32]

That felt really portentous and made her feel goose bumpy. It was as if she was meant to find the card for some reason. What was her real purpose, her destiny? She certainly felt like a fool a lot of the time, but what did that mean? She flicked through the book and found where it described The Fool as the naïve individual entering on a journey of discovery. She knew intuitively it was all tied up with her journey to North Feasgar, that somehow this was about the inner life the card referred to. Was this another nudge towards her need to return?

It was time for first period, so she put the book and cards away and rushed off to class, trying to put it out of her mind, but during the morning the urge to return grew and a half-formed plan started to emerge. What if she went to Hannah's in the first week, retrieved the wall plate she'd used to get to North Feasgar from storage at her house, and then tried to find her way back for a week or two before going to Jas' place? Her parents wouldn't miss her. Her entry to North Feasgar was different to Tom's, or the Birches, probably because while theirs had been physical, hers had been through her imagination. She'd just have to figure out what would happen to her physically while she was there. Last time her grandparents had taken her to hospital, thinking she'd slipped into a coma. Would her physical body need to be taken care of again? It was complicated—she'd have to trust it would work out.

"Sarah, stop daydreaming!" She was jerked back to the reality of maths—so *not* her favourite!

***

In the dinner break Sarah returned to her room to Skype her parents. Even though her mother's text had indicated a truce of sorts, she still found she had a knot in her stomach and her hands were a bit shaky with anxiety. It was so stupid! Why did she have to react to them like that?

"Hi Mum, hi Dad. How are you?"

Her dad moved into the view of the camera.

"Hi Peanut, how are you? You're looking healthy and tanned." He hadn't called her that since she was little…

"Yes, it's quite summery here already. I guess it's the same pretty much all year for you."

"It's horribly humid at the moment. I'd love to have the chance for a bit of cool weather. Going to work in my suit is ghastly!"

"Where's Mum?"

Her mother came into the frame.

"Hi Sarah, I'm here." She looked a little awkward and there was a pause before her dad cut in.

"So when would you like me to book your tickets for?"

She let out her breath. She hadn't realised just how uptight she'd been—thank goodness, it seemed as if they'd listened and were letting her make some of her own plans.

"Well, I thought I'd go to Hannah's first so I can see Gran and Grandad. Jas has invited me to stay with her too, so I'd like to go there next—we're going to go camping with her family," *stretching the truth a little...* "That means I can have the last two weeks with you before the end of the break. Does that sound okay?"

"Oh Sarah, I'm not sure about that. We don't know Jas' family. How do we know they're reliable and that it's okay for you to be there?" her mother queried.

"Mum it's fine. Jas has checked with her parents and they're really happy to have me as company for her. That means they can have some time together while Jas and I explore."

"Well send me their contact details so I can make sure you're safe."

"But you can get me on my phone. That's why you got it, remember? And anyway, if we're camping up in the hills we may be out of mobile range. I'd rather you didn't get anxious just because you can't get in touch with me."

"Sheryll, we need to trust that Sarah is growing up fast and needs a bit of space. Let her be," her father added in the background. Her mother's face blanched and kind of twisted somehow and she moved out of view. Her dad came onto the screen.

"That's fine, honey, but please keep in touch with us. And we'd love to talk to Gran and Grandad on Skype if you can set it up with them. They don't like using it, so we only get to talk to them once in a while by phone."

"Sure Dad. Is Mum okay?" In the background she heard a door closing and she guessed her mother had left the room.

"Don't worry about her. She's a bit uptight at the moment. I'll sort it out. I'll send you your tickets by email—just give me a couple of days. We're really looking forward to seeing you!"

When she finished the call, she slowly closed the computer and sat for a minute, not sure how she was feeling. It was all so confusing—why did she wind her mother up so much, just by trying to be herself? Maybe because she was reminding her that she was no longer a kid. Maybe because her mum couldn't get her to think the same way as her any more. With a start she realised it was the end of the dinner break. She grabbed her PE gear and left her room, running down the stairs to meet Lara and Jas. PE today was athletics. She quite liked that, just so long as she didn't have to do high jump!

Chapter II

Strangers

"Mary!" Tom yelled as he barrelled through the door. Mary was sitting at the table, reading, when he appeared, looking flustered.
"It's the third day in the past week that a man's been standing by the side of the road under that tree with the weeping branches, just near the house. I think he's watching us."

"Let's find Arthur—he's in the mill room. I doubt it's anything we need to worry about, but best to be sure."

They found Arthur sharpening some tools. His brow furrowed as Tom repeated what he'd noticed on his return from school, and he quietly suggested that he'd go out the front door to the road, while they went out the other door, through the field, to come out onto the road on the other side of the tree. They went out quickly, but the roadside was empty. Whoever had been there had already gone, leaving no sign of their vigil.

"How could he have just disappeared so quickly?" Tom asked.

"Well I don't think we should get too worried about it," Arthur said, glancing pointedly at Mary.

"It's likely to be someone fooling about, but nonetheless, I don't think any of us should go out walking alone until we've seen whether it happens again. What did he look like?"

"I couldn't really see much. I imagined it was a man, he was tall... The branches of the tree stopped me getting a decent look. He was dressed in black and was just standing there, really still. Do you think it was someone watching us? Or more likely, me, since he left as soon as I got home?"

"It may be someone keeping an eye on our movements," said Mary, being careful not to give any credence to Tom imagining it was about him, "but I can't imagine why. The only person who could have a grudge against us would be Willard and we've not seen anything of him in quite a while now. Then again, it could just be someone sheltering from the rain."

"But it wasn't raining when I got home today... And where did he go?"

Tom had been living with the Birches for a little more than two years now. It was so very different for him—no yelling, no violence, no anxiety, once they'd gotten rid of Morwyn and Willard. And they were so kind to him! He wondered from time to time about his mother and Leah, but mostly he'd settled in to life in North Feasgar like a duck to water. He went each day to school in Hunterdale and he'd even made a few friends. It was too far to cycle and they'd left Morwyn's car back at the tree house after they'd returned from the labyrinth, none of them wanting anything more to do with her, so he'd helped Arthur design and build a three-wheeled motorbike. Well, Tom called it a motorbike, because it had a small motor on the back, but it didn't look much like the ones he'd been used to in New Zealand. It had two smaller wheels at the back and one large one at the front, with handlebars like Tom's bike at home, only a bit bigger. Tom sat on a seat in front of the rear wheels and controlled the throttle by twisting one of the handlebar grips with his hand, and the brake with his foot. The motor ran off a battery behind the seat that Arthur recharged every few days. It was covered by a wooden box with a padded top, which could be used by a second passenger, although Tom had never tried to drive it with someone on the back. Constructing it had been fun and it made the trip to Hunterdale really easy.

Lately there had been talk of unrest in North Feasgar. Strangers had been reported, a lot more than the few kids like him who'd come through from his world, though no one he knew had actually seen any of these strangers, and no one seemed to be able to say much about them. Mary and Arthur had been wondering whether people were deliberately stirring up unrest for some unknown purpose. People had started to cluster together behind closed doors for meetings about how to protect themselves, even though they didn't know what from. What was the feeling of threat that was starting to seep into their community? Even the weather had been a little odd lately. Nonstop rain, on and on, making everything seem soggy and bleak, even though it wasn't all that cold.

He'd always known that sometime things would change—it was clear from when he was in the labyrinth with Sarah that both of them would be involved in something dangerous together in the future, along with the Birches, but he wasn't ready to have to start worrying again. Though of course, it would be great to see Sarah. How would they 'summon' her when it was time for her to come back? And how would they know when the right time was?

Later in the afternoon Hermione wandered in and found them still sitting around the table. Sensing something from the expectant way they were holding themselves, she padded over to Tom, sniffing the air.

"What's going on?"

"Hermione, where have you been?"

"I went up the river, making the most of the rain stopping for a while. The river is swollen—it's almost up to the level of the stepping stones. Why, has something happened?"

Tom told her about the man. She hadn't seen him—she'd been lying low during the rainy spell. She really didn't like getting wet! She asked him to take her to where the man had been standing, and when they got close, she started making a scary, growling noise in the back of her throat and the fur down her back stood up on end. She turned and walked determinedly back towards the house. Tom had to jog to catch up with her, watching the way she slunk low to the ground, with her tail whisking from side to side as if she was clearing trouble out of their path. It freaked him out that she'd reacted so strongly, much more so than what actually seeing the man had done.

"Hermione, what is it?"

"I don't know, but it doesn't feel right. It feels bad, evil!" she hissed, and Tom shivered. Once inside, Tom told Mary and Arthur what had happened and they calmed her down, stroking her as she sat between Tom and Arthur on the couch, while they planned how they would keep a watch on the house and each other. They decided it may be safest for Tom to be driven to school for a while.

"I hate the feeling of being caged in because of the behaviour of others, but I think we also need to lock the millhouse if we're ever alone here, and at night, just until we have the measure of what's going on," Mary reluctantly suggested.

The others agreed.

"Hermione, do you think the time may be approaching when we need to contact Sarah? And how would we do that?"

"I think we wait a while longer. If strange things keep happening, I'll call her through her dreams. We won't want to call her too soon, because the timing might not be right for whatever it is we need to do. I also don't know how easy it will be for her to understand my message and to actually get away from her world, so timing is everything and I'm going to have to trust my intuition," Hermione responded.

Tom translated for the Birches and they agreed to watch and wait. Secretly though, Tom worried about what would happen if Sarah didn't want to come back—what would happen to the prediction about the four of them having important work to do for North Feasgar if Sarah wasn't here? He tried not to think about it, but worry started to gnaw at him. He could feel it starting to crumble the edges of his new life…

***

The following week, although they hadn't seen the man again, Mary dropped Tom at the school gates in Hunterdale. As he got out of the truck, he noticed a couple of students, a little older than him, lounging on the wall near the gate, looking as if they'd always been there, but he was sure they were new. He glanced back towards Mary, but she'd already driven off. Walking through the gate, they broke off their conversation and stared at him, following his progress, with their eyes penetrating him in a way that made him shiver. If he was Hermione, the hairs on his head would have stood on end!

When he got to class, he was surprised to see them both sitting across from him, towards the back of the room, looking as if they'd always been there. The teacher didn't introduce them and no one else seemed to even notice them. By the time this was repeated in all six of his classes, he felt more and more uneasy. They always seemed placed so they could see him clearly and he felt their eyes boring into him, though when he turned to catch their eyes, they didn't acknowledge him at all. It was weird how everyone seemed to take their presence for granted, so that he started to doubt himself... He felt increasingly anxious and perplexed, especially when he mentioned them to his friend Alan in the lunch break. Alan just looked at him blankly, and when he pointed them out to him as they leaned on the corner of the school building, he looked puzzled and said he didn't know who he was pointing at, there was no one new that he could see. It was about this point that he realised that he couldn't describe them. It was a bit like a dream, the way it can be really clear one minute, then just kind of slip away as you try to remember it. As he tried to recall their appearance, details evaporated or dissolved in his mind, until all he could remember were indiscriminate features—they were males, a little taller/older than him, they may have had dark hair and they somehow appeared to be 'very casual', leaning and watching, but no other aspects of them would come to mind.

At the end of the day he lingered before leaving the school grounds to see whether they would leave before him or wait to see him go. Mary was waiting when he got out to the road, and he couldn't see any sign of the boys. As he slid into the passenger seat, he must have looked anxious, because straight away Mary asked what was up. He did his best to explain as they drove back to Riverstone. Mary checked in the rear-view mirror that they weren't being followed and by the time they got back he began to wonder whether he'd imagined everything.

When they talked about it over dinner, Arthur suggested that tomorrow he should try to be first out of school at the end of the day and he and Mary would be waiting so they could try to follow them when they left. Strangely, he felt even more concerned that they weren't making light of it, that they were seriously considering that the boys posed some sort of menace.

The following day they were there again, ahead of him. Interestingly, Mary could see them too—so what was it all about that his classmates couldn't? He decided to experiment during the day, but that just made it even more confusing. First period he went to class early, only to find them already there. Second period he made a point of taking a seat on his own at the last unoccupied pair of desks, even though his friends sent him enquiring looks. But when the boys came in and looked around, suddenly another student moved to sit beside him, leaving a pair of desks vacant for them to sit, again watching him. Wondering if that was a coincidence, he tried the same thing again, with the same result. It was as if the boys willed the students to move, even though they were probably unaware of why they did. When he asked the girl who'd moved the second time to sit beside him, she looked at him blankly, as if he was mad, and said she didn't know—what was he talking about?

At the end of the day, feeling quite shaken, he hurried out ahead of the other students and squeezed into the front of the truck alongside Mary. A short time later the boys emerged, looking nonchalant, clearly in no hurry. Both Mary and Arthur could see them. They wandered over to where a green car was parked, and with a shock of recognition, Tom realised it was Morwyn's car! It pulled out onto the road and Arthur followed, waiting for another car to take the space between them. Once they got over the bridge, Arthur kept his distance and they drove at moderate speed for about fifteen minutes, at which point they weren't surprised to see the car turn off to the right towards the tree house. They worried all the way home about what it might mean.

"But she can't have come to life again, can she?" Tom asked in horror.

"No, she's well dead and buried, as you saw. No coming back from that! But someone must have moved into the tree house. I think we should wait until evening and come back to take a look," suggested Arthur. "We could leave the truck off the side of the road in the trees and walk the last bit so we can hide up and see who's there."

After dinner, the three of them, plus Hermione, set off in the truck, all squeezed in the front. It was a cloudy night, but at least the rain was holding off. After a couple of days of respite, the river was not quite as swollen and the ground was less boggy underfoot. As they turned off from the main Hunterdale road towards the tree house, Tom shuddered. He hadn't been here since he and Arthur had come back to bury Morwyn more than two years ago. Arthur and Mary had returned her car when he and Sarah were in the labyrinth—that seemed such a long time ago! The road was as potholed and bumpy as ever, so they jolted along over about half the distance to the tree house before Arthur found a spot off the road in the trees where they could leave the truck with enough cover in the almost dark so that it couldn't easily be seen. *Lucky the ground had dried out a bit,* Tom thought, or they would have had trouble getting the truck out again when they headed home.

Setting off on foot up the road, they listened intently for the sound of anything approaching. Hermione led the way, her body on high alert, ears up, head swivelling at any sound, walking with the smooth grace of a leopard. In the midst of worry, Tom registered that she was magnificent! They walked around the sweeping bends leading up to the tree house, but suddenly stopped as Hermione lifted one of her front paws in warning.

"Off the road and into the bushes," she said to Tom, who translated for the others. "I can hear voices in the clearing."

They moved forward as quietly as they could through the trees and undergrowth, holding their breath each time a twig snapped, until Hermione stopped again. She made a quiet hissing noise.

"Look," she pointed ahead. They could see a vague shimmer in the air.

"What is it, Hermione?" asked Tom.

"I sense it's some sort of force field. See its energy flickering?" They could see a ripple of soft blues and purples across their path and stretching up in the air above the trees. It looked as if it was forming a dome, enclosing the whole clearing, including the five trees and tree house.

"Wow, it looks like it's magical."

"Yes, you're right. The question is, how has magic come to North Feasgar?" Hermione wondered. "It was banished and the barrier was set up to keep it contained in the south. I'm afraid that this may mean that the barrier has been breached."

"So why is the field there? What happens if people start to wonder about it? Wouldn't they, whoever they are, be better to keep out of sight since they must have a secret purpose in being here?" Tom asked.

"Have you considered," Hermione said carefully, "that maybe no one else can see it? Think about the boys at school—no one can see them other than you and Mary and Arthur. What's the thing you have in common?"

"What? Coming here from our world?"

"Yes. Maybe people in North Feasgar had the ability to detect magic taken away from them when the divide was created. It would make sense that that's why you and Sarah and Mary and Arthur are needed."

"Wow, I see what you're getting at! So, what's the magic field trying to protect and how do we get to take a look inside? I need to tell all this to Mary and Arthur." Tom translated the conversation, with the Birches getting more sombre as he spoke.

Arthur put his arm around Tom. "This is looking very serious. I think we need to take some time to think it through carefully. First though, we could establish now what happens if something or someone encroaches on the field. What would happen if one of us walked into it?"

"I wouldn't suggest you do that. They obviously know you're different to the others in North Feasgar or they wouldn't be keeping an eye on you. If you walked into the field, it might harm you, or you might not get out," cautioned Hermione.

"Why don't we throw something into it instead? Something that could naturally come into contact with it, like, if the wind blew something into its path. Or what if an animal or a bird bumped into it?" Tom asked.

"They wouldn't! We can see things you humans can't," said Hermione, with the slightly superior tone she sometimes used.

"What could we throw at it? A stick? It needs to be something that would make an impression."

"Maybe that's not such a good idea. It might call them to us. It's unlikely that wind would blow something into its path when it's not actually windy," Hermione remarked drily. After Tom had passed the conversation onto the Birches, they paused to think for a while.

"How about…" Mary reflected, "we get Ryder to drop something on it? He said he'd only be gone a few days, so he should be back any time now."

"Great idea." Arthur started steering Tom away from the shimmering field, back towards the truck. "I think that means we get to go home now for a cup of hot chocolate and bed, don't you?" He wondered just what they were getting themselves into, and whether Tom was resilient enough yet to face the darkness he sensed was approaching.

***

The next day Tom slept in—it was the weekend and the tension of the week had totally wrung him out. They all had a slow start to the day, and it was when he and Mary went out to the garden in the early afternoon to clean out the herb beds that they saw Ryder approaching, gliding in on a current of air. He sunk gracefully down to the ground and landed close to them. Tom still found it hard to understand his rough, scratchy language, so he called to Hermione, who strolled out and started a long thought conversation with him, filling him in on all that had happened over the past few days.

Ryder waited until early evening before flying to the tree house and over the dome, observing the way it seamlessly encapsulated the clearing. When he'd passed over its smooth surface, noticing the way the light glancing off it rippled with soft colour, he turned and flew back in the other direction in a long, lazy spiral, over and around the shimmering field. Just before he cleared it, he dropped the pine cone he'd been holding between his claws. It fell, hitting the dome. The next instant an enormous wall of energy that felt like an explosion blew upwards and caught Ryder, pushing him up and to the side. He started to spin, pushed off his flight path, and disoriented, he plummeted towards the ground. Struggling to right himself, he pulled out of his nosedive, feathers ruffled and heart pounding, and just managed to miss the top branches of a tree. He flew on shaken and dazed, not stopping until he landed heavily outside Riverstone, his shoulders heaving and his breath coming in short gasps. Tom and Hermione rushed outside when they saw him and asked what had happened, but he couldn't speak. He started grooming his feathers, taking his time to collect himself. It was some time before he could communicate with Hermione, and shortly after, he disappeared to recover in the trees by the river. Hermione looked very worried, her head up on full alert, tail swishing, and told Tom to talk to the Birches. She was going to go and try to communicate with Sarah.

"It's time. Everything feels wrong and suddenly menacing. I might take a while—I don't know whether she'll understand what I'm saying to her, or how long it will take for her to get here, but all my instincts say that I need to call her now." She slunk off through the garden to find a quiet place to curl up and concentrate.

***

The next morning when Tom awoke, something felt strange. It took a while before he realised that everything was silent. Like *really* silent. No birds, no wind, none of the ordinary noises that were so usual that he didn't even consciously notice them. And it was still almost dark, even though he was pretty sure it was time to get up. He got out of bed and pulled the curtains back—there was nothing there! He couldn't see the trees, the garden, he couldn't see anything at all. Racing downstairs, he called to the Arthur and Mary and opened the front door. Hermione was there, on the steps sniffing the air.

"What is it Hermione?" Outside he could see that a fog surrounded them, so dense he could only see as far as the bottom of the steps. It felt thick and heavy, making everything eerily quiet, muffled, almost lifeless. It clung to the garden, the trees, sparing nothing. Tom felt like he was breathing in water and his hair was damp and heavy. Shaking his head, little droplets of water flew away from him into the air, joining the fog and disappearing. A greenish, grey colour, it was so close he felt like he could reach out and touch it as he would an object, and it seemed to carry the smell of foreboding and darkness.

"It's like a pea soup," said Mary, appearing beside him. "I've never seen a fog as heavy as this one. It doesn't quite feel right, does it?" she said with a shiver.

Hermione flicked her tail and returned inside. She'd been in a funk since she tried to contact Sarah, worrying about whether she would receive and understand her summons. She was feeling more and more anxious about what was happening, and this fog wasn't helping. It felt threatening, and it was clear that something was wrong when the natural order of things started to change.

The fog never dispersed, but it gave way later in the day to a heavy rain that was so steady and insistent that it felt like damp was getting into all the corners of the house. Luckily it wasn't cold, or it would have been really miserable. As it was, it felt like they were going slowly mouldy! The bad weather set in and, over the next few weeks, little changed: going to school, being watched, sloshing through puddles, avoiding the mud and watching the water level of the river steadily rising. The stepping stones above Riverstone were now submerged and Arthur was worried that if the river level rose much higher, water would start to spill either side of the waterwheel, which would mean it would flood the mill.

They were all feeling cooped up and tetchy. But the stranger didn't appear outside the house again. Tom wondered whether he was somehow 'known' now—what he (and the others) looked like, his location, his patterns. He was under surveillance at school, and maybe somehow, in whatever way he was perceived to be a threat, they thought he was currently under control. It brought his stepfather, Gerald to mind—the way he'd tried to manipulate Tom into being compliant and subservient. What Gerald never realised though, was that in a strange way, while appearing helpless on the outside, he was freed up to go to places in his mind that Gerald could never control. Maybe that was the answer here. To give the appearance of being 'normal' when they were in public, go about their business and keep under the radar while they waited for Sarah to join them.

Chapter III

The Pull of the Cavern

Kayla was roused from her sleep when she heard the front door close at about five in the morning. Someone lurched along the downstairs corridor, bumping into the hall table and swearing. The person resumed an erratic path and slowly climbed the stairs. On reaching the landing outside her bedroom door, there was a solid thump and a loud exhalation of air as the person fell and was winded. She wasn't going to get out of bed and check this time. What sort of daughter did that make her, to have got past caring about her mother? She turned resolutely to face the windows, pulling the bedcovers further up under her chin. The door across the landing opened, then after a minute or so it closed again. Good for Jonnie, he'd made sure she was okay. Closing her eyes, Kayla drifted in and out of a light sleep until her alarm went off at seven-thirty. Getting out of bed, she gathered her school uniform and bag, taking them with her as she stepped over the inert form of her mother, lying spread-eagled in a congealed pool of vomit. She got dressed in the bathroom and went downstairs. How bad was it that part of her might not have cared if her mum had fallen on her back and drowned in her own vomit?

Downstairs, she opened the fridge and took out a carton of

natural yoghurt and the other half of the apple she'd started yesterday. Carefully, she measured out exactly 100 grams of yoghurt, putting it in a small container, and diced the apple up into small pieces that went into a matching container. Filling a bottle with cold water, she was out the door on the dot of eight-thirty walking briskly in the direction of school, sucking on a piece of apple, seeing how long she could extract flavour from it before it disintegrated in her mouth.

Her mother would be out for the count until the middle of the afternoon and would wake in a foul mood, and her brother Jonathan would probably stay in bed until lunchtime. Since he'd dropped out of school he'd kept very lazy hours, only emerging in time to go and hang around at the bike park with his mates, or to the local cafe where, heads together, they shared goodness only knows what on their mobile phones. Jonnie was pretty good to her, but he got a bit strange when he was with his friends, all sort of smart-mouthed and pretending he didn't care about her, that she was somehow embarrassing, but she knew that deep down he looked out for her. He was all that was worth going home for these days, though he did go on about her eating a bit. She didn't think she was anorexic exactly, something she'd heard people saying about her. She didn't think she looked fat or anything, it was just that she always felt worried and bad about herself and most of the food her mum bought just clumped in her mouth and tasted awful—it was like trying to swallow horse chaff! She liked the feeling of being tall and lean and hungry. The school counsellor wondered if it gave her a feeling of control, being able to decide what she ate and what she didn't, and there was maybe a bit of that—it drove her mum mad that she couldn't make her eat! The counsellor had also suggested that it got her attention—that maybe it was better to be noticed for doing something seen as dysfunctional than to be ignored; to be a martyr saying unconsciously to her mum, 'look at me, I'm becoming really unwell because you don't take care of me and if you don't watch out, I might die—then you'll be sorry'! She didn't think she'd let it go that far, though there had been a really odd moment recently when she'd gone all faint at school and had been taken to the doctor. It turned out that it was just that she'd been sipping on her water bottle too much and her sodium levels had got so low she'd passed out. When he checked her out, the GP told her that there were other serious things that could go wrong if she didn't eat more, something about anaemia or possibly even heart problems? And if she didn't take more care she'd have to be hospitalised. Since then she'd taken a lot of care planning out just enough food to keep her away from his notice and giving her enough energy to get through the day.

***

Kayla left school at the end of an uneventful day and hurried straight home. A cool wind had sprung up and she thrust her hands deeply into her blazer pockets, pulling it tightly around her. Arriving home, she let herself in and made her way upstairs, hoping her mother would be asleep in her room. She'd left the spot where she'd fallen earlier but hadn't bothered to clean up the carpet. Kayla stepped over the patch of vomit thinking there was *no way* she was going to be the one to clean it up. It was disgusting! Dumping her bag on the floor in her room, she shut the bedroom door and threw herself on the bed, trying to contain her fury with her mother. It was always like this. If she thought back far enough, she could remember times before it had got this bad, but even then, her mother had always been wrapped up in her own problems, along with being a martyr, having to work to keep the family going. As if they'd chosen to be born! Jonnie's dad had stayed around for a while but had disappeared when Jonnie was about one. She had no idea who her dad was. It seemed she was the product of a one-night stand one time her mum had been out drinking (that could obviously be any night of the year)! She still chose to have her though, rather than get an abortion or have her adopted, so why did it seem to somehow be her fault that she breathed the same air as her mother? Why did she feel guilty for making her mother's life difficult? It's not as if her mum worked that hard—she wasn't capable of holding down much of a job, but when her grandfather died twelve years ago, he left them this house so all she needed was to earn enough for food and bills.

Kayla realised she was lying on the bed shivering, partly from dredging up the same old stuff again, partly from lying still for too long... *God this house is cold in the winter*! She got up and pulled on a pair of jeans, warm socks, an old pair of boots that had seen better days, and an oversized, baggy, blue jumper—a discard of Jonnie's that still carried a vague smell of him that was comforting. She pulled the sleeves down over her fingers, scrunching them up to hold them in place, then braved her way downstairs to get something to drink.

Opening the living room door, she saw her mother sitting, slumped and dishevelled on the couch in front of the television, which was tuned in to a games programme. Her hair was lank and greasy, hanging in strings around her pale face, her eyes bloodshot and puffy. Kayla's heart sank. All she wanted to do was get through to the kitchen, but there was no way she'd get away with that now.

"Mum…" There was a pause.

"Kayla," her mother eventually replied, on a weary exhalation that sounded like a sigh. Kayla struggled not to get pulled into the sigh's sticky web that left her unable to think or speak. Her body registered high alert—this was when she became the fly, trapped and paralysed, awaiting the vicious approach of the spider, knowing she was about to be attacked. Taking a deep breath, she moved towards the kitchen.

"Come here!"

Kayla slowly, reluctantly, turned and walked towards her, against her will but unable to stop herself.

"Mum, are you okay?"

"Please don't start!"

"I just wanted to know if you'd like a cup of tea."

"Tea? At this time of day? Don't be silly, girl." She was looking Kayla up and down with a sneer on her face.

"Come closer!"

As she approached, she could smell her mother's rank, unwashed body. She imagined staleness oozing out of her pores.

"Your skin looks wretched—it makes you ugly. Aren't you eating or washing properly?" she almost spat at her, her breath cutting the air between them, sour and fetid, a repulsive force that made Kayla take a step backwards. *Ugh, hasn't she even cleaned her teeth since she was sick?* She suddenly felt like gagging and ran to the kitchen, pouring a glass of water and took large gulps. There was no point getting upset—her mum picked on her appearance every time she saw her, so why did it still hurt? And how could she look after herself properly when her stomach was always in knots and there was no decent food anyway unless she found money to buy it herself?

"Kayla, stop being a drama queen and come back here. I need you to vacuum upstairs, then go to the shops and buy some bread for dinner. We don't have much in the cupboards, so you'll have to be inventive."

"Mum, I've got a test tomorrow to study for, and some maths homework to do." *Vacuum upstairs? As if that's how you clean up sick!*

"So? You can do that after dinner!"

"No, that's not fair! I'll run to the shops to buy what you need when I've done my homework, but I'm not going to clean up your mess upstairs!"

Her mother's face changed in front of her into an angry mask, diffused with splotches of red.

"How dare you talk to me like that, you ungrateful girl! Get upstairs at once and do what I say."

Kayla stood her ground, though her legs were starting to shake and she'd broken out in a cold, prickly sweat. A second later, something hit her ear and glanced off, ricocheting into a porcelain vase that had been her grandmother's. It fell and smashed into fragments as it hit the ground. The TV remote control landed on the tiles and skidded to a halt, the battery cover shearing off, batteries careering across the floor until they were brought up short at the carpet edge. There was a deathly silence, then Kayla's mother threw herself at her with a howl, like a wildcat, all teeth, hair and claws. To protect herself, Kayla rolled up into a ball as her mother lashed out at her, screaming like the wild thing she'd become. The front door slammed and broke her mother's focus. Rolling off her, she lay on her back on the floor keening and muttering.

***

Jonnie came through the door and dumped his backpack on the floor in the hall, wondering at the noise from the lounge. The sight that confronted him left his blood boiling, but he tried to be super-calm as he carefully unrolled Kayla and helped her to an armchair. A tea towel from the kitchen staunched the blood streaking down her face and shoulder from deep nail gouges, and he found ice to pack inside paper towels for her to hold to her cheek to stop it swelling. Meantime, his mother was still lying on the floor murmuring incoherently and tossing herself sporadically from side to side. He leant over and grabbed her arm, hauling her unceremoniously to her feet and dragged her to the couch, where she collapsed in the corner, hugging a cushion to her chest.

"Mum, what have you done?"

"It wasn't me! Kayla broke your grandmother's vase." She sounded sulky, like a little girl.

"No I didn't! You threw the remote at me and it hit the vase."

His mother started to argue, calling Kayla vile names.

"Stop it! That's enough! I only came home to get a jacket. I'm going out with Mike and won't be back until tomorrow. I need you to tell me you'll leave Kayla alone."

"Oh no you're not! You're not going with those losers when I need you here."

"Yes I am Mum. You have to sort out your own mess."

"If you go, don't bother coming back—you won't be

welcome."

"Not sure what you'll do to stop me if I do want to come back to this poxy hole." He strode out the door and grabbed his jacket from a hook in the hall. Kayla launched herself from the chair and ran after him.

"Please, please, take me with you. I don't want to be alone with her."

"Okay, get your coat. We'll drop you back later when she's calmed down."

As they headed for the front door their mother ran up the stairs. They heard her open the window and by the time they got outside she was firing his clothes out the window onto the grass.

"They're only clothes. Come on, let's go." He grabbed her hand and pulled her to the car waiting beside the front verge. He opened the back door and clambered in beside his friend, Mike.

Kayla slid into the seat beside him in the back of the old, beaten-up black car. Mike was in the back seat – she knew him – he nodded at her, acknowledging her presence. His other friend Peter was driving, but she didn't know the other guy in the front passenger seat. Jonnie introduced him to her as Dan. As he turned to say a brief "Hi," she noted that he was really good-looking, with dark eyes, maybe part Maori.

They didn't seem too curious about why she was there, with Mike just saying, "Having some mother troubles then?"

"Yeah!" Jonnie slumped beside her on the back seat, staring morosely at nothing in particular in front of him.

Peter drove the car fast but skilfully, through their suburb, heading west. By the time they reached the next suburb and began to meander through an increasingly rural New Zealand landscape, Kayla realised they were probably heading for one of the West Coast beaches. The car climbed up over a range of hills, on a road that wound through native bush, then down the other side. As the road straightened out again, the sun was dropping and the landscape became trees and long shadows, with a strip of grey/blue sea on the horizon. Everything seemed to go quiet. All she could hear was the noise of the tyres on the road and their breathing inside the car. It was a bit like leaving bedlam, climbing up to the top of the world on an inhalation, and then slowly releasing, exhaling, on the other side. She sighed and relaxed, leaning against Jonnie. In the quiet she mused about how little conversation they seemed to need. Like they accepted the situation without any need to talk about it. Weren't they curious, or did they know Jonnie so well they didn't need to communicate with speech? Or were they just sullen boys, as their mother would have it? It didn't feel like that, there was no tension, they were just there, hanging out together.

Arriving eventually at the beach, they piled out of the car, pulling up their jacket collars against the sharp wind. They had to lean into it to walk across a small bridge that spanned a reedy stream, up a sand dune, and then the stunning vista of a wild beach with black sand was spread in front of them. Large waves crashed onto the shore, releasing plumes of spray into the air. To their left, at the headland, rocky cliffs jutted out into the water and waves exploded into them, sending up great jets of water that fell again to break up on the rocks and eddy through deep fissures created by the age-old tidal rhythm. They walked towards the rocks and found pools of water out of reach of the tide, still and dark and deep. The boys stopped in the lee of some rocks out of the full force of the wind, pulling out packets of cigarettes and shielding their lighters behind their hands as they struggled to get steady flames to light them. Kayla watched them for a while, then wandered off on her own towards the cliffs.

"Hey K," yelled Jonnie, "don't go too close to the blow hole and don't go into the water—there are rips out there."

She nodded and carried on, feeling drawn to being solitary with her thoughts and feelings, in such a beautiful but ferocious landscape. As she walked, her boots sank into the black sand making it feel like she was perpetually walking uphill. She scooped some up in her hand – it was so fine and soft – it clung to her fingers even when she let it fall through them, and she tried to brush it off. So unlike the golden sand of the East Coast. Somehow much more elemental.

For a while she was absorbed tracing patterns in the sand with a stick. Great spirals, starting wide and working their way inwards, then looping, connecting to the centre of a second, then a third, stacked like a pyramid. She was vaguely aware that she'd seen a pattern something like that before, maybe a Celtic symbol, but hers was connected through the centre rather than the outside. She loved drawing—it was something about putting marks out in the world, things about herself that no one else understood, a way of expressing how she was feeling that she didn't have the right words for.

Ahead she could see a dark, vertical slash in the face of the rocks jutting out into the sea. As she got closer it resolved into a large opening, a cavern. She heard a yell in the distance and turned to see Jonnie walking towards her, gesturing for her to wait. She waved at him—she wasn't about to do something stupid and turned back to the cave and kept walking. She was drawn to it, curious and fascinated by the pounding waves, magnificent and terrifying. As they passed their peak and crashed, spray and foam floated through the cold air, salty and tangy on her tongue and stinging her eyes. It caught up in her hair, whipping strands across her face, obscuring her view so that she grabbed it up in one hand, twisting it into a rope out of the way.

Her attention was drawn back to the cave. She could now make out that it was quite wide at the entrance, but not enclosed. It had a narrow slit of light in its depths, where it opened out to the ocean. Standing in front of it, the sand sloped down towards its mouth, pulled by the motion of the waves. Near her feet, incoming waves reached a few metres in front of its mouth. She watched it, mesmerised by the push of the waves as they swirled up the slope towards her feet, then pulled back into the cavern, followed soon after by a dull thump as the outgoing waves hit the narrower outlet to the sea. In and out, in and out. She heard her name called again, but stayed facing the cave, lulled by the motion and the sound of the breaking waves. They had such a tremendous, natural power that she felt small before it, but not in the horrible way she did with people who wielded power over her.

To the right of the cave, on the rocks, something sparkled. Straining her eyes, she thought it looked like a necklace, draped over a rocky ledge by a small pool of water. She calculated that the sea between her and the rocks was only a few centimetres deep when the waves were out, and she'd have plenty of time to reach it and get back before the next one. She waited for the tide to pull away and then quickly moved over the sand. A part of her registered running feet behind her. She'd just reached the rock and put out her hand to pick up the necklace when two things happened at once: Jonnie reached out and grabbed the hood on the back of her jacket; and a large, oversized wave crashed through the cave, catching them both and instantly transforming the shallow water into a seething, frothy melee of angry water that swirled around them thigh deep.

For a moment it seemed as if everything would be okay, but the wave, having crashed on the shore, reversed its hold and sucked ferociously backwards, catching them off-balance, pulling their feet from under them, plucking them up and carrying them back through the cave in its turbulence. Initially they were swept along on the surface, but the next moment the current pulled them under, tumbling and twisting their bodies until they had no idea what way was up or down, Jonnie still clutching Kayla's jacket, with his arm feeling almost pulled out of its socket. Images of being smashed against the rocks at the exit flew through Kayla's mind and a wild panic set in. She flailed, desperate to get her head above water. Just as she felt her lungs would burst, her head surfaced, closely followed by Jonnie's, both coughing and spluttering. It took them a minute to realise that, while they were still being drawn rapidly through the current, they were now outside the cave. In fact, they weren't even in the sea. They were in a fast-flowing, swollen river, rocketing towards a building with a waterwheel.

As they were carried swiftly down the river, remarkably, Jonnie managed to keep hold of Kayla. With the waterwheel getting closer, they started panicking. The current was too fast for them to be able to strike out for one of the banks.

"Just keep your head up K, we'll be all right. I'm sure we can find a handhold to the side of the wheel," Jonnie yelled, trying to be reassuring. Kayla felt as if she was hyperventilating; her head felt light and fuzzy and she was unable to think beyond her fear about what to do. Suddenly something large and solid, hidden under the water, thumped into Jonnie's chest, knocking all the air out of his lungs. Instinctively he threw his free arm out and found himself holding onto something like a large, rounded, submerged stump or post. His arrested movement threw Kayla around the downriver side of it so they were both left with their arms straddling the post, holding on tightly while the river carried on flowing past.

The only thing they could do was yell for help. First Jonnie, with a reedy voice, but then joined by Kayla, becoming louder as they realised the immediate danger was over and their panic subsided. After what felt like a lifetime, with their voices becoming hoarse, they saw three figures emerge from the building—up close it looked like a mill-house. They started running over the field towards them, a boy about their age in the lead, followed by a girl and an older woman, the boy yelling back to someone out of sight to bring a rope.

Chapter IV

Sarah's Return

The countryside rolled by as the train traversed through lush fields, belts of trees, rivers, small villages and then on to the sprawling brick and concrete of urban centres. Through the backyards of houses, poky gardens with ramshackle sheds, decaying cars in an enclosure waiting to be scrapped, washing hanging on lines flapping in a light breeze, pretty courtyard gardens, small shops with overflowing rubbish—dogs fossicking for scraps; past allotments, graffiti on walls pronouncing the overthrow of the bourgeoisie, Matt's love for Alice, anti-racism; over bridges; miles relentlessly gobbled up as Sarah sped towards home.

She was aware of feeling kind of embarrassed that until she'd had to travel on her own to school, she'd always assumed somehow that her own upbringing was what living in England was like. Small village, enough money to live on, good schools, a few family issues, but basically good parents who did their best for her. Going to North Feasgar had somehow made her so much more questioning, and she looked at things differently now. Actually, it wasn't just her experience in North Feasgar that had changed her, it was also her increasingly difficult relationship with her parents. She felt as if their disagreements had let her see herself as separate to them and she'd had to grow up fast. She now wanted to know about things below the surface, why things happened, why people were the way they were. And with her eyes more open, even something as simple as a train trip showed her that so much of England and how people lived was *not* like her experience of it. While her school was fairly multicultural, she had to acknowledge that everyone there was privileged compared to so many. Her parents could afford the fees, as could everyone else's parents other than the few girls who were there on scholarships. Lara was on a scholarship. She was really clever, but she never wanted to talk about her family. She seemed embarrassed, or maybe ashamed of them, and had never suggested they meet up with her in the holidays, or go to her place…

As Sarah's mind wandered, she was slumped in a seat, facing the right way, thank goodness, looking out the window to try to prevent motion sickness. Here was a garden littered with debris from a lifetime of lack of care; there was a pretty garden planted with English garden flowers, incongruous against the harsh lines of the brick terraced house, but at least someone was trying. The rails clicked rhythmically, hypnotically, until the sudden whoosh of an express train passing in the opposite direction gave her a fright, the carriage swaying sickeningly. They passed a school, children playing on a jungle gym, then suddenly they were back in the countryside, and before long she dozed off…

Nearly an hour later she woke, aware of the sound of bells, and looked out to see the train pass through a crossing, cars waiting patiently (or not) in a queue. She recognised the approach of the town her grandparents were picking her up from and tried to rouse herself by taking a few mouthfuls of water. Smoothing down her hair, she got out of her seat, lurching a little as she walked down the swaying corridor to where her bag was stored in the luggage rack. She yanked it down and waited while the train slowed and pulled in at the station.

Clambering off the train with her bag, she walked towards the barrier and could see her grandparents waiting expectantly on the other side. She made her way towards them quickly and ran the last few yards, allowing herself to be enfolded in a big hug from her grandad. Tears came to her eyes at feeling his comfortable and familiar presence. She hugged her grandmother, thinking about how good it was that they were always so pleased to see her.

"Sarah! You've grown again! What a beautiful young woman you've become. Are you hungry? We thought we'd take you for lunch and a catch-up before we take you to Hannah's."

"Thanks Gran, that would be great. I only had an apple on the train."

They walked off to the car and a short drive took them to The White Horse, a small pub with a garden bar where they could sit in the sun and talk.

While they were waiting for their food, her grandmother asked her about school and her friends. Sarah answered, but it felt awkward, as if there was something sitting between them that was getting in the way.

"Sarah, are you all right?" her grandfather asked.

She found herself at a loss for words. How she was feeling was too big and she didn't know where to start.

"From what little we know, I think you and your mum may have had a falling out—is that what's bothering you?" her grandfather asked.

Sarah's eyes teared up and she nodded her head.

"I bet it's been hard for you over the last couple of years. You had that scary time in hospital and so soon after that your parents went off to Singapore…"

"Oh George, leave it be. If she wants to tell us she will," her grandmother interjected.

"Louise, why don't you go and see what's happened to our drinks—I'd have thought they'd be ready by now."

When she left, her grandfather took her hand, saying, "She's a bit too much like your mum isn't she? Doesn't like anything emotional! Now tell me what's going on. Don't feel awkward—your mum is our daughter, but you're part of us too, and we love you."

Sarah hesitated… "I just feel so alone sometimes. They're so far away and it feels like they're not interested in me any more. Even when I went to visit, I had to fit in around them. They weren't really interested in me at all other than to make sure I was doing well at school. It feels like I've grown away from them, and that's scary."

"You changed a lot when you were in hospital – I'm not sure why it was so profound – it was as if you really grew up. I imagine your mum was confused and worried."

"Well so much happened to me and I couldn't stay a child bound up with them forever." *Oops,* she thought. She'd nearly said too much. She still hadn't decided whether it was wise or foolhardy to take him into her confidence. How could he ever believe her? Her grandad didn't seem to have picked up on her slip though.

Over lunch they chatted about her friends and how she was getting on at school, and she listened as her grandmother talked about what they'd been doing at the retirement village and the day trips they'd been on visiting historic places in neighbouring areas. It felt like her gran was trying to fill all the space between them, but eventually she ran out of steam. In the short silence that eventually fell, her grandad finally had the chance to ask what was still on his mind.

"So, what can we do to help? Louise, we had a quick chat while you were inside and Sarah's been struggling with her mum and dad being away."

"Oh George, it's a lovely day, just let it be—she'll be seeing them soon enough. When are you off to Singapore, Sarah?"

Sarah caught her grandad's eye, with a resigned look on her face.

"Louise," he said impatiently, "things aren't okay just because you want them to be. Give her a chance to speak honestly—the world won't collapse if she's not happy."

With a sideways glance at her grandmother, Sarah started to talk about how difficult it had been since her parents had gone, how she felt abandoned and as if she wasn't important to them any more. While her grandad listened as intently as he had before, her gran was looking very uncomfortable.

Once she interjected with: "Do you think you might be overreacting a little? They're just trying to rebuild their relationship."

"But Gran, I'm meant to be part of their lives too, but they don't think about what's best for me!" At that her grandmother got up and walked inside, saying she was going to order coffee.

"Sarah, don't mind your gran—she loves you very much, she just finds dealing with feelings, especially talking about them, really difficult. Her own Mum was the same. She had a tough upbringing and no one to teach her how to deal with how she felt, and I guess she didn't know how to do that with your mum either. That's probably why your gran and I do well together—I'm 'safe' and process all the difficult things for her, and she's been a wonderful partner for me in so many ways. I've tried to moderate things for your mum too, but I wasn't around a lot when she was really little. In those days women gave up their careers for a time when they had children, so I had to work hard to support us."

"So… if you process things to make it easier for Gran, who does it now for my mum? Dad's too busy and he doesn't think that way anyway. I only just realised how alone she must have felt through all that time when she was depressed and Dad was going to leave her. And she must have been worried about me on top of it all!" Sarah felt horrified that she hadn't been more support for her mum. Her grandad seemed to anticipate where she would go with that.

"Sarah, don't go there. You were just a kid—you still are, mostly. And it's not your role to take care of your parents! It's interesting though that you've learned so much about emotions. Your personality is more like mine than either your gran or your mum or dad, but something seemed to happen to you when you were in hospital. You grew up somehow and I've always puzzled about that."

Sarah took a deep breath. It was now or never… "That's something I want to talk to you about actually, Grandad." She petered out as she saw her gran approaching from inside the pub. "Can we meet up sometime, just us, over the next couple of days?"

"Yes, of course. Why don't you spend the day with Hannah tomorrow and I'll pick you up on Monday morning—we can go and find somewhere to have coffee and a chat."

***

It was wonderful seeing Hannah again. Part of her wished she'd been able to stay and go to high school with her, but another part of her recognised how important it had been for her to have to travel outside her comfort zone and meet new people and make new friends. It was just as if they'd never been apart though—it was so easy to be with her and her family, in her house, in a comfortable way she didn't experience in her own.

On Sunday afternoon, Hannah had to go and visit her grandmother who was in hospital, so Sarah decided to go to her family house and see if she could get her grandparents' plate out of storage. It was really weird—somehow so familiar yet strange at the same time. An unknown car in the driveway, unkempt garden and lawn, a child's bicycle propped up by the front door. Hesitantly she approached the front steps and knocked on the door. She waited, but there was no response. She could hear the TV blaring in the front room, so feeling exceedingly awkward and intrusive, she banged on the door again, loudly this time. After what felt like ages, she heard footsteps moving towards the door and it was opened a crack with the snib chain in place. A woman's face looked her up and down.

"What do you want?"

"I'm Sarah. This is my house that you're renting." Sensing the wariness on the woman's tired-looking face, she was quick to add, "Sorry to bother you, but I need to find something my parents stored in a box in the garage. If you could just let me in for a moment, please, I won't be in your way for long."

The door was closed in her face and Sarah stood there at a loss, wondering what to do now. A short time later though, she heard the garage door opening. The garage had been organised with space down one side for a car and the family's storage boxes piled on the other side. She was glad for the way her mother had methodically labelled them all. Hers were grouped together, and in the second box labelled 'Miscellaneous' she found the plate, carefully wrapped in towels to protect it. She felt an enormous surge of relief to have it again.

As she left the garage she called out, "Thank you!" And by the time she was walking back down the path the garage door was closing behind her. Not exactly friendly then, but maybe she was just scared—what a horrible way to live!

Back at Hannah's she sat on the bed and carefully wiped down the plate, tracing the raised surface with her fingertips. As she ran her index finger over the water tumbling down from the waterwheel, she started to feel a tingly sensation, and she quickly took her hand off, deliberately looking away. Too soon. She didn't have things in place yet... For now she needed to think through what she'd say to her grandfather tomorrow!

***

The day was overcast. Little flurries of wind puffed dust and leaves along the pavement outside the cafe. Sarah watched them out the window, avoiding her grandfather's concerned gaze. They'd already had a coffee, but Sarah didn't know where to start, how to start. Her voice had deserted her and her tongue felt rough and dry and too large for her mouth. She took a deep breath and another swallow of water.

"I can see you're really struggling. What's going on?"

She moved her gaze from the window but didn't know where to look. He had such a kind expression on his face, she thought she might burst into tears if she held his gaze.

"You're never going to believe me," she finally managed to whisper.

"Try me. What's the worst that could happen?"

"If you don't believe me, you'll think I'm really stupid, or crazy, and I'll be all alone..." A silence stretched out between them, then Sarah felt his warm hand on hers.

"Why don't we go for a walk? Sometimes it's easier to talk into the air than across a table."

Once outside they crossed over a stile, to a public walkway that ran through fields alongside a wood. It felt much better to be outside. Although it wasn't sunny, it was warm and very peaceful once they moved away from the village. Eventually she found the courage to start.

"Grandad, it's about the time I stayed at your place and ended up in hospital. I need to tell you a very strange story." She told the story of a young teenage girl, afraid and confused about what was happening between her parents, thinking it was somehow all her fault and not knowing how to put it right. She didn't know what to do, so she escaped into her imagination and found herself in a different world.

An hour later, her story had petered out and her grandfather still hadn't said anything. They'd found a bench to sit on and were side by side, looking out across the valley, a peaceful scene, totally at odds with the tale she'd just told.

"Grandad, say something, please."

"Well, you know, I was completely pulled in—you tell a powerful story. But I just don't know what to make of it. I've had a lifetime of having it drummed into me that everything in medicine has to be based on evidence; that there is always a logical, rational answer to everything. But to be frank, sometimes that's been at odds with my instincts. I've always waged a bit of a war between the two and I find myself really wanting to believe you, but not knowing how to. Just sometimes I'd like to believe there's more to the world than what we can directly perceive."

"Well at least you haven't straight off told me I'm crazy!" She managed a watery smile.

"So, if I heard you right, you're thinking that there is a parallel world separated from here by a rift. It seems as if kids who are troubled somehow have the right energy to be pulled through it, like this Tom you speak of."

She had a sudden thought, "Oh yes, of course, I can show you something! His disappearance from New Zealand was in the news for ages. I've saved some newspaper articles on my phone." She opened her phone and pulled up information about Tom's disappearance and what had happened to his family in the intervening two years. She also pulled up what little she'd been able to find out about Mary and Arthur, at least enough to know they had actually existed in England in the past. The look on her grandfather's face grew very serious as he read.

"Well, although it appears inconceivable, it would answer a lot of my puzzlement about you and the way you changed. Just say I go along with this, what would you like me to do?" There was a long pause as Sarah considered his question.

"I'm the only one of us I know of who's gone there through my imagination. That means my body stays behind. The others seem to go completely—don't ask me how that works, because I certainly seem to be completely embodied in North Feasgar. I even injured myself while I was there! So, I would need someone to take care of me here so I wouldn't have to go back to hospital and my parents wouldn't find out."

"So, you'd need me to keep you hydrated for how long? A week again?"

"Yes. It couldn't be any longer because I have to go to Jas', then to Singapore for the last two weeks of my break."

"I'm curious now—can the others come back?"

"Evidently, through the labyrinth, as I did, but I don't know of anyone who has. It made Tom and me wonder about all the children who go missing and are never found. It would be quite nice to think of them in a parallel world rather than being abducted or killed!"

"I'd have to tell your gran of course – don't know how I'd do that – she'll never let herself believe it, and I'm sure I'd have to do it against her will... Okay, let's say we do it. I have plenty of supplies still in storage from my practice that I kept just in case... Hmmm, I'm just thinking... I wonder whether your phone would go with you if it was in your pocket? Photos would be one way to prove it!"

They chatted on for a while, planning out what would happen if something seemed to be going wrong; at what point he would contact her parents. Sarah knew he wasn't totally convinced about her story, but he seemed willing to go with it for now and see what happened. That was a huge part of what she loved about him—he didn't criticise or dismiss her and he treated her as if she was worthy of being listened to.

She was meant to be staying with Hannah for the next ten days, so they agreed to meet again for coffee at the end of the week. Her grandfather was going to wait for the right time to talk to her gran. They walked back to the village talking about a book she was reading for English, Sarah feeling relieved that she'd talked to him, and knowing all she could do now was wait and trust in what would happen next.

She met her grandparents again the following Saturday. Nothing was said about North Feasgar, so Sarah assumed her gran hadn't been told about it yet. It was a relief in a way—she'd been feeling really tense when they picked her up, worrying about what would happen if her gran tried to stop her plans. When her gran went to the bathroom her grandad quickly told her that he hadn't managed to think of a way to broach it, and wondered whether it might be best for her just to visit them, and if she did manage to go through the rift, he'd tell her about it then...
"No need to upset her if it's not needed." That told her that he was dubious about her story and thought it was unlikely to happen, so why rock the boat? Well she could go with that...she wouldn't be there to worry about it when her gran found out anyway! They agreed that he would invite her to stay for her last night, ostensibly so she could get the train the next morning to Jas' place. They had a small spare room they used as an office, with a couch that folded out to a bed that she could sleep

in.

Everything went as planned. She had fun with Hannah and her other old friends, and the evening before she was due to leave, she had a Skype call with her parents that was reassuring. Her mum said she was looking forward to seeing her and confirmed that they'd be at the airport to pick her up. The next day she made her way to her grandparents' unit in time for her favourite dinner—her gran's famous chicken and mushroom pie. She was wearing jeans and a T-shirt, and when she went to her room after saying goodnight she put on a cardigan and a jacket—she didn't know what to expect in North Feasgar, but she remembered that last time when it was winter in England it was quite warm in North Feasgar, so now it might be the other way around. She'd charged her phone over dinner and now switched it off and zipped it into her jacket pocket. There was no point taking her charger – who knows what power supply and sockets they had there – she just wanted it to show Tom what had happened to his family and to take a couple of photos for her grandad. She decided not to try to take anything else—the Birches would take care of anything she needed and she was better to 'travel light', if travel was what you called moving between parallel worlds.

There was a knock on the door and she let her grandfather into the room. He saw her dressed to go and the plate sitting propped up on a low table. He looked serious, with worried frown lines on his forehead. Moving towards her he enveloped her in a big hug and whispered, "Good luck!" and that he loved her, before going out and quietly shutting the door.

Sarah sat on the floor with her back to the bed, looking at the plate and feeling a mixture of emotions that were hard to pull apart. She loved her grandad so much! Tears tracked down her face, but at the same time a knot of worry was gnawing at her insides as she thought again about her parents. She wished so much that they hadn't left her. She didn't even mean leaving her to go to Singapore; somehow, they'd left her long before that, and they didn't seem to want to understand her, or even really *see* her. They had their own life now and she was definitely on the outside of it! Mind you, she wouldn't have found North Feasgar if they'd stayed a close family, and if her parents weren't happy with each other, she probably wouldn't be leaving now because she'd feel like she had to be there to care for them!

Leaning forward, Sarah lightly ran her fingers over the plate as she had the week before, and sure enough she felt a responding tingle. She leaned back against the bed and let her eyes wander across it, her mind loosening from her surroundings and merging with her memories of the mill. Letting go of the tension she'd been holding, she let her imagination take her to how the air smelt, the feeling of the breeze on her skin, the sound of the bubbling water and its coolness on her feet. She found herself beside the water below the millwheel, her toes just touching its wet surface. Where last time it had been bubbling over stones, now the water level was higher and she couldn't even see the stones. The air felt grey and damp. Vaguely, in the distance, she could hear a woman's voice (her grandmother's maybe?) calling her name, but at the same time she saw Hermione at the top of the steps and she started walking up them excitedly, being careful not to slip on their wet surface, then hurried over the landing to gather her up in a hug.

She buried her nose in her silky fur, remembering her particular scent, hearing the rumble of her purr.

"It's so good to see you again!" Hermione nuzzled her under her chin and licked her neck with a raspy tongue, making Sarah laugh.

"That feels like sandpaper! Oh Hermione, I've really missed you." She carried her to the door and pushed it open. The living room looked warm and inviting and smelt of the familiar presence of people she cared for, but there was no one inside and Hermione told her that they'd gone to Hunterdale on an errand and should soon be back. They walked together through the house and out the back door.

The garden was looking cared for and there seemed to be a new raised bed behind the lavender with herbs in it. When she checked, she saw them all carefully labelled with neatly written tags. As she bent over to pluck a bit of lavender to crush and smell, Hermione told her that Mary and Tom had decided to grow them for when she returned, replicating all the main ones found in the concoctions she'd brought back from Morwyn's, plus a few others. *How amazing*, she thought, feeling overcome with emotion at the way they'd remembered and held her in mind while she'd been away. She moved on down the path and out the gate. The ground was soggy, as if there'd been a lot of rain. Her shoes squelched as she walked towards the river, which was swollen, running high up its banks. She couldn't see the stepping stones—they must be completely covered. She turned around and saw that Hermione hadn't followed her—she was waiting back by the gate, licking her paws. Of course, there's no way she'd want to get her dainty feet muddy if she didn't need to! She wandered back and scooped her up to carry her back along the path to the house.

Just before she got to the door, it opened and Tom appeared. Somehow it was Tom and yet not Tom; someone familiar and expected, and yet a stranger. She registered a sense of oddness, of awkwardness, just as he saw her. The look of surprise and happiness on his face was very funny and gratifying at the same time. He yelled out to Mary and Arthur as he ran to her and flung his arms around them both. Hermione tolerated it for a minute before meowing and wriggling out of the tight space between them. Sarah was then enveloped by Mary and Arthur, and she felt herself smiling so widely that her face ached.

"You got Hermione's message then—we wondered if you'd come!" exclaimed Tom.

"Goodness Sarah, look at you! You've grown! You're a young woman now." Mary was holding her hand, looking warmly at her.

"Well so has Tom! He used to be shorter than me and now look at him!" It had been quite strange embracing him. She felt unexpectedly self-conscious. No longer a slightly weedy, frightened looking boy, he was now quite a bit taller than her and looking healthy and strong. His green eyes had lost had their hooded, distrustful air and part of her noticed how good looking he was, but she pushed that thought away as they excitedly caught up on the past two years.

It was mid-afternoon in North Feasgar. They had plenty of time to talk and renew their connection. They wanted to know how

Sarah had got back to England, whether she'd been missed and how her parents had reacted to her return. She also told them what she'd found out about Tom's disappearance. She turned on her phone—obviously there was no signal, but she showed him the information she'd saved from the New Zealand Herald. He read it with a worried frown as he thought about his mother and Leah, but whooped with laughter at the idea that Gerald had been through such a hard time when the police thought he'd been responsible for Tom's disappearance.

"Couldn't happen to a better person," he spluttered, as he tried to control his laughter.

As soon as he could, Arthur grabbed the phone, turning it over and over, aghast at how such a small device could be a phone, take and transmit images, and be a source of unlimited information. It was more than he could comprehend and Sarah had to stop him from trying to take off the back cover. Instead, he passed it to Mary, who was similarly puzzled. Sarah took it back to take photos of the two of them, of Tom and Hermione, then thought to go outside and take one of the mill-house and river, from an angle similar to the plate. Switching it off, she put it safely back in her zippered pocket—she didn't want it to get damaged now it had served its purpose!

While Arthur and Mary were preparing dinner, Sarah suggested that she and Tom go for a walk along the river. Tom looked inquiringly at Arthur.

"I guess that's okay, there are two of you, just don't go out of shouting distance." Sarah must have looked puzzled, because he added, "Tom you need to catch Sarah up on what's been happening here and why we called for her. In short, there are strangers around who are behaving oddly, so we have a new rule that we don't go out alone and we always make sure someone knows where we are." Sarah exchanged an enquiring glance with Tom, but decided to ask him more when they were on their own.

They walked across the sodden field to the river and made their way along the river's edge. It felt so good being with him again—she hadn't realised quite how much she'd missed him!

"The water's really high," she noted. "Has it been raining a lot?"

"Yes, Arthur says they've never seen anything like it—it's been raining most days for the past few months. It's a bit spooky; it feels like something's stirring up trouble. First the disturbed weather patterns, then the strangers appearing. What's really weird though is that although they're being reported on, no one can recall what they're like or what they're doing. They've created a lot of fearmongering—groups of people are meeting secretly and everyone is really watchful, but no one can give any details about them. And even though Mary, Arthur and I can see them more clearly than anyone else, we can't recall their appearance precisely." He then added what was worrying him more: "They're watching us though. Two of them have turned up at school and seem to be keeping an eye on me. But it's really odd; the other kids kind of move out of the way for them but don't notice them! And someone's been watching us here. We wondered if it's something about us coming from outside the land that allows us to see them, but that also attracts them to us."

"That sounds really worrying. It'll be interesting to see if I can see them…" Sarah replied.

"We followed them last week and they seem to be staying at Morwyn's treehouse, but they've put up a protective barrier around them so no one can see what they're up to." He paused for a moment as they found their way across a slippery patch of ground. It seemed the natural thing to do to take her hand.

"We've heard stories too about Greyvyn starting to show some signs of activity and everyone's hoping it doesn't erupt. It's evidently been dormant for about 500 years. Folklore says that an old woman guards the underworld and that it can be accessed beneath Greyvyn. Some say that there's treasure there, others that she's guarding whatever it was that created the barrier to keep the black magic in the south. If that's true, I can only imagine that the rumbling of the mountain is a sign that's somehow linked to the strangers. Arthur and Mary wonder if they've somehow got through the barrier, because they seem to have magic that hasn't been in the north since Feasgar was divided."

They were silent for a few minutes while Sarah thought about what Tom had said.

"So, what do you think I'm meant to do while I'm here; what are *we* meant to do?"

"I don't know. I guess we just need to trust that whatever it is will become clear over the next few days."

They were now walking over a rough patch of ground near the river, where tree roots had tangled their way towards the water. Sarah stood on a tuft of grass that must have been covering a root and slipped. Tom grabbed her quickly, pulling her towards him so she didn't slide into the water. For a moment they stood chest to chest and Sarah felt her face suffuse with red, and embarrassment at her reaction made her quickly pull away. Tom straightened up, not saying anything and turned to go back to the mill-house. Why had she reacted like that? She felt awkward and stupid, and hurried after him as he strode ahead. They finished the walk back in silence. When they were sitting down to have their dinner, Mary caught Arthur's eye across the table—he gave her a half shrug, as if to say *Don't ask me...* and they did their best to keep a casual conversation going about the mill, Hunterdale and what Tom had been studying at school.

After dinner, Sarah said she was tired and needed to go to bed. Mary had made up the bed in her old room and laid out some pyjamas. When she went into the room, it felt familiar and welcoming. There were fresh wild flowers on the windowsill and she could see that all the jars of herbal remedies she'd brought back from Morwyn's were still sitting on the bookcase where she'd left them. She managed to stay awake long enough to clean her teeth, then fell into bed, falling asleep immediately, utterly exhausted with an overlong day and the impact of all the emotional worries she'd gone through in getting there.

She awoke in the early hours of the morning with her heart pounding from a dream. It felt like it was important, like the one she'd had when Hermione called her back, so she went over it in her mind before she fell asleep again, not waking until she heard the others moving around downstairs. Over breakfast she told it to them.

"I had this really weird dream last night. It felt really important, but I've no idea what it meant: *I was in a small clearing with trees around and soft foliage underfoot. It felt safe. There were three of us in the clearing: a boy (maybe Tom), me and an old lady. She was wearing a white robe and had long, silver/white hair. The atmosphere she created was one of wisdom, knowledge, warmth and caring. She was teaching us things that felt familiar, as if they were about things that had happened recently in our lives. She kept giving us the message that 'All is one'. We were then underground, but it was a palace-type setting, very beautiful and wealthy-looking. Everything was a silvery white. There were now four of us—we'd been joined by a beautiful, slim young woman, maybe the princess of the underground palace. She radiated a sense of beauty and completeness. She asked for a platter of precious things to be brought to her. Out of these she selected a beautiful ring. It was simple—silver with a strange pearl-like lustrous stone set in it. When it was turned it sometimes looked red, like it was a ruby, but at other times looked like a pearl. After selecting the ring, she asked that all the other precious items be given away—they were no longer needed. She then gave the ring to the old lady as a gift, putting it on the ring finger of her left hand. Each of us in turn placed our finger on hers within the circle of the ring, as she said to each of us 'All is one'."*

They were silent, thinking about the dream, each of them feeling strangely moved by it. Mary broke the silence: "What a wonderful dream. Whatever it means, it feels like it's portentous somehow."

"Yes, I had the feeling it was something to do with tasks we have to achieve while I'm here; Tom and I together, just like the pool in the labyrinth told you. It's funny though, that's the third dream I've had about being underground—the scary one when I was here before, then the one when Hermione called me, now this... And, even more weirdly, the older woman reminds me of a tarot card that recently turned up out of the blue—The High Priestess, Persephone, the queen of the underworld. I'll show you later."

After they'd eaten, Sarah helped Mary clearing away the dishes and Tom muttered that he was going for a walk.

"What's wrong with him, do you think?" Mary asked. "He's been very quiet since yesterday."

Sarah could feel herself going pink again and became very busy clattering plates. "I don't know, maybe it's just strange the way I reappeared so suddenly."

They were wiping down the bench when they heard someone yelling.

"Arthur, Arthur, quick, bring a rope!" It was Tom. They rushed to the door, calling Arthur on the way past the mill room in case he hadn't heard, and raced outside. Tom was running towards the river, and as they followed him, they could see in the distance what looked like two figures, people, in the river, clinging to something in the fast-flowing current. One of them, a boy, was yelling at them to hurry. Arthur ran to join them with a rope. When they got to the side of the river, they could see that he and a girl must be holding onto one of the submerged stepping stones, which was all that was stopping them from being carried down the river to the mill wheel. He called out to them and threw the rope. It fell short, so he hauled it back in and threw it again. This time it fell slightly below them in the river, so he tried again, this time aiming it further up the river so that the current would carry it down to them. The boy managed to grab it and clumsily tied it around the girl's waist, then holding onto the loop around the girl with one hand and the rope's end with the other, he yelled out to Arthur to pull them.

They all stood in a line behind Arthur to secure the rope from their end as Arthur hauled the rope to the bank.

Chapter V

Betrayal

Arthur used his weight to anchor the rope near the edge of the river. The others were behind him, feet struggling to get a good grip in the muddy ground, their hands and backs taking the strain as they pulled, fingers burning against the tension of the rough rope as they walked it hand over hand behind them. It was hard going and Sarah and Tom could feel the wet fibres imprinting themselves into their hands, forming blisters. Neither of them was used to such rough work. Eventually the two bedraggled figures were hauled to the bank, and Arthur remained as the anchor while Tom ran to the side of the river to help pull them to safety. He took the girl's hand and dragged her up onto the reeds. Despite her heavy, water-sodden and over-sized jumper, she somehow felt as fragile as a bird. She murmured something that sounded grateful and slumped on the grass. When he turned to the boy though, he brusquely brushed him aside and pulled himself up onto the edge beside the girl.

While Tom and Arthur stayed behind to gather up the rope, Mary helped the girl to her feet and led her away towards the house. She had long, dark hair and a thin face. She was all angles jutting out even beneath the heavy jumper. The boy got up and followed them, a few steps behind Sarah. She tried to engage him in conversation, asking him his name and where he came from, and after a while he fell into step beside her. Tom noticed and didn't like the way he so obviously looked her up and down before deciding to walk with her. It made him feel uncomfortable in a protective way that he wasn't used to. The boy was good looking if you liked that slightly 'bad boy' style—he seemed to be somehow casual, but confident, with a bit of a swagger, and so different to the way Tom felt about himself. How did guys like that find it so easy with girls? Why did girls get sucked into them?

Once inside, Mary took them straight upstairs to warm up in the bath and change into the clothes she'd accumulated over the past two years for Sarah's return, and others she found in Arthur's wardrobe, since the boy was taller than Tom. Sarah filled Arthur and Tom in on what she'd managed to find out. They were called Kayla and Jonnie, and noticing that their accent was similar to Tom's, only stronger, she hadn't been surprised to find out that they were from New Zealand. From Auckland, in fact. They'd been swept into a cave by a wave and found themselves in the river above Riverstone. She hadn't said much to Jonnie about where they were, as she thought it needed to be a discussion they all had together. Although he'd been nice to her, he seemed to be struggling with what had happened, coming across as confused and angry.

When Mary came back downstairs, she apologised to Sarah and Tom for having to let Jonnie and Kayla use their bedrooms to change in and to wait for each other while they bathed. She'd found Kayla quite subdued, probably in shock, cold and shaky.

"She didn't really want me to help her getting changed—

she seemed self-conscious, but I did notice that she's very thin, just skin and bones. Jonnie seems quite... maybe... belligerent? Seems to have a bit of a chip on his shoulder. He bristled at any suggestion that I could help him. He's very protective and concerned about Kayla though—she's his sister. I found out that she's fourteen and he's seventeen. He's demanding to know where they are, so I suggested they wait until they're both changed, then we'll talk to them together over something to eat."

Arthur went off to the kitchen to make scrambled eggs to go with Mary's freshly baked grainy bread. When Jonnie and Kayla came downstairs, Jonnie tucked in as if he was famished. Kayla looked at her plate suspiciously, then cut one piece of toast into little squares. She cautiously put one piece, with a bit of egg on top, into her mouth and chewed it for what seemed like ages. Mary fully expected her to find a reason not to have more, and was surprised when she continued eating, a strange expression on her face, as if she suddenly realised she was hungry and wasn't used to how that felt. She didn't eat a lot but told Mary it was the nicest food she'd had in ages.

Hermione wandered into the room and went straight over to jump up on the couch between Sarah and Arthur, looking Kayla and Jonnie up and down. She'd watched them being hauled out of the river, keeping her distance for a while to see what happened.

"Don't like cats! Keep it away from me!" Jonnie said. Kayla looked a little afraid of her, her body language pulling away so that she looked even more turned in on herself than before.

"She won't hurt you, she's really friendly," Sarah said, stroking Hermione's head.

"Sarah, Tom, *don't* tell these two about Ryder or me," cautioned Hermione. "We don't know yet whether they can be trusted. The less people who know the better!"

Sarah sent back a thought message affirming that they'd be careful, wondering what Hermione was picking up from them.

When the conversation paused, Jonnie abruptly asked, "So where are we then? This is really weird. We were at the beach, then suddenly we find ourselves here, in the countryside, being fished out of a river."

Tom hesitantly replied, "Well you'll find this hard to believe—I did too. You're not in Auckland any more, you've somehow slipped through a rift into a parallel world to a place called North Feasgar. Sarah and I both came here, me from Auckland and Sarah from England, a bit over two years ago. The Birches came here years ago from England."

Jonnie frowned and kicked Kayla under the table. "Sounds like a right story."

"No, it's true," Sarah added. "Tom fell down a bank and hit his head on a rock in a stream, and I found him unconscious on the edge of the same river you were in. The Birches came through an opening in a hillside." She didn't say anything about her own arrival and hoped they wouldn't ask. It was even harder to explain how she'd got here through her imagination and she didn't think it would help them at all in trying to accept the situation. They were both looking really dubious and confused as it was. There was a long pause, with no one knowing what to say next.

"Yeah right… pull the other one!" said Jonnie sarcastically.

"Now tell us where we really are and how we can get out of here!" When no one answered him, he pushed his chair back angrily, screeching its legs on the floor, and stomped out of the room and out the back door of the house. Kayla went to follow him, but Mary put a hand on her arm to stop her.

"Kayla, leave him be. He'll have to work this out in his own way and he won't thank you for interfering."

***

A couple of hours went by, with Mary doing her best to make conversation with Kayla, while Tom and Sarah helped Arthur to stack more firewood. Kayla looked like she'd break if she did any physical work, so Mary encouraged her to help with cooking dinner and was surprised to see how adept she was.

"You've obviously done this before," she commented.

"Had to—I had to look after myself or starve. I wasn't going to eat the rubbish my mum sometimes thought to eat, so I did anything I could to make the budget stretch to healthy food."

"Sounds like you've had a difficult time?" Mary invited, but Kayla self-consciously clammed up and wouldn't say anything more.

When they were ready, Mary sent her off to find Jonnie. She wandered outside and along the river bank, eventually finding him sitting on a rocky outcrop—he seemed to be carving a piece of wood with a knife he'd probably taken from Riverstone.

"I didn't know you could do that!"

"Dan showed me how. Makes me feel better." He held out

his hand to reveal a small figure that looked like it was going to be a man.

"Hey, that's good! Come on, I've been sent to fetch you for dinner."

"Kayla, what are we going to do? We can't stay here!"

"Why not? At least until we work things out. The Birches are nice."

"Suffocatingly nice! And I don't want to be out in goodness only knows where in the countryside. What are we supposed to do? How do we get back?"

"Why do you even want to go back? There's nothing for us there, just a grubby suburb and no decent place to live. No one cares about us!"

"My friends do!"

"But you can't stay with them forever. And how would you earn enough to rent a place of your own?"

"At least whatever I do there is my own choice. I never asked to come here!" With that, he got up and strode off towards Riverstone, Kayla trailing behind him wondering how to persuade him to calm down and give the place a chance.

He was silent throughout dinner and wouldn't respond when the others tried to draw him into the conversation.

"We want the two of you to know that you can stay here as long as it takes for you to sort something out, to get your bearings," ventured Arthur. At that, Jonnie gave an exasperated exclamation and left the table again, slamming the door as he left the house.

"What's up with Jonnie? He seems so tense," said Tom.

"I don't really know. I think he's just confused. He'll probably tell me later. I guess he's never been in a household with guys in it before. He's gotten used to telling me and my mum what to do. Maybe he feels awkward, or he's lost his sense of where he fits."

As Jonnie walked down the path, he felt restless and agitated. He paced backwards and forwards outside the gate for a time before striding across the field towards the river. He could feel something rippling inside him that it was hard to describe. It felt like he was being stifled, trapped and he had a huge impulse to run away, to get out, to scream. His whole body felt enraged and he didn't know how to contain it. He was *so* angry! He didn't know what was taking him over, but it was all focused on the Birches—they were trying to trap him with their 'niceness'. He wanted to knock their contentment and complacency away from them. He wanted to hurt them! He wanted to hit something, but instead kicked a fallen tree, yelping as his toes screamed at him, with pain searing through his foot and up his leg. He grabbed his foot, hopping around trying to rub away the pain, but lost his balance and toppled over onto the soggy ground. Shit! He sat on the ground, suddenly deflated and feeling sorry for himself. He wanted to cry but he forced it away—he wouldn't be a wuss, a girl! He sat there, on the wet ground until he thought everyone would have gone to bed, then slowly made his way inside. There was no sign of anyone. He changed into the pyjamas left out for him and crawled into his bed made up on the mattress on the floor of Tom's room.

***

The next day he emerged, subdued, and did his best not to interact with anyone. His silence was leaden and eventually they could no longer bear it.

"Arthur, why don't we take them for a drive to Hunterdale," Tom suggested, "then they can see we're in a different world, that it's nothing like New Zealand, and not much like England either, even though the houses look a bit more like they do there. The market's on in Hunterdale today."

"Okay, good idea, let's go now before I get engrossed in work. Make sure you all have jackets—you four will have to ride on the back of the truck. Mary, do we have some spare?"

Arthur went off ahead to the truck while Mary locked the doors. In the back, Kayla huddled against the cab, not saying much. Jonnie looked around him as they drove, asking questions. He was sitting by Sarah, and made a point of addressing her, not Tom. Tom felt himself getting more and more cross and decided to try to draw Kayla into conversation.

"Kayla, are you okay? You look like you're cold."

"Yeah, I'm all right. It's so weird though, I'm just taking it in and trying to make sense of it."

"Will you have people worrying about you at home?"

Kayla gave a short laugh that came out a bit like a bark. "Hah, no chance! My mum had more or less kicked Jonnie out and I didn't want to stay without him. It'll be a couple of days, if she manages to be sober for a while, before she even notices I've gone!"

Tom grimaced. It sounded all too familiar. Another dysfunctional family to add to their ideas about who slipped through the rift. "That's pretty much like me. My mum would have noticed but wouldn't have done anything about it until my stepfather said she could. Too late if I'd actually been harmed! He'd think good riddance anyway. I had to leave my sister behind though…" His voice trailed off as he thought about

Leah. He still felt sad about her and how she'd have worried about him, but he was grateful to know from Sarah that she'd moved away from home – a long way out of reach – and had a boyfriend.

They'd just driven past the turn-off to the tree house and Tom heard Sarah talking to Jonnie about it. *Don't say too much,* he thought. He didn't trust Jonnie—he looked like a bit of a chancer, a chancer with a chip on his shoulder, though he could see, knowing a fraction more about them both from Kayla, why he might be like that. All 'bluff and bolshy.' Where did that expression come from? Maybe his grandparents? He watched Jonnie putting his hand on Sarah's arm as he made a point and felt a wave of jealousy. Sarah was *his* friend! And she'd only just come back—he hadn't even had a real chance to talk to her himself.

***

The town was bustling with market day buyers and sellers. With the truck parked a few streets away from the town square, they walked together towards the centre. Jonnie and Kayla's heads swivelled as they checked out their new surroundings, fascinated by the steam escaping through vents in the gutters.

"It reminds me of Rotorua!" remarked Kayla.

"Yes, but it doesn't seem the same as the really smelly sulphur in Rotorua, it's more like it's just steam," Tom added. When they got to the market, Mary and Arthur left them with instructions not to leave the square and went off to do some business elsewhere.

"Why did they insist we stayed here?" Jonnie asked after they'd gone. "Looks like a pretty harmless, bland sort of a place to me."

"They have their reasons—we've all been warned about the arrival of some strangers lately," Tom replied.

"Oh no, not strangers!" said Jonnie sarcastically. "How upsetting for a peaceful little backwater!"

"What, so where you're from is so much more exciting is it? What suburb did you say you lived in? Somewhere out in west Auckland?"

"Stop it you two," Sarah broke in. "Tom, I've just spotted Corrin and Gwynn at that stall over there. You know, the ones I told you about who helped me on my way back to the treehouse. Come with me and I'll introduce you... If they remember me!"

"Think I'll go for a wander on my own," Jonnie announced, breaking away from their group and leaving Kayla to tag on and follow the other two.

Sarah led the way across the square to a stall selling leather goods. A slight woman with fair hair was behind the stall, while a stocky man was reaching up to hang leather bags from hooks arranged around the frame of the stall.

"Gwynn, Corrin, do you remember me?" Sarah called out to them as she covered the short distance between them. Gwynn dropped the things she was holding and rushed over to her, giving her a hug.

"Do we remember you? We've so often wondered what happened to you and whether you were all right! Look Corrin, it's Sarah!"

Corrin gave her such a hug that she was swept off her feet.

"Well you're looking in a much better state than the last time we saw you, and so grown up!" he exclaimed.

Sarah introduced them to Tom, then Tom hurriedly included Kayla, wondering at Sarah forgetting her. As Sarah talked animatedly to them, Tom drew Kayla away, saying to Sarah that he'd show her around and they could meet up on the other side of the square. The smell of food was enticing and Tom asked Kayla if she'd like anything. She frowned and looked away. Tom drew a breath and decided to risk saying something.

"Hey Kayla, I'm not sure how to say this right, but are you okay about eating? Can I help at all? I've had my own problems around eating."

"Really?" her attention caught, "What do you mean?"

"Well, when I was at home, it always felt unsafe, so I made kind of rituals around eating. Like, what I had to do before I ate anything, when it was okay, when it wasn't, and developed sort of magical thinking around it that I linked to being safe or not safe. I didn't really realise until I got here how obsessive I was getting."

"Yeah, well my place was shit. And that's what food in my house tasted like! I can eat stuff I choose myself, good food, but not the stuff my mother dishes up!"

"So, something like food being about your mum—bad mother, bad food?"

"Yes! And I got so used to it and trying to control how much shit I had to take in that when I got here I was completely shocked at how good that egg tasted. I think I'd forgotten how to actually taste anything and it caught me by surprise!"

"Mary and Arthur are really good, kind people. They'd have been brilliant parents if they'd had children. They've kind of adopted me and I think they're wonderful."

"I only have Jonnie and I don't really know what's he's up to most of the time, though he always looks out for me."

Soon after, the Birches reappeared with Sarah, who was talking excitedly to them about Corrin and Gwynn. They set out together to find Jonnie and spotted him on the other side of the square. Tom thought that he looked almost reluctant to join them.

***

Jonnie had wandered through the stalls. The waft of the smell of food from a pastry stall made his mouth water, and before he really realised what he'd done, he slipped a triangular pastry into his pocket. He sauntered away from the stall and stuffed it in his mouth – an apple turnover – it was so good; tart and flaky! He walked on past a place that was selling barbequed meat on skewers. He managed to grab one while the stall owner was serving someone else, but almost dropped it. Clumsy! He managed to stop it hitting the ground and quickly covered it with his jacket. The next minute he felt a heavy hand grabbing the back of his collar.

"What was that about?" A tall, rangy man with grey streaked hair was holding him with a steely grip. Jonnie mumbled something incoherent. "You can do better than that," the man added. "Watch and learn!" He wandered past a stall selling loaves of bread, 'accidently' knocking against a pyramid of small bread rolls, sending some of them tumbling onto the bench. "Sorry!" he said to the stall owner, while at the same time, as soon as her attention was on the rolls, palming a small loaf of bread. As he walked off, he tore it in half and tossed a piece to Jonnie. "If you're going to steal, do it with finesse, and don't get caught! Haven't seen you around these parts before. Where are you from?"

"Auckland," Jonnie replied.

"Where's that? Up north somewhere?"

"In New Zealand?" Jonnie said hesitantly.

"Never heard of it! Where are you staying?"

"We just arrived, my sister and me. We fell in a river and Mary and Arthur Birch hauled us out, so they're the only people we know here so far."

"Hmmm, the Birches... Do they have any kids staying with them?"

"Sarah and Tom?"

"Yeah, they're the ones. Bad lot they are. You'd do best to move on from there..."

"Why?" Jonnie asked, "They've been kind to us."

"That Sarah, she stole something very valuable from me, and they all helped her to keep me from getting it back. Arthur is a brute—he's violent!"

Jonnie looked puzzled. That didn't sound like the people he'd met. "But we don't know anyone here, so we don't have anywhere else to go."

"You can stay at my place for a bit if you want. I live on my own and could do with some company. You can bring your sister if you like—you'd have to share a room mind; it has a single bed and a mattress. You couldn't say anything about it to the Birches though, there's not much love lost between us!"

Jonnie felt flattered that the man was asking him to stay. He was a tough looking man and was really dextrous and strong, the kind of man he admired.

"Why don't you come back tomorrow with your sister and come to my place. All I'll need you to do for your keep is a few errands when I need you to. Nothing you can't manage easily. Can your sister cook? Could do with someone to look after things."

"Yes, she can, but don't put it like that to her, or she's likely to say no. She can be a bit stroppy. She'll be happy to do it though if she thinks it's her idea. How do we find your place?"

"I live at 55 Cross Street—see the Town Hall over there? That's the street running along the side of it. Willard's the name." He looked about him, then suddenly said, "Got to go!" and walked away quickly. A minute later Jonnie noticed the others come into view, clearly looking for him.

Jonnie felt confused. He didn't feel comfortable staying at the Birches, they were too old and 'parenty', too nice, too ordinary, and he thought staying with them would be boring. He felt a bit bad about his overreaction yesterday though—he'd been caught up in something he wasn't sure about, and it had been scary, like a bottomless rage. Yet here was this man saying they were thieves and violent. He didn't have too much problem with that, but it didn't add up. The man, Willard, though, was appealing. He offered something enticing and exciting. He couldn't quite put his finger on it, but it was like a pull to something dark and powerful that might mean he didn't have to live the hard and small life he'd had at home. He'd never had anyone to look up to and he thought maybe Willard could teach him a thing or two about how to get on in this strange world. It was completely weird being in this place, but maybe it was a chance to create something new for himself. He didn't think for a moment that

Kayla would fit into a life at Willard's though. She was too anxious, having been so damaged by their mum, but he'd worry about what to do with her later. He wouldn't just abandon her until she had somewhere where she'd be okay.

***

That afternoon back at Riverstone, Jonnie tried to find time to talk to Kayla alone. Annoyingly, she seemed to be sticking close to Tom and repeated attempts to extract her didn't work. He grew more and more frustrated. Tom seemed to have it all. The Birches clearly adored him, Sarah liked him, even the cat was all over him and now his sister! The more he thought about it, the more he wanted to do something nasty like kick the cat, but even the cat was onto him and hissed when he walked past.

Eventually, just to rile everyone, he waited until Sarah walked past, when he knew Tom could see and he grabbed her and kissed her. She was so shocked she didn't know what to do. She put her fingers to her lips as Jonnie sauntered off, her face flushed. She turned and saw Tom watching and went bright red with embarrassment. Seeing the thunderous look on his face, she awkwardly tried to tell him it meant nothing, but he wouldn't stop to listen and walked off, leaving her words hanging in the air.

Jonnie went outside and found Kayla leaning on the gate at the end of the garden path, looking distractedly over towards the river.

"What's up?" he asked.

"Isn't this weird?" she responded. "I don't know what to

make of it. It's so hard to believe what we're seeing, that somehow, we've slipped into a different world. I keep moving between wanting to be really happy that we're out of that dreadful house, and complete overwhelm that makes me want to curl up in a corner and pretend I don't exist."

"Well don't get too comfortable here with the Birches. The four of them are wrapped up together and we're obviously intruding—Tom and Sarah don't want us here. Sarah doesn't like you and Tom's just being nice to you to get Sarah jealous."

"How do you know Sarah doesn't like me?"

"She told me," he lied.

Kayla's face went still and she swallowed nervously, feeling even worse suddenly than before. She'd thought that she'd be safe here for a while until they knew what was happening to them—the Birches were kind to her.

"Don't worry though—I think I have a solution. I met a guy at the market today who told me some things about them that I don't think you'd like at all, and he seemed to think he could help us out."

"Like what sort of things?"

"He said they'd stolen something from him, and that Arthur was violent! I didn't get the chance to ask for details because you all came along and he left, but not before he asked whether we'd like to stay with him for a bit. He said he could find me some work."

"Really? Well that'd be good. We're going to have to find something to do if we can't find our way out of here, but I'm not sure I'm ready to leave the Birches yet. I don't believe for a minute they're like what that man says."

"Well I've decided to go and I want you to come with me. We have to stick together—we're all we have from our past."

"Can we wait a few days?" she replied nervously.

"No. He told me to meet him tomorrow. I don't want to miss the opportunity. I just came to tell you that I'm going to go early tomorrow morning, before the others are up—you'll need to decide by the time we go to bed tonight so we can plan. And don't say anything to the others!"

Kayla felt a bit sick. Everything had happened so fast and she didn't feel like she was keeping up with all the changes. On the one hand Jonnie was the only family she had, other than her wasted mum, and he'd always looked after her; on the other, she instinctively knew that staying with the Birches was safe, and being part of any of Jonnie's schemes was never that! While she was thinking about it, he'd wandered over to where Tom's bike was parked close to the house and was looking it over.

"Jonnie," she called over to him. "If I go with you and it doesn't work out, can we come back?"

"Of course we can. When we've got away, we'll send the Birches a note and thank them for saving us and ask whether we can keep in touch." He had no intention of doing anything of the sort, but he'd worry about that later. "I only want to leave secretly so they don't put pressure on you and talk you out of it."

***

At dinner that evening Kayla felt too anxious to eat.

"Kayla, are you okay?" Mary asked, seeing her huddled in her chair, head down, looking at the floor.

"I don't know…"

"Why don't you have a little to eat?"

"I don't feel well. I'm really worried about where I am and what happens now. I don't want to be at home, but I have nowhere here that's mine... Can I go back if I want to?"

"Well, there is a way, but I suggest you think carefully before deciding. Like, what if Jonnie doesn't want to go too? What would that be like for you? What would you be going back to? People coming here seem to be ready to leave some aspect of their life. Do you want to go back?"

"No. It's awful there, with my mum. But then, maybe... I don't have anything here either, only Jonnie. At least there I have my room, my things, my school, things that I know. I really don't know what to do."

"Look Kayla, we'll work something out with you. You can stay in Sarah's room for now, but we'll work out something more permanent if you want to stay in North Feasgar."

"But Sarah doesn't want me in her room."

"Whatever makes you say that? She's a kind girl and would never want you to be left with nowhere to go."

Jonnie, sitting beside Kayla, overheard this conversation. He felt agitated and restless. He wanted Kayla to go with him but was getting increasingly impatient with her for being scared. If she didn't want to go, what would he do? He didn't think he could just leave her, but neither did he want her to stop him from doing what he wanted. Why didn't he ever have it easy? He was so sick of how things had turned out for him and of feeling powerless to change them. He always had anger simmering under the surface, eating away at the corners of his self-control. He'd really lost it a few weeks ago over something so stupid that he felt ashamed to even think about it.

He'd been at the mall waiting for Mike in the carpark so he could have a cigarette when a car with a souped-up engine had cruised past. A bunch of guys were hanging out the windows, yelling insults at him, pretty indiscriminate and stupid, like 'gay boy loser'. But the one thing that really got to him was being called Palagi in a derogatory way. Something about being labelled as a white boy, implying privilege, thinking too much of himself, thinking he was superior, not knowing what it was like to have a hard time… Having just come from an awful row at home, yet again having only breakfasted on abuse, rage overtook him. They had no idea about him or his life! How dare they see him like that! He'd tracked where they parked their car, and when they went into the mall, he'd found it and scraped deep gouges into the shiny black paint with his keys. He felt full of adrenalin for a short time, but then suddenly he'd deflated. What had he done? He'd vandalised someone's car, in a way that would cost a fortune to repair. He'd given into the chip on his shoulder and had proved to them he was worthy of their contempt. He didn't even know if they were judging him in that way—he was totally capable of doing that to himself! He couldn't even leave a number or anything so he could make amends—he couldn't pay for it if they rang and didn't want them to trace him and take revenge.

He'd got out of there quickly, texting Mike to say he couldn't make it. He'd gone to the park and just walked, trying to quiet his guilt. He hated being out of control like that, like he'd been last night. It was really scary, and deep down he knew he'd stepped over a line from the stupid things he'd done in the past, to something that he really felt shameful about.

He didn't want to rethink all this now. His foot was jumping up and down on the floor and he found his hands clenched into fists beside him. His breathing had become fast and shallow. He got up from the table abruptly and went outside, where he sat on the bottom step and tried to calm himself by watching the shades of the sky shifting into darkness, settling into a deep indigo. It was too overcast to see the stars, but the air felt pure and fresh. He breathed in the silence deeply—so different to his suburb at home.

It took him a while to notice a dark shape circling overhead. It descended lower and lower until he could make out the shape of a large bird. It called and he saw a shadow moving near him, making him start, before he realised it was just the cat. It was as if she was responding to the call. How odd. The bird sank gracefully down to land beside her. It looked like an eagle, maybe a hawk, something large anyway. He'd never been very good with birds, not having much more than sparrows in his neighbourhood. It was weird the way Hermione seemed to be communicating with it. He went back inside to tell the others.

"Ryder," exclaimed Sarah, running for the door. As she and Tom raced out to talk to the bird, Jonnie watched on, outwardly sneering at the fuss they were making of him, but inwardly wondering at the connection they seemed to have with both the bird and the cat.

***

Tom woke up early the following morning, instantly alert, as if something had pulled him out of his dreams. Everything was quiet though, and he tried to get back to sleep. But his mind kept wandering to think about Jonnie and Kayla. Something was niggling, jostling to find its way into his consciousness. Eventually he turned over to where Jonnie had his mattress on the floor, only to see that the bed was empty. That was odd, where could he be at this hour of the morning? He got out of bed and walked down the corridor to Sarah's room, quietly opening the door, and poking his head around it to look inside. Kayla's mattress was empty as well!

"Sarah, Sarah, wake up!" he whispered. Sarah mumbled and turned over, her back to the door. He went into the room and shook her gently.

"What is it?"

"Shhh… It's just me, Tom. Jonnie and Kayla seem to have gone somewhere—do you know where they might be?"

"What?" She sat up, suddenly wide awake. "But they went to bed last night and Kayla and I were talking about finding her some books to read today. Maybe they've gone down for an early breakfast."

"Come downstairs with me and we'll look," said Tom. "Arthur will be up soon anyway, so we don't really need to worry too much about waking him or Mary."

They went quietly downstairs, but the lights were out and there was no one there. They heard scratching at the door and Tom let Hermione in.

"What are you two doing up so early?" she asked.

"Jonnie and Kayla have gone out early, which is a bit odd…" said Sarah.

"So maybe that's why your bike has gone Tom—I thought it was strange that it wasn't in its usual place."

"What? What are you saying Hermione? I haven't loaned it

to them. Are you telling me it isn't in the back garden?"

"No, it's not there. I've just come back from the river, in through the garden."

Tom ran through the house and out the back door. Sure enough, the place he parked his bike, on a square of pebbles by the path, was bare.

"How dare he!" cried Tom. "After us pulling them out of the stream and making them at home—how dare he steal my bike! And Kayla! I thought she liked me!" Right at that minute, that felt like even more of a betrayal than Jonnie—at least he knew Jonnie had no time for him.

Sarah and Hermione had joined him in the garden and a few minutes later Arthur and Mary appeared, still in their pyjamas, looking rumpled, having woken up when Tom cried out. As he explained to them what had happened, he suddenly realised what had been bothering him since the previous day... There had been a man walking away from Jonnie when they found him in the market – tall, a bit rough, unruly grey-streaked hair – could it have been Willard? Could he have been talking to Jonnie? That would make some sort of weird sense out of their disappearance. He didn't say anything out loud right then because it seemed a bit far-fetched, but it oddly sat with him as a kind of 'knowing'—the sort of thing Sarah sometimes felt. Mary and Arthur went inside to get dressed, saying they would talk over breakfast.

As Tom and Sarah walked slowly back to the house, Tom couldn't help himself voicing some of his annoyance about Jonnie.

"You didn't know anything about what they were

planning?"

"No! Why would I?" Sarah responded indignantly.

"Well you and Jonnie have been looking pretty cosy…"

"What about you and Kayla then?"

"I've been trying to talk to her because you and Jonnie are so obviously into each other and I think she's been feeling left out."

"We haven't talked that much…"

"So, do you like him then?" It was like he had to know, even though he didn't want to.

"What do you mean by that? He's easy to talk to and I guess he's good looking… But I hadn't thought any more about him than that. What you saw yesterday was a complete surprise to me. I think he did it to annoy you!"

"He doesn't like me. He won't even talk to me directly."

"I think that's something to do with having had no father, or any other male to grow up with. Suddenly he's in a household with both you and Arthur and he doesn't know what to do with that. He's probably trying to find his place."

"So, is it a bit the same with you and Kayla?" Tom asked. "You don't talk to her."

"Well, maybe. But she's weird, and she's so skinny like a stick insect!"

"That's really mean, she can't help it—she's had a tough time and you shouldn't pick on how someone looks!"

"So, because she's had a hard time, you think you can 'help' her," Sarah said sarcastically.

"Well at least I can be nice to her and try to understand."

Sarah flounced off quickly so Tom wouldn't see the redness of shame suffusing up her neck and over her face. He was right, she was being mean having a go at Kayla's appearance. But there was something about her she really didn't like; Kayla got under her skin and Sarah hated it that she brought out the worst, bitchy side of her. Maybe it was something about the way Kayla drew all the attention to herself by making people feel sorry for her. It didn't feel very 'clean' somehow, though Sarah didn't really know what she meant by that. And she had to admit that maybe, just possibly, she didn't like the way Kayla was taking Tom's attention away from her when they hadn't even had a chance to reconnect with each other.

Tom was left standing on the garden path with Hermione.

"Goodness, you two need to stop bickering!" She looked up at him with an expression he could swear looked smug and somehow knowing, and sauntered off towards the field to continue her morning hunt.

Inside, when they were sitting around the table, Tom talked to them about thinking he may have seen Willard the previous day.

"What do we do now?" he asked.

"What *can* we do? I suppose we could drive past his place and see if we can see Jonnie and Kayla there?" suggested Sarah.

"What good would that do? I'll bet they won't be leaving the bike outside so I can take it back again."

"Don't forget," said Arthur, "that they don't know that we've made the connection between them and Willard. They won't even be thinking that you may know where they are."

"Actually, we have something more important to think about. I mean, it's a pain about the bike, but I had another dream last night that was really insistent. I think we're being pushed to act sooner than we thought; or at least, I know that I hadn't really thought through that we wouldn't have much time once I got here." Sarah looked really serious and the others focused on what she was saying.

"Tell us your dream Sarah," Mary encouraged.

"Well, Tom and I were being chased, I don't know what by, but it was scary. We found a path into some woods and ran deeper and deeper until we realised everything had gone quiet. We couldn't hear anyone chasing us any more, all we could hear was our breathing. We walked a bit further and found a small clearing that had two tall stone pillars in it. Suddenly an apparition appeared between them – I think it looked like the woman on my tarot card – the High Priestess. She told us that we had to hurry, there was no time for delay because our task was urgent. She told us to find the tunnel—when she said that, I could kind of pick out an image in the background behind her of an opening in a rock face and had the idea it was a mountain. She said once we found it, to enter, not to linger anywhere, no matter what we saw. Each time there was a choice of direction we were to take the left, and to be brave. As her image faded, I woke up..."

"Do you remember anything more about the mountain?" Arthur asked.

"Not really... the thing about the mountain was just a sort of thought picture—I think it was a mountain on its own, so it wouldn't be the mountain range up north. That means it's probably Greyvyn unless there are others I don't know about."

"Well Greyvyn is more or less on the border of North and South Feasgar, so that would make sense if there is a threat to the barrier. Why don't we send Ryder to have a scout around and see if he can see anything that looks like a tunnel entrance?"

"Good idea!" Mary agreed. "Sarah, can you call him and let him know that we might have to make a trip there in the next few days and to keep a look out for us?"

***

"I think we need to be really careful with Jonnie and Kayla," Mary said to them later in the day. "If we see them again, and I wouldn't be at all surprised if they come back, we need to keep everything about the two of you being here for a purpose, to ourselves. It's highly likely that Willard will send them to find out what we're up to and report back to him."

"I don't know that he has anything to do with those strangers, but I wouldn't trust him not to be working with them," Tom replied.

"I don't think Kayla would knowingly get caught up with him, but I reckon Jonnie would; he's impressionable, and Kayla will go along with Jonnie," said Arthur.

"She doesn't have anyone else, and as she's said, he's the only one who's ever looked out for her," added Tom.

Sarah reached out and took Tom's hand. "So, it's up to the four of us then, together, just as we always knew it would be. Oops, sorry Hermione, the six of us!"

Tom felt a lump in his throat at Sarah's touch. Unexpected emotions welled up inside him, and he knew that he and Sarah didn't need to talk any more about how they'd been feeling since she arrived—they'd be okay. He swallowed, and as he looked up, caught Arthur and Mary exchanging a knowing look. He wasn't sure what that meant, but he suddenly felt warm and accepted, and let out a big sigh.

Chapter VI

Working for Their Keep

Kayla tossed and turned all night. She felt horribly conflicted. She'd felt safer with the Birches than she'd ever felt before, even though she didn't have a clue where she actually was. She also realised that she only knew the half of the scrapes Jonnie had got into in the past, so she had no reason to trust that he was making the right decision for them both. But at the same time, she couldn't bear the idea of him going without her, of him leaving her, being left with no connection in a strange land. And what if she never saw him again? What should she do?

It didn't feel as if she slept at all, but she probably dozed off, because she was woken at first light by a light touch on her shoulder. Jonnie put his hand over her mouth to remind her to be quiet and looked questioningly at her in the pale morning light. She hadn't come to a decision during the long night, but suddenly, with him there beside her, she knew she had to go with him and she nodded. Clambering up off the mattress, she gathered her meagre possessions—the clothes she'd arrived in and the ones Mary had given her yesterday. While Jonnie waited downstairs for her, she went silently into the bathroom to change out of her pyjamas, and took one of the cloth laundry bags hanging on the back of the bathroom door to put her clothes in.

She carefully went down the stairs, trying to be as quiet as possible. There was no sound of anyone waking. Jonnie was standing at the bottom of the stairs, having already raided the kitchen for some bread and fruit for them to take for breakfast. No sign of anyone, including the cat! They noiselessly let themselves out the back door—Kayla looked at Jonnie questioningly as he made his way to Tom's bike.

"Well we have to get to Hunterdale somehow, don't we?" Jonnie whispered. "Don't worry, I'll give it back to him later." As quietly as he could, he wheeled it down the path, through the gate and out onto the road. The pebbles of the path scrunched under the wheels, but there was still no sign of any movement from the house.

They pushed the bike a little way down the road before Jonnie tried to start it. It had a push button that he figured must be the starter button—how weird! He pushed it a couple of times and eventually it coughed and belched before settling into a quiet whirr, unlike any bike he'd ridden before. He was glad none of his mates were here – it was more like a trike really – they'd have laughed. Swinging his leg over at the front, he sat on the seat, while Kayla clambered up onto the box at the back, which seemed to house the motor, sitting on it with one leg either side of Jonnie. She held onto him tightly as he worked out where the brake and throttle were. It didn't take him long to sort it out, and he let off the brake and started off down the road—it drove smoothly, gathering momentum as he turned the throttle on the handlebar.

Although the road had a gravel surface, it wasn't difficult to ride on. It was packed down hard through frequent use, making it an easy drive through the half-light to Hunterdale. By the time they approached the town, the sun was starting to come up and it looked rather beautiful as it illuminated the dark shapes of the buildings and trees, with whisps of steam eerily drifting, pearl grey, up into the lightening sky. Kayla automatically raised her wrist to glance at her watch, but she'd forgotten that it was dead from being dunked in the sea yesterday. It wouldn't have helped her anyway. The time had to be different here, since they'd left their world towards evening, but had arrived in the afternoon.

Hunterdale was strangely quiet. They'd only passed a couple of vehicles. Maybe they didn't have the market every day, or there would have been people arriving to set up their stalls. They drove through to the village square, which was empty—such a contrast to the bustle of yesterday. Jonnie drove the bike across the square and parked it near a bench nestled between the square and a copse of trees. They sat side by side on the bench trying to catch up with all that had happened to them in the last twenty-four hours.

"Look, isn't that the bird that was at the watermill yesterday?"

"Well, it's a hawk, but there are bound to be plenty around with all the mountains and forests," Jonnie replied.

"Wasn't it odd though, the way it seemed to be communicating with the cat?" asked Kayla. "I thought birds and cats were aggressive with each other, though I wouldn't be surprised if a hawk came out better rather than the other way around. Did you see its talons?"

"Everything in this place is odd, especially how we even

got here! Why don't we walk around the town and check it out—we can't go to Willard's too early."

They pushed the bike into the cover of the trees and set off on foot. There were now a few people around and some of the shops surrounding the square had lights on and were showing signs of opening.

They found Cross Street easily and wandered down the road to locate Willard's house. The curtains were still pulled across the windows, and the house—a grey stone bungalow with a dark-blue door, looked like it was sleeping. They walked on, turning right, heading back parallel to Market Road, past a park, where they sat for a while on some swings before continuing. Eventually the road took them to the river where there was quite a bit of early morning activity. A few boats were heading off down river and canoes were being dragged out of a shed onto the river bank by a burly looking man, dressed in a heavy woollen jumper and waterproof trousers. Kayla shivered as she imagined how cold the water in the river would be.

Heading back towards the square down a different road that they found on the far side of the bridge, they came across a school. It looked like a high school, with a few students wandering towards it, bags slung over their shoulders—Kayla imagined it would be the school Tom went to. As they got close to the gates, she noticed a couple of boys leaning against the wall staring intently at them.

"Well that was freaky," she commented once they'd walked past.

"What was?" asked Jonnie. He hadn't noticed anything—he'd been looking in the opposite direction, at a bakery on the other side of the road. His mouth was watering at the enticing smells wafting towards him and his stomach rumbled.

When they got back to the centre of the town, they wheeled the bike over the rough cobbles of the square to Cross Street, then once again along the road to Willard's house, parking it outside. Jonnie walked up the steps and rapped loudly on the door. They waited... No response. He was about to try again when they heard footsteps and the door was suddenly yanked open.

"What is it? What do you want?" Willard's voice was aggressive, but when he recognised Jonnie, his grim expression softened a little. "Oh, it's you. Come in then."

Jonnie walked into the house, ignoring Kayla, who was tugging on his sleeve and whispering that she didn't like it—she didn't want to go in. He shook her off quite roughly and she ended up reluctantly following him.

The living area was dimly lit by a rectangle of light coming from the partly open door of the kitchen. The curtains were still pulled across the windows. Willard turned to face them and Jonnie introduced him to Kayla. He put out his hand and Kayla, again reluctantly, extended hers, pulling it away again as soon as his rough clasp released her. She felt a strong physical repulsion to his shambolic appearance and the stale smell coming off his skin and abruptly turned away, looking around the room to cover her consternation. In the half-light it felt oppressive and Willard's tall presence in it was menacing.

He led them down a corridor, opening the door of a room and switching on the light. It was a bedroom minimally furnished with a single bed, a chair and a wardrobe. It smelt stuffy, as if it was rarely used, the skirting boards were dusty and the worn carpet sported unattractive stains she really didn't want to think about!

"I'm not set up for visitors, but I'll bring a mattress. You can draw straws for it!" He clapped Jonnie on the shoulder – he already appeared to Kayla to be seduced by the attention of the older man – it was as if she ceased to exist as soon as the introductions were over. When Willard left the room, Kayla walked across and opened the curtains. The window looked out onto a path leading down the side of the house, with a hedge running down its length. She turned to talk to Jonnie, but saw that he must have followed Willard, so she dumped her belongings on the bed and sat on it, deciding to stake her claim on the bed in a silent protest at being there, and at Jonnie's immediate withdrawal from her.

Pushing her dark hair away from her face she drew in a long, deep breath and let it out, trying to release some of the tension she felt in her body. She then heard a knock on the front door. Willard didn't respond. The person knocked again more loudly and Kayla poked her head out the door. No sign of Willard or Jonnie—they must have gone somewhere further down the corridor to get the mattress. After a moment of battling with her nerves – should she answer it or not? – she went through the living room and opened the door. A very tall man, dressed in some sort of long overcloak, was standing on the top step. She thought maybe she saw or imagined a flicker of surprise when he saw her. He stared at her intently and handed her an envelope that he said was for Willard. His voice was very deep and resonant—it made her ears buzz and her skin tingle. It was all she could do to stop herself from clapping her hands over her ears. By the time she registered how uncomfortable she was feeling, he'd turned and walked away, so quickly and silently it was like he glided down the path and back towards the market square.

As she closed the door and turned, she jumped to find Willard standing closely behind her.

"Oh," she exclaimed, "this is for you," handing him the envelope and hurrying back to her room, where she found Jonnie arranging the mattress beneath the window.

"Who was that at the door?"

"Just a man with a message for Willard. He was odd—he looked at me a bit like those creepy boys at the school did."

"Well, we went down to the basement. Willard's got a full workshop down there. It's really cool, and it has a bedroom and bathroom."

"A bedroom? In the basement? Why?"

"Dunno, extra space for visitors I suppose."

***

Willard opened the envelope and extracted a single sheet of thick parchment-type paper with spidery writing on it in ink. Ah, a bit of luck was coming his way at last. It looked like he'd been inspired when he'd spotted Jonnie in the market and had taken the chance of pulling him in to work for him. It looked like the boy was going to be his way of getting back at the Birches and those other two kids, and at the same time getting a foot in the door with whatever it was the strangers were bringing to Hunterdale. Jonnie and Kayla had been spotted earlier today and were 'of interest' to them. And now, thanks to

Kayla opening the door, they knew they were under his roof. He'd been asked to find them and befriend them, and send one of them to the man. They'd now know he was a step ahead.

As he was standing thinking about what he'd just read, he looked down and saw the note starting to fade. It was as if it was dissolving in front of his eyes. Then the paper started to crumble until all that was left was a pile of soft dust, like ash, on the floor at his feet. He hoped he'd read the message properly—he felt quite disconcerted, but excited at the same time. Changes were coming – he could smell them – and he was going to be riding their waves, right at the front of them. He rubbed his hands together and the last of the ash-like, powdered paper drifted to the floor.

***

During the day Willard kept Jonnie and Kayla occupied with errands and chores. In the morning he'd given them a stodgy bowl of something that looked like porridge but tasted like watery horse chaff to eat. Actually, that was being kind; to Kayla it was more like slime with bits of chaff swept up from the floor of the stables floating in it, and it made her want to retch. When she could only manage the smallest morsel, politely saying it wasn't the sort of food she usually had for breakfast, he said that food wasn't his thing and if she wanted something better, she could take on the job of shopping and cooking for them for her board. Even though she still felt super wary of him, she thought at least by agreeing it would mean she wouldn't starve. It would keep her busy, and would be a novelty getting to buy stuff she wanted, and hopefully be given enough money to do it! Jonnie, too, was sent off to buy some things Willard needed, do some chores, and drop off messages to various merchants around the town. He was eager to help—it was the first time in his life a man had trusted him to do things and he wanted to prove himself.

Later in the afternoon, Willard told Jonnie he had a special task for him. There was a man he wanted him to meet who could be very important for them in the future. He was to meet him at the wooden bench at the back of the village square in thirty minutes. He was to listen to him carefully, be polite, answer any questions as best he could, and agree to anything he was asked to do.

"What do you mean by 'anything'? What if it's something I don't want to do?" Jonnie asked.

A look of annoyance crossed Willard's craggy face. "Don't be difficult. Just go along and see what he wants."

A bit later Jonnie headed along Cross Street to the square. Sure enough, there was a man in a dark cloak sitting on the bench he and Kayla had shared earlier. As he approached, the man remained sitting, so he sat down beside him, and not knowing what to say, cleared his throat.

"What is your name?" the man asked. His voice was smooth, almost oily and somehow lacking any accent.

"Jonnie."

"And the girl you are with?"

"My sister? Kayla."

"Where do you both come from?"

"New Zealand."

"I do not know this 'New Zealand'. Where is it and how

did you get here?"

"We're not entirely sure. The Birches say we slipped through a rift from our world to here. Tom is from New Zealand too; Sarah is from England."

"Ah, the other boy we've been watching. Willard told me there might be a girl too. So New Zealand and England are different places in the same world?"

"Yes."

"How long have you been here?"

"Kayla and I came here yesterday. I'm not sure about the others. I think Tom said he and Sarah came about two years ago."

"And you can see me?"

"What do you mean? Of course I can. I'm sitting right beside you!"

"And can you still see me now?"

Jonnie looked at him again. Something undefinable about him was a little different.

"Yes, though you're kind of blurring a bit at the edges. What are you doing to make that happen?"

"It doesn't matter. You can be useful to me. I'd like you to find out some things for me."

"Like what?"

"There is a meeting tonight that many locals will be attending in the town hall. Willard will not be made welcome there, so I want you to go. When they start talking about 'the strangers' in town, tell them that you've met them and that they come from the mountains in the north and are here to trade their stone products. Get to know them. Find out what they're afraid of. If they say something about a barrier, find out more about where its centre is located and who controls it. Report back to me here tomorrow at noon."

"Okay… when is the meeting being held and who do I say I am?"

"That's for you to work out. Listen well and you'll be rewarded. I'd also like you to keep an eye on those others from your world."

"But when we left them I took Tom's bike!"

"Fix it. We need to know whether they could harm our presence here in any way."

"Why would they do that?" Jonnie asked. "They're just kids, and the Birches are only ordinary people."

"But you come from another world, and you may be capable of things you're not yet aware of."

When he got back to Willard's he was bursting to talk to him about his encounter, but found that he was out, so he talked excitedly to Kayla instead.

"So, the locals are afraid of the strangers because they freak out when they see them, then lose their sense of them, and they don't know who they are or why they're here; and the strangers are wary of us for the same reasons. And everyone is watching everyone. Why would we get involved?" Kayla asked, "It's not our business!"

"Because Willard says he'll look out for me if I do what this man wants."

"And me? Where do I figure in this? And why would you trust Willard?"

Jonnie didn't answer. He kicked aimlessly at the edge of a mat on the floor. He wasn't sure himself; he just knew that Willard fascinated him and that he didn't want Kayla telling him what he should do. He'd known it was a mistake to talk to her about what the man had said, but he needed someone to talk to—he wished Mike was here. He really hoped Kayla wouldn't be difficult.

After dinner, cooked by Kayla (*and not half bad either*, he thought), Jonnie went back to the market square and hung out where there was a good view of the town hall. After about thirty minutes, people started arriving in twos and threes, slipping in the side door quietly. No fuss, nothing advertising what was happening from the outside. He waited until a youngish man approached the door, and sauntered over to go through it immediately behind him, as if they'd arrived together. He found himself in a large room with a high wooden ceiling and a wooden floor. The walls were white-washed, with framed portraits of officious looking people hanging on them. People were sitting in rows of seats before a platform at the front, which held a lectern, a small table and three chairs. After about ten minutes, two men and a woman made their way to the platform. One of the men, with an air of importance, stood and called people to order, waiting for their talk to subside before starting the meeting by welcoming them all and thanking them for coming. He said that they'd called the meeting to discuss their growing concerns about a number of strangers reported to be in their midst and invited anyone who'd had contact with them to speak.

Several people started murmuring to each other, with some saying that they'd seen people they didn't know in the town. But when questioned further and being asked to describe them and what they were doing, they were strangely unable to recall any details. One woman became quite agitated, saying that she'd definitely seen unknown men around, but realised she couldn't hold any memory of what they were like and wondered if there was something odd in the way her thoughts about them kept disappearing. Jonnie decided now was a good time to interject.

"Well I've met one and he was perfectly friendly. He told me he was from the north, in the mountains, and was here to trade stone for timber."

"That's interesting," the woman replied, "and here we were thinking they were from the south and had somehow breached the barrier."

"The barrier? How would they have done that?" asked Jonnie.

"The keeper grows weary, and the power from the south is getting stronger," a man replied.

"Say no more Joseph. No one from around these parts would be asking those questions," a burly looking man warned. All the heads in the room turned to stare at Jonnie and several others murmured their agreement. Jonnie felt scrutinised and squirmed, realising that he'd said enough to raise their suspicions of him.

"Who are you anyway?" the woman demanded.

"I'm a friend of the Birches," he replied.

"Oh right," she relaxed a little. "I'd heard there was someone else staying, but I thought that was a girl. So, you know young Tom then?"

"Yes, that's right."

"He's a good lad, even though he's not from these parts either."

They seemed to lose interest in him then and the conversation returned again to the woman, who seemed to be called Elena. She continued to express concern about losing her memories of the strangers. She could hold enough in mind to know she'd seen people who didn't belong, but like an evaporating dream, she couldn't keep a grasp of what she'd seen and found it really scary. It was elusive and slippery and freaked her out. Others affirmed her experience, nodding in agreement as she spoke. Elena suggested that they should write down any encounters as they happened to try to hold a memory of them. Some seemed to think she was overreacting, especially if the strangers really were just there to trade, but she seemed to have the sympathy and agreement of a sizeable group. Other than deciding that they would report anything unusual to the woman on the dais and making a date for the next meeting in a week, not much else of importance was discussed, and it wasn't long before people began to drift off home again.

Jonnie left too, and after thinking about what to say to Kayla and Willard on his short walk back to the house, he went inside to find Willard slumped at the kitchen table, pitcher of ale and a large pottery mug by his hand. It looked like he'd had a lot to drink—he lifted his head from the table to look at Jonnie with bleary blood-shot eyes—he didn't even ask about the meeting before dropping it heavily back down onto his arms, looking so unconscious that Jonnie went straight to his room. To Kayla, he merely said he'd met some locals, who seemed to know Tom and the Birches. She didn't ask him anything—she seemed to have decided she didn't want to know what he was up to, which suited him just fine.

***

Waking in the morning, Jonnie and Kayla went to the kitchen to find Willard staring moodily at a mug of tea. His brow was furrowed and he looked like he'd had a rough night. Kayla recognised the signs of a hangover and decided to keep out of his way, as she had with her mother. How was it that she'd already found herself back in a place with the same kind of pattern? She felt sick looking at him, worrying about how he'd behave, realising just how much time she'd spent in her past being scared and anxious and vigilant. It wasn't okay just to replace one bad environment with another so similar. Why didn't Jonnie get it? She could tell he was itching to talk to Willard, so she busied herself making tea and toast and took hers back to the bedroom.

He joined her a little later, telling her that he was going to the marketplace for a while and that they'd be going back to visit the Birches in the afternoon so that he could take the bike back. She looked at him warily. Why would he do that? He hadn't given her any reason to believe he had a conscience about it, and Willard certainly wouldn't be encouraging him in that regard. There was obviously something in it for them both. Still, she'd rather be there than here, so she kept her thoughts to herself.

After Jonnie left, everything seemed quiet. Kayla didn't know whether Willard was still in the house, so she wandered along to the kitchen and found him sleeping, head on his arms, at the kitchen table. She backed out of the room quietly and set about exploring the house. There wasn't a lot to see. The first room down the hallway was Willard's bedroom, fairly neat other than unfolded clothes strewn about, not much furniture, same stale smell as its owner; a smell of sweat and unwashed clothes; then their room was on the opposite side. Further along the corridor there was another door that must lead downstairs, where Willard and Jonnie had gone for the mattress. She opened the door to darkness and fumbled with her hand around the corner until she found a light switch. Stairs going down into a basement area lit up. It seemed to be fitted out as a workshop, much as she'd expected from what Jonnie had described. She walked down the stairs and poked around, checking out the bedroom and wondering what use he would have for it. Over in the corner of the space there was a large cage—goodness only knows what that was for! She turned and wandered back towards the stairs, stopping to check out a piece of equipment that looked like a motor with a seat attached. Just as she was bending over to look at it more closely, the light suddenly went off. She was left in the dark, eyes temporarily unable to see a thing, until they adjusted with the help of the thin sliver of light coming down from the slightly open door at the top of the stairs. As she looked up, she gasped to see a large shape moving down the stairs towards her. She turned to find a place to hide, but smacked the soft part of her thigh into a piece of metal protruding from the motor. She gasped and rubbed her leg to try to ease the sharp pain biting into her flesh. Just as she was about to move again, a rough, strong hand grabbed her by the back of the neck and pulled her hard against him.

"What are you doing down here?" The voice was gravelly and menacing.

"Nothing," Kayla managed to squeak through her fear. She was immediately cross with herself for showing she was scared and managed to clear her throat and add, "I just came down to look at the workroom Jonnie told me about. He was really impressed with it."

Willard didn't say anything, but roughly turned her around to face him. Even though she was tall for her age, her face was pressed hard into his jacket at chest level, her cheek painfully gouged by a metal button. His clothes smelt sour, of stale sweat etched into unwashed clothes and skin. An overlay of putrid alcohol on his breath washed over her, reminding her suddenly of her mother, causing her to retch. He clamped a hand over her mouth, while the other one moved down her back and caressed her buttocks. His breathing became hot and heavy and ragged. Her body went rigid as he roughly started to force her backwards towards the bedroom. She suddenly let her body go limp, and when he checked his movement in surprise, she bit down hard on the finger across her mouth, tasting the saltiness of his blood, while at the same time lifting her knee as hard as she could into his groin.

"Aargh!" he yelled, letting go of his grip on her and doubling over.

She lunged away from him and moved as quickly as she could up the stairs. When she got to the top, she flicked on the light switch to see him doubled over on the floor, swearing and moaning.

"You little bitch! I only came to check for intruders," he spluttered.

"Sure, that's why you had your hand on my bum," she retorted.

"As if any warm-blooded man would want anything from you, you skinny little runt." At that, she switched off the light abruptly, backed out and slammed the door. There was no key in the lock, or she'd have locked him in. As it was, it would take him a few minutes to get himself together and back up the stairs in the dark, so she ran to her room, grabbed her few possessions and raced out of the house.

She ran as fast as she could up Cross Street to the market square, starting to feel a little less afraid as she drew nearer to the people who filled the square. Of course, market day. She ran until her chest was heaving, her breath ragged, stopping suddenly by the town hall to bend over and vomit into the gutter. She stayed bent over, hands on her knees as her body started to shake all over.

"Kayla, isn't it?" a woman's voice asked.

She looked up and saw the woman she'd met with Sarah and Tom the day before yesterday. She couldn't remember her name.

"Are you okay?" she continued, putting a hand on her shoulder.

She nodded mutely, not trusting that she would be able to speak. The woman gently helped her upright and gave her a bottle of something, telling her to take a mouthful. It was sweet and fruity and helped her to feel better, taking the sour taste of vomit from her mouth.

"Thanks," she managed.

"What were you running away from?" the woman asked.

"Willard! Do you know him?"

"Oh yes, he's a nasty piece of work. How do you know him?"

"My brother Jonnie met him when we were here the other day and he invited us to stay. He seems to be doing some work for him. I need to find Jonnie because I can't go back there again!" She started to cry and the woman put her arm around her shoulders and led her towards her market stall, sitting her down on a stool until she calmed down.

"I think I've seen him. I'm pretty sure I saw him talking to someone, over on the bench by that stand of trees." She pointed in the direction of the bench on the far side of the square.

"Thank you so much. I'm sorry, I can't remember your name."

"Gwynn. Please be careful, and if you need any help from Corrin or me, we live above our shop down by the river. It's the one with the blue door—we sell leather goods."

Kayla smiled at her, got up and walked shakily across the square, her legs feeling like her bones had turned to jelly, wending her way between the stalls and around people who were standing in groups talking and eating. They sounded so cheerful—why wasn't life like that for her?

Gwynn watched her walking away with concern. She looked so vulnerable. Thin and still so child-like somehow. Dark hair hanging about her narrow face, hunched forward in worry, with her shoulder blades protruding from her slight frame, looking a bit like wing buds. She had the feeling she'd be seeing her again…

Ahead, Kayla could see Jonnie sitting on the bench, talking to a tall man wearing a dark cloak. Was he the one who'd come to the door yesterday? She drew a deep breath—she didn't want anyone seeing how rattled she was just now, so she practised feeling centred like her school counsellor had taught her, before standing as tall as she could and walking over to them.

"Hi Jonnie, who's your friend?"

"Oh... Kayla... This is someone Willard knows." He turned to him, "I'm sorry, I don't know your name." He looked at him expectantly, but the man ignored him.

"Hello Kayla, I'm very pleased to meet you. We were just talking about how you could both help me to get to know your friends Sarah and Tom, and the Birches. He's feeling bad about the bike though, so I'd just suggested that you both take it back today and apologise."

Oh, he's good, thought Jonnie. A reason to go back, that she'd buy, at the same time totally nailing her worries, even though he'd hardly said anything about her to him.

Kayla looked them both up and down. She didn't know what felt wrong, but something did. She caught the eye of the man and he gave her a slight nod that conveyed without needing words, that he was acknowledging that it was a ruse, and was somehow daring her to say something about it. At the same time, creepily, she felt the pull to collude with him, making Jonnie out to be the one being used by not seeing the dynamics at play. She was also aware of a sick desire to be the clever one, the 'special' one, understanding something Jonnie didn't. *He's playing with my mind,* she thought. *And I bet he's done the same to Jonnie. But somehow, I know he's doing it?* It was a bit like the in and out groups at school and the way kids manipulated each other so some felt special and others felt excluded. She responded by giving them both a bland smile.

"Well we'd better get going then." She turned abruptly and walked off, leaving Jonnie to stand up and apologise before hurrying after her.

"What was that about?" Jonnie demanded when he caught up

with her, grabbing her arm to slow her down. Suddenly it seemed clear to her. He was trying to turn the tables from feeling intimidated in the man's presence to blustering with her, the bully in control, to shore himself up. How come she could suddenly see him so much more clearly than in the past? Part of her wished she could still see him as her caring older brother who looked out for her against her mother, rather than this flawed and susceptible guy who would betray people if it suited him. She felt a bit sick and wanted time to process how she was feeling.

"Jonnie, I can't go back to Willard's house. While you were gone, he tried to grope me and I ran away. You'll have to go back and get the bike alone."

"He tried to grope you? Are you sure? Why would he want to do that?"

"Well I can take that two ways. One is that you can't see that anyone would *want* to touch me; the other is that you're incredibly misogynistic and think that I must have asked for it somehow, or at best misinterpreted it. I'm not going to accept either from you. Just leave me alone, go get the bike and meet me back here in half an hour." She walked in the opposite direction before he could bluster. It was the first time she'd ever talked to him like that and she felt a confusing mixture of being empowered, but also a sort of coldness, of not feeling good about him.

Jonnie looked after her retreating back for a moment before continuing on his way to Willard's. What did she expect him to do? Why did she always make things difficult for him? He couldn't imagine for a minute that Willard would bother with a kid like her, but then she was scared of her own shadow sometimes and maybe it was all in her imagination. What if he did have a bit of a fumble? Didn't all guys do that? Dan was the only one of his friends who'd been with a girl. Mike had snogged one at a party, but they mostly just watched girls from a distance. Didn't mean he didn't fantasise though... Anyway, he'd seen his mum with heaps of men doing what they liked to her and she didn't stop them. Almost enough to put him off for life—sex with a drunk woman must be a bit like sex with a corpse! Disgusting! Well he wasn't going to say anything to Willard. He'd pretend he hadn't seen her.

Willard had given him a key, so he let himself in. He could hear him banging about in the kitchen. When he went in, Willard was standing at the bench making himself something to eat.

"Hi," Jonnie said breezily, "I just saw that guy. He told me to go back to Riverstone and check out what they're up to. Where's Kayla?"

"Don't know." Willard looked pissed off. "I heard her go out about half an hour ago."

"Oh! Well should I wait for her or go without her?"

"Just go. When she comes back I'll keep an eye on her."

Part of Jonnie wondered what he meant by that, but dismissed the thought—Kayla wouldn't be alone with him here anyway, because he'd be picking her up on his way through the market.

"I don't know how long I'll be—the man said I might need to stay a night or two if I have to get their trust before they'll talk openly. What's the guy's name anyway?"

"I don't know, he's never said."

Jonnie went to his room and picked up a change of clothes, shoved them in the bag he'd brought from Riverstone and yelled out "Bye" as he went out the door. He heard a grunt in response.

Retrieving the bike from the shed, he wheeled it along the path to the front of the house and set off down the road. Sure enough, Kayla was waiting by the town hall and he stopped for her to clamber on before setting off for Riverstone. As they drove, Kayla tried to sort out her confused feelings about her brother. He'd always looked out for her and she'd thought that meant he loved her. Maybe he did, but she'd been forced since they got here to see him differently. Strangely, at home he was the top dog in the household and managed to do what he wanted; he held the power—both she and her mum were more fragile in their different ways and she hadn't really seen him outside their family environment before. She'd ignored any hints that didn't fit with him being the strong one, or on her side. The thought that he might actually be vulnerable himself was scary—he might be vulnerable to being manipulated by someone stronger than him! She knew he cared for her, but sometimes caring wasn't enough. It was about values too, and knowing yourself, and what was right to stand up for—or not!

Jonnie was all she'd ever had that was good enough to keep her from falling to pieces, so she'd clung onto the idea of him out of fear. But she didn't really know him or what he wanted. Had that stopped her from working out what she wanted to be, or could be? She didn't know what that would even look like, though she was starting to realise since she got here that although she was physically fragile, she had other reserves to draw on that she hadn't known she had in her... She leaned into him on the bike and held on just that bit more tightly, not wanting yet to let go.

***

As they drew near to Riverstone, they could see that the truck wasn't parked in its usual spot. Jonnie put the bike back where he'd found it and they walked up the steps and knocked on the door. There was no reply. He tried the door handle but it was locked. He jiggled it angrily until Kayla told him to stop. She drew away from the house, but he really wanted to get into it, as if it had been locked deliberately to keep him out! He walked around it testing the windows, until he found one that wasn't properly fastened. Heaving it open, he pulled himself up and over the stone sill, sliding forwards on his stomach into the kitchen.

"What are you doing?" demanded Kayla from outside. He ignored her. Picking himself up, he walked through to the living room. The house felt deserted. Everything was clean and tidy, other than a piece of paper lying on the table. He picked it up—it was some sort of hand-drawn map that he recognised as being a rough copy of the one he'd taken from Tom's room before they left, thinking it might be useful later. It showed Riverstone and Hunterdale, and a more heavily drawn road to the south of Riverstone to a mountain called Greyvyn. The road had been drawn over a few times as if to accentuate it, and had an asterisk marked on the near side of Greyvyn. He wasn't sure what to make of it, other than that was probably where they'd gone.

He let himself out the door to where Kayla was anxiously hovering. "We have to go back to Hunterdale. They aren't here."

"So why don't we wait for them to return? They won't mind us being here… If we stay outside the house," she added pointedly.

"No, no point wasting our time. We'll go back and return later."

"You mean you want to report back to Willard and that man so you can find out what they want you to do next?"

He gave her a withering glance, but she thought that underneath it he looked a bit embarrassed, probably because he realised she'd rumbled him.

"Jonnie, I don't want to go back to Willard's."

"Don't be daft. You'll be okay, I'll make sure you're not left alone with him if that's what bothers you. Anyway, it won't be for long—I'm sure we'll be back here soon." He walked off to the bike and Kayla had no choice but to follow him.

***

When they got back to Hunterdale, Jonnie realised he didn't know how to contact the man outside of their timed arrangements. He'd been going to turn up late afternoon tomorrow or the day after, depending on what he'd found out. He didn't want to go to Willard first—the stranger was at the top of the pecking order. However, he needn't have worried. As he drove into the emptying market place, he saw that the man was sitting on the bench, as if he knew he was coming. He parked the bike and told Kayla to stay with it, while he walked as casually as he could over to the bench.

"Well?" the stranger asked.

"They're not there. They've gone somewhere and I found this on their table." He extended the map. The man took it and scanned it intently. After a moment's thought he folded it carefully and gave it back to Jonnie.

"Go back to Willard and tell him to take the car – he'll know which one – tell him he'll find it at the school, and to drive with you to Greyvyn. Find them, see what they're doing, and if it is anything to do with what we discussed, he'll know what to do."

"Why can't you go, since you know what you're looking for?"

"My powers are muted in this landscape and will remain so until we break the spell that holds the barrier in place. It took tremendous energy from our most powerful mages to create a small rift to get me here with a few young helpers."

"The barrier?"

"No more questions. If you do well, you'll find out in time." He extended his hand to Jonnie and dropped a car key into it. Standing up, his eyes sought out Kayla and when he saw her standing across the square, nodded at her and raised his hand in a kind of half salute before walking off.

It took every bit of Kayla's self-control not to salute him in return. *He's playing with my mind again,* she thought, and was determined to stand tall and not respond. She thought she caught a slightly ironic smile on his face as he turned away. Jonnie came up beside her and told her they were heading back to Willard's and were going to go by car to find the Birches.

"There's no way I'm going into his house again," Kayla said forcefully. "I'll wait outside while you get him."

She waited outside, leaning on the fence for about ten minutes before a slightly dishevelled looking Willard appeared with Jonnie behind him. He walked past her with a scathing look on his face and spat just to the left of her feet. She watched the globule of slime sliding off a cobblestone and felt a wave of nausea. He was already striding off down the road, though she noticed that he wasn't terribly steady on his feet. Jonnie told her to get a move on as he moved past her to follow him. They had to walk quickly to keep up with him, as he walked the route they'd taken the previous day to the school (*was it really only yesterday?*) where he opened the door to a dusty green car and gestured to Jonnie to get in beside him. *Well, I know my place*, she thought, as she slid into the back seat behind her brother.

"We'll head south down the river road," Willard said to Jonnie. "That'll make up a bit of time. They've probably had at least a good half day on us." He started the car, which was remarkably silent after the engine had fired and settled, and they pulled out onto the road into the small amount of afternoon traffic that preceded the school finishing for the day.

As they drove south along the River Dearth, the landscape became increasingly remote and craggy. The lush green landscape that surrounded Hunterdale gave way to scrubby trees and undergrowth, with their splotches of green stretching progressively further apart. They could see a mountain in the distance, and the river to their right became increasingly windy, with white water bubbling around stretches of rapids. They passed a number of kayaks or canoes though, and the occasional small boat, so it was navigable and used maybe as a trade route for the town. Eventually, when the landscape was almost entirely rocky, with just small tussocky-looking shrubs to break its greyness, they saw the road angling up to a small stone bridge that traversed the river. The car advanced up and over the bridge, and they could see the river tumbling over large rocks and disappearing into the distance in front of the mountain, in such a way that it looked as if it was diving under it.

"Does the river go under the mountain?" Kayla asked.

"Don't know," was the surly reply. It was the first time Willard had spoken since she'd suggested earlier that he slow down a little, being concerned that maybe he'd been drinking and shouldn't be driving. He'd barked at her then and she'd retreated further into the back seat, keeping any other thoughts to herself.

On the other side of the bridge they dropped down into a village. Clusters of houses and businesses jostled for space alongside the river and lined a criss-cross of small streets surrounding a market square. A narrow road seemed to lead straight towards the mountain through a band of trees and undergrowth that stretched around its base. The green vegetation looked intentionally cultivated against the bleak backdrop, with neat gardens tucked behind houses, and further from the village, organised plantings of crops and trees. A jetty jutted into the river and a small vessel looked like it had recently moored and was discharging a handful of passengers. People were sitting outside a low building at rough-hewn tables, drinking ale—probably the local pub. Even though it wasn't very warm, at least it wasn't raining, and it looked friendly and inviting.

Willard stopped the car by the road to the mountain and asked Jonnie for the map. He pulled out the hand-drawn one and also Tom's one that he'd picked up from his room in Willard's house when he went back to get him. He laid them out side by side.

"It doesn't look like this is where the asterisk is," Willard said. "It's on the far side of the mountain, not directly in front of it." Jonnie agreed, so they started the car again and continued along the main road. As they drove on past Greyvyn, there was no sign of another turn-off. Eventually they realised that they'd now gone too far towards Riverstone. Willard was getting increasingly tetchy. Frustrated, he stopped the car and turned around. As they drove back, looking more carefully at the side of the road, Jonnie saw a hawk wheeling across the sky to the side of the mountain.

"Look, there's a hawk—I wonder if it's that one that hangs around Riverstone?"

"Not likely. There are a lot of hawks in these parts, but keep your eyes focused."

Shortly after though, driving slowly and carefully scanning the roadside, they saw tyre tracks turning off to the right, just to the west of the mountain. Willard turned the car onto a rough patch of ground and slowly followed the tracks a short way to a clearing in front of a band of trees. They stopped the car and got out to look around. Jonnie quickly found the truck carefully hidden behind foliage.

"Here," he yelled. Willard came over to him, and Kayla reluctantly got out of the car to slowly follow them. To the side of where the truck was hidden, they found a narrow track leading to the westerly side of the mountain. Willard indicated that this was the path they were going to follow and they set off in single file, Willard, then Jonnie, then Kayla bringing up the rear.

Chapter VII

Under the Mountain

Galawand stretched on her narrow pallet bed and reluctantly roused herself. She felt so weary—no amount of sleep could alleviate her deep exhaustion. She felt a dullness wrapping itself around her entire body, making her limbs so heavy that it was all she could do to right herself, hauling herself up into a sitting position on the edge of the bed. She looked around at the deep cavern, with its naturally vaulted ceiling that stretched up into the darkness above her. The rock walls at her level had their recesses filled with candles that cast a beautifully soft glow, illuminating the rich tapestries and silk hangings she'd brought with her to make her long vigil bearable. Over the years, candlewax dripping down from crevices had created a beauty of its own—long, creamy, voluptuous rivers of wax trailing down the cavern walls to create pillars on the floor.

The floor was strewn with vibrant rugs in deep reds and blues, and the sparse furniture (all they'd been able to manoeuvre through the narrow tunnel passage) was made of warm-hued timber. She loved her surroundings, but was beginning to suffer from not having the energy to get herself out to the fresh air each day as she used to. Looking down at her hands, she thought they looked frail, maybe because they were now so pale, but also because her depleted energy prevented her from getting much physical exercise. Friends regularly brought her fresh fruit and vegetables, but that didn't compensate for being able to get outside and smell the air, hold her arms up in the sun, see the sky and the clouds and the trees, and walk vigorously in the daylight. Her body was beginning to waste away and she knew she couldn't last much longer without help. Her hopes were pinned on the stories she'd heard of a boy and girl from another world who had arrived—the prophecies had always spoken of them, but her magical powers had all been channelled into maintaining the barrier and she hadn't been able to detect their arrival. She was aware that changes were afoot though—dark changes that were draining her energy, but also a positive feeling that there was hope yet. More intuition than mystical powers, she had to give it credence to give her the will to keep going.

Her eyes were drawn to the centre of the room, to the purpose of her extraordinary confinement. A block of solidified lava formed a natural platform, a table, rising up in an almost circle, waist height above the cavern floor. Arranged on the table surface was a ring of stones that was illuminated with a deep red, interconnecting glow. The glow was dim this morning, waiting for her to revitalise it. With a heavy sigh, Galawand pushed herself to her feet, feeling the sense of responsibility weighing her down. Even after a good night's sleep it was becoming more and more difficult to get the circle to light up in the way it had in the past. She knew from what her friends told her that alongside the weakening of the barrier, 'strangers' were arriving in North Feasgar. Presumably they'd found a way through and it was only a matter of time before they tried to find her and destroy the barrier entirely. She'd been holding out against the dark magic from the south for many years now—she had to find a way to keep defending their land.

For now, she walked over to the ring of stones and placed her left hand within them, palm down on the flat surface of the circular rock. She gathered her inner energy and visualised herself as standing tall and whole and centred, until the red circle started to glow more intensely, then slowly grew an overlay of silver. She hung on for long enough to see a kind of double band illuminated, silver and red, then had to let go, half slumping onto the ground on her knees beside the table, gasping, hand on her racing heart, feeling drained and exhausted. That was all she could manage for now. Hopefully by the afternoon she could try again once she'd eaten and had some rest. In the past she only had to restore the power of the ring once a day, leaving her free to meditate and read and spend time outside. Now she was merely limping along, just coping, and hoping for help.

***

Sarah wandered along the riverbank, her mind churning over and over the last couple of days, worrying about what would happen next and how she would know what to do. The river was high—the stepping stones still submerged. Suddenly she felt a shock reverberate through her chest and she gasped, putting out a hand to steady herself. It wasn't anything physical—she had suddenly remembered that there *had* been another part to her dream last night. Everything had happened so quickly that the whole dream had completely gone from her mind, even though it had been scary and confusing. She turned quickly and walked back towards the mill house. At the end of the garden path, Hermione was sitting on the bottom step.

"What's happening?" she asked, sensing Sarah's agitation.

"I just remembered another part to my dream from last night. I'm not sure what it means, but I'm feeling really scared. It's as if something or someone is telling me it's getting really urgent and is pushing me to hurry."

"Do you want to tell me about it?"

"I need a bit of space to try to put it all together and remember it as a whole."

"Why don't you sit here and think it through while I go and find the others. I'll bring them back in about ten minutes."

Sarah sat on the steps in the watery sunlight and let herself slip back into a dreamy state. At first, she couldn't get rid of the anxious chattering going around and around in her head, but gradually she found herself relaxing and finding her way back into the dream: *she and Tom were going deeper and deeper down into the mountain. It was dark—they only had a flickering lantern to light their path. The walls narrowed until they felt like they were going through a tunnel and her breathing started to become more and more desperate. Just when she wondered whether she could handle it without screaming, the passage opened and they entered a cavern that had water running through it. It looked cold and dark and fast-flowing. It was really clear that there was no going back and the only way forward was across the river...*

When Tom and the Birches joined her, she reminded them about the first part of the dream, "And... the other thing I just remembered, I think, was that I had the idea of water, very deep water, that we had to cross somewhere down under the mountain…"

"The River Dearth runs under Greyvyn," contributed Tom.

They sat in silence for a moment thinking…

"If we have to cross the river, we'll need to plan out how we do it before we leave. I think we need to put together the things we'll take today and leave tomorrow morning," Arthur said.

"Yes, if we take our cues from the dream," added Mary, "we'll need lights—we can take a lantern each and some spare candles; food and water, and suitable shoes and clothing, preferably with a change to go into a waterproof bag in case we end up in the river. It can hold the matches and candles too. Don't look at me like that Sarah," she smiled, "It's not going to happen, I'm just thinking of the worst case so we're prepared."

"How will we cross the river?" asked Tom.

"What was it like Sarah?"

"Well, it wasn't that wide, but it looked deep."

"What was on the other side?" asked Arthur. "I presume the sides were rocky, but was there a flat place to cross to?"

"Yes, I think so. I remember the rock walls, a fairly flat area with rocks scattered around."

"So, we'll need a rope and some sort of hook to snag a rock on the other side, unless any of you can think of an easier way to get across. I don't have a grapple hook, but maybe you can help me make one, Tom?"

Hermione had been sitting between Sarah and Tom on the couch, listening. She put a paw on Sarah's arm to get her attention.

"Hey guys, Hermione wants to say something."

Through her, Hermione told them that Ryder had reported back to her just before Sarah had come back from the river. He'd been watching the marketplace at Hunterdale and had picked up on Jonnie and Kayla exploring the town, then going to Willard's place.

"So now we have a definite link between them!" exclaimed Tom.

Ryder had waited and had seen a man with a strange energy going to the house. As she reported this, the fur down Hermione's back rippled and stood on end, as it had when she'd encountered the scent of the man who'd waited outside Riverstone. Sarah stroked it down again, soothing her until she resumed. He'd then later tracked Jonnie going to the market and meeting the man there just a short time ago. He'd flown straight to them to let them know.

"What're they up to, I wonder?" mused Arthur. "Hermione, there's nothing we can do for now, but could you ask Ryder again whether he'd fly ahead of us to Greyvyn to check out whether there's a track around our side of the mountain and any sort of tunnel opening? It feels more urgent now than when we thought of it before, and if he could give us any idea where we might be headed in advance, that would be really helpful."

"He's gone off to hunt tonight, but said he'd be back at first light," reported Sarah, "so Hermione says she'll ask him then."

While Tom and Arthur disappeared into the mill room to try to fashion something to attach to the end of the rope, Mary prepared two bags, one between each couple, in case they ended up in a narrow passage where they wouldn't want to be struggling with a pack each. Instead, they could push and pull it between them. Sarah blanched, remembering the narrow, panicky spaces from her dreams, adding to the habitual feeling of claustrophobia she experienced in small spaces.

***

In the morning, after Hermione had caught up with Ryder, Sarah went upstairs to find Morwyn's map. It wasn't there. She looked through her room—she was sure she'd left it on her bookcase when she was there the last time, but no luck. Running downstairs, she asked if anyone had seen it and Tom said he'd borrowed it a while back. He went up to his room to get it, but it wasn't there either.

"It's not there. I know I had it on the table by my bed. Jonnie must have taken it. What a dumbass!"

Sarah thought for a minute before going to find some paper and a pen so she could try to redraw it. She remembered thinking that their part of North Feasgar looked a bit like a kite. A short cross piece linking the West to East, and a longer one from North to South, intersecting in the top third of the map, near the labyrinth. She located Riverstone to the west, the treehouse to the north, Hunterdale to the east and Greyvyn in the south, placed at the four points at the ends of the crosspieces. She drew in the road to the labyrinth just south of Riverstone. She then highlighted the road from Riverstone, south past the labyrinth turn-off, then down to Mt Greyvyn, marking with a cross the point slightly west of the mountain where Ryder had indicated they would find the path they had to take. It wound around its base, with the entrance to the tunnel a bit further around than south-west.

"South-south-west," Tom said.

"What?"

"That means south-south-west," he repeated.

"Okay—"

"Didn't you do geography?"

"Come on you two—we're off," said Mary, heading for the door. They rushed to pack a change of clothes in their bag, called Hermione, locked the door and joined Mary and Arthur in the truck. They scrambled onto the back of the truck while Mary opened the passenger door for Hermione to jump in between her and Arthur. Starting the truck, Arthur drove it out of the property, turning right onto the road. The road south wasn't used a lot; most traffic headed for Hunterdale, and anyone heading south to Greyvyn normally went by boat from the town via the River Dearth or travelled on the road that followed the river.

They hadn't travelled far when Sarah realised with a start, that she'd left the map behind on the table. She was really cross with herself, but then realised it didn't really matter—by drawing it, she had it etched in her mind anyway. They knew where to look out for the track to the tunnel, and Ryder would be hanging around waiting for them.

As they drove past the turn-off to the labyrinth, Sarah grew quiet as she started to worry about her next return to her world. What if the pool in the labyrinth didn't work for her this time? What if she stayed here, with her body in a coma in England—would they take her off life support? Would she stop existing here if she died in England? What if she was seriously injured, or died, here—what would happen to her body in England? What about her poor Grandad? He would feel dreadful—she couldn't do that to him! How on earth did that whole body thing work anyway? It was beyond any sort of rational reasoning... If she came back again, could she do it the way the others did? Find a rift that she could go through body and all? Then at least it would be her own decision whether or not she returned. She couldn't even think about making that decision while other people were involved. She felt sick even raising the idea in her mind.

She suddenly felt something like a soft feather stroking her skin. *What on earth?* She looked around and saw Hermione standing up on her back legs, looking at her out the cab window. *Oh, thank you Hermione.* She sent a thought message back— Hermione knew she was feeling worried and was soothing her somehow with her thoughts. When Sarah acknowledged her, she turned and dropped back down onto the front seat again. Sarah carried on feeling much calmer and incredibly grateful to her, even if communicating in that way with a cat would have been really freaky in her other world. Here it felt right!

They continued their drive south to Mount Greyvyn. They could see it getting larger in the distance, looking forbidding in the overcast sky. Arthur had told them that although it was a volcano, it was dormant and hadn't shown any sign of activity that he was aware of. It wasn't about to erupt on them while they were in the tunnel, though Sarah was thinking that was the least of her problems—merely going into the tunnel was going to be a challenge. She'd always had trouble with claustrophobia. The last time she'd been here she'd had that frightful experience hiding in the blanket box in Willard's bedroom—she was really proud of herself for not falling to pieces and screaming, but now she wondered how she'd even done that; and yet it paled alongside the feeling of fear she'd had in her recent dreams. She took some comfort from knowing she had good people with her—they wouldn't let her do it alone! Just then Tom reached over and squeezed her hand. Her heart gave a flip that she hoped wasn't audible! It was just a gesture of support, he could obviously pick up that she was worried... But maybe part of her was trying to make it into something more? And what would that mean?

The remaining trip towards Greyvyn was uneventful. The road became a little rougher, with potholes slowing their progress. They didn't pass many other vehicles and Tom and Sarah both felt as if they were somehow travelling to the other end of the earth—it felt so far away from their other world. The only thing Sarah felt at home with was the dull weather, while Tom looked at the approaching mountain with a sense of familiarity—Auckland was full of volcanoes, just not in such a different landscape. Arthur slowed the truck as they drew near to its westerly side, looking for signs of the road, or track, they were to take. Finally, Sarah spotted Ryder. He swooped down suddenly from a grove of trees and flew low over the truck, rolling and turning like a plane in an aero show.

"Show off!" exclaimed Sarah.

He then straightened out a little ahead of them and they settled into a steady following speed. A few minutes later he veered to the right and Arthur carefully manoeuvred the vehicle over a flat, gravelly area to where Ryder was waiting on the branch of a tree.

"Doesn't much look like a track," Tom muttered as they drew to a stop.

"Well, I guess there might be reasons why it has to be kept out of sight?" Sarah retorted.

Climbing down from the back, they went over to Ryder. Sarah still had trouble tuning into his scratchy form of thought speech, but Hermione helped to translate. He told them to lift the canopy of the nearest trees and drive the truck beneath them, then to break off and drape foliage to disguise the gap. They did this quickly and silently. Now they were close to the mountain, a sombre feeling was descending on them. It suddenly felt like something important was happening for which they were responsible. Sarah shivered and pulled her jacket more closely around her. Mary, noticing, put her arm around her shoulders.

"Be brave. We'll be okay, I'm sure we'll be looked after. We have each other, and we have all the good forces of North Feasgar behind us."

Sarah swallowed and tried to dispel the feeling of dread that was knotting her stomach. She busied herself finishing their camouflage work and then pulled their pack onto her back.

"I'll take the first shift with this, Tom," she said, walking towards where Ryder was waiting for them just beyond the initial band of trees.

Ryder led them to a track that they would have missed if he hadn't been there to start them off on it. Arthur led them, with Tom in the rear. Hermione scampered on and off the path to investigate the undergrowth, and goodness only knows what else. Nose in the air, head swivelling, she was like some sort of finely tuned instrument, reading the environment with an instinctive ease that demonstrated her nature as far more than a domesticated cat.

It was easy enough at the beginning, but rapidly became hard going—slippery with the recent rain, and in places there had been slips that had sent rocks tumbling onto the path, over which they had to clamber. They started off walking through tree cover, with branches flicking back and whipping them in the face as they walked. Small, biting insects attacked their hands and necks leaving welts, and a cool wind cut through their layers of clothing, even though their bodies were hot from walking. It seemed never-ending, through boggy patches, over rocks, then the landscape gradually changed to become barer of vegetation as they circled the mountain and got closer to its base. The ground was rougher, with the rocks looking porous and spiky—Tom told them it was volcanic, obviously the side where an old eruption had deposited its lava. At one point he slid, landing on his hands to save himself and grazed his palms quite deeply. They bled and stung like mad, settling into a dull ache, which reminded him of the time back in New Zealand when he came off his bike on a gravel road and grazed his knees and hands. He tried to put both the pain and the reminder of home out of his mind.

They reached a small stream and Arthur signalled them to stop. Dropping the packs, they sat on some rocks and had a few mouthfuls of water. The stream was only narrow, but it had grown in volume after all the rain, from being a small outlet for excess water down a mountain crevice, to a stream with definite flow, creating runnels in the soft ground either side of its usual pebble and stone path. It wasn't deep, but they were going to get their feet wet crossing it.

Getting back on their feet, they swapped the packs over to Mary and Tom. Arthur again led the way, picking out a path over the stream, across stones and firmer bits of ground. Mary followed, stepping carefully to find solid footing. Suddenly something startled the birds in a tree nearby and they flew, shrieking, up into the air. Mary's concentration was diverted, just for an instant, and her right foot landed awkwardly on a stone, slipping and wedging itself against the one next to it, turning her ankle as her body weight continued moving her forward. She cried out, and Arthur turned to catch her. Sarah, coming up from behind, slid her pack off her shoulders and Arthur lifted her, carrying her to the far side of the stream.

"Are you okay?" Sarah asked anxiously.

"I'm sure it's just a sprain." But she was clearly making light of it. Arthur pulled off her shoe and sock and already a diffuse mottled red colour was spreading over her ankle and it was looking a bit puffy. She could move it, with difficulty, and it didn't feel as if anything was broken, but it had been a violent wrench.

"I think we need to bind it," contributed Tom. "I did something like that once playing soccer and my coach bound it up to help prevent it swelling."

Mary nodded her agreement. "Help me back to the stream, Arthur. I think it would be good to put it in cold water for a bit first."

While she was soaking it, Arthur tore some strips off the bottom of his spare shirt, then he and Sarah wrapped them firmly around Mary's foot and ankle and tied them up. They pulled her sock back on, but couldn't get her shoe on over it, so they put it in her backpack. Arthur and Tom helped her to her feet.

"I'll have to walk on your right side," said Arthur, "so you don't have to put much weight on that foot."

Gingerly she tried to put her foot onto the ground, but a sheet of white fire erupted up her leg, making her cry out in pain.

"Okay, so that's not going to work!"

"How about I make a crutch from one of those spindly trees over there?" Tom asked. "There isn't enough room to walk three abreast on the track, so we need something else to support her. With you on one side and the crutch on the other, she won't need to put her foot down." He set off for the trees and disappeared from sight.

Mary suggested that it might be better if she hid out in the trees while they continued without her. Then they'd get there much more quickly.

"No!" Arthur and Sarah said in unison. They were in it together, and she was just as important to them as whatever it was that lay ahead.

With Arthur's help, Mary sat down on the side of the path and they waited in glum silence for Tom to return. He came back a few minutes later.

"Look what I've found," he said with a big grin. In his hand he had a stout stick with two broken branches forming an open Y at one end.

"Wow," Sarah exclaimed, "that's brilliant!"

Tom swelled with pride, though he tried to hide it. It felt wonderful to hear Sarah say something positive about him.

Mary got up with Arthur's help and tried the makeshift crutch. "You're right Sarah, he's brilliant," she said, smiling at Tom. They resumed their journey, picking their way along the track in a slow, plodding walk. It seemed interminable. Each of them wandered off into their own thoughts. Mary focusing in on herself, registering the deep throb of her foot, but trying to take herself mentally away from it so that she could cope and keep moving. A bit like the way she'd removed herself from her parents' arguments when she was a kid…

Arthur had also plunged back into old memories. He was thinking of a time soon after he'd met Mary when they were teenagers. They'd gone for a walk in the countryside and had come across a rocky outcrop. He'd started to climb it, knowing she would try to follow, even though he knew she was afraid of heights. She'd managed to get halfway up, to a narrow ledge, but had then frozen. She couldn't make herself go either up or down. He'd helped her down, and seeing the terror on her face, had decided right then never to do something like that to her again. Maybe he'd been trying to see what power he had over her; or maybe he wanted to be her knight in shining armour and rescue her so she thought he was wonderful. But really, it had all been about him and it had been a cruel thing to do to someone he cared so much for. And yet here they were again. He'd led them into danger, not just Mary, but Sarah and Tom as well. Another part of his mind came in though, and reminded him that they'd made the decision together and that it was for some greater good, even if they didn't know what that was yet. Besides, Mary would never allow them to leave her behind because she was afraid; the only way she'd ever stay behind would be if she thought she was holding them back from something important. Well, if that happened, he'd be staying with her!

They heard a distant rumble of thunder that made them look up out of their reveries. The sky had darkened to a deep, sombre grey and the threat of rain was in the air. They had no idea how much further they had to go, but it looked like they were going to get a drenching. Stupidly they hadn't brought rainproof gear. It had been raining for so long, that the reprieve they'd had recently had lulled them into forgetting just how persistent it had been. They put their heads down and continued their progress along the track as quickly as they could manage, with Arthur and the stick supporting Mary, and Sarah and Tom carrying the two packs along behind them.

"Tom," Sarah said, as they trudged slowly along the track. He moved forward to walk beside her. "What do you want to do when you leave school?"

"I'm not sure—I really like being creative and making things, like Mary and Arthur do, practical things we can use. It's fun. But maybe what I'd really like to learn more about is geology. It's fascinating – like, even though today is hard going, I keep looking around me at this landscape – just look at that volcano and think about the forces that created it!" There was a moment's pause while Sarah thought about how that was one of the things she wanted to keep furtherest from her mind when she was going to have to go inside it! "What about you? Do you know yet?"

"Well, I'm still not really sure, but since I was here last time I've thought a lot about using natural remedies for healing—you know, herbs, plants, spices, and I think just talking to people at the same time. It seems to me that human kindness is as useful as anything when people feel bad. That's what I get from my grandad—something about his presence and the way he listens."

"Wow, that sounds really interesting, and like it's something you'd be good at."

"Yes, but my parents won't have a bar of it! Not good enough for their girl. I have to be a doctor or a lawyer or something, just because I do well at school. I know I *could* be a doctor first, then move into what I want to do later, but I'm afraid that all those years of studying, in that particular way, would make me lose something about me. I sense things, I know things; intuition, I guess. And I trust that. But med school is all about facts and having evidence. Both my grandparents are GPs—my Gran is lovely, but very stuck in the black and white way she sees the world. My Grandad is a lot like me, but he talks about how hard it is to let himself believe in the things his gut tells him. I had to get him to help me to get here this time, and because he loves me, he made himself let go of his disbelief – he wanted to believe me – but he said he'd been taught to only trust things that had 'proof' through research or because they were factual. He wants to believe that there are things that exist that aren't like that – that's why I brought my phone – to take a few photos for him, to show him."

"So…you could always do it here," Tom ventured. "Morwyn wasn't a good person, but she had real skills that people went to her for and no one seems to have taken her place." The silence stretched out for a long while.

"…I know, I know…" Sarah trailed into silence. "I've been thinking about that. But how do I make a choice to never see my grandparents, or my parents again? What would it do to them to have me go missing? Though it's really my grandad I'd miss, and he knows what's happening, even if he doesn't quite trust yet that I'm okay."

"Well at least you have parents who are interested in you, in wanting the best for you."

"Even if it's all about them, not me? Anyway, you have Mary and Arthur now. For them, you're their son."

Tom felt his eyes beginning to water and swallowed. Before he came here he'd felt so much shame. Shame for being bad, deserving to be bullied and hit; shame for being pathetic and not standing up for himself; and even worse, shame for being unlovable—otherwise his mother would have stood up for him. It had taken two years of patience and care from Mary and Arthur to unpick the threads of that shame, so that he could start to feel how it might be different. So that he knew that no one ever deserves to be abused, that children who feel frightened and powerless need love and protection, not punishment. He'd never thought he'd find what he had here in North Feasgar, and he wasn't about to let anyone or anything destroy it. He wondered again what they were about to face and knew he'd follow through with it, no matter what.

It was well into the afternoon before Ryder flew down to let them know they were near their destination. Knowing it wasn't far now, they suddenly felt exhausted – the tension of worrying about Mary, the slow, stumbling walk and carrying the packs – they were completely over it.

"Come on, not far now," urged Arthur, and they wearily picked up their pace. For some time, the path had been steadily gaining height as they traversed the base of the mountain. It now became steeper, and the path was strewn with smaller rocks that had fallen down the mountainside. It took another twenty minutes before they reached the point where the track bifurcated, one path becoming a set of rough steps, steeply rising directly against the mountain face, while the other continued around the mountain.

They set Mary down on the bottom step, dropped their packs and stretched. Looking up the steps, they realised Mary would never make it with her stick.

"I'll piggyback you," said Arthur.

"No," said Tom, "I'll give it a go first and you can take over when I get tired." He passed his pack to Arthur and helped Mary onto the second step so she could get directly onto his back without him having to bend down. He set off up the steps in the lead, so that if he slipped there would be some chance of Mary being caught by Arthur, who followed closely behind, with Sarah bringing up the rear. It didn't take long to realise it was going to be a slow and painful process. Each step up felt like he was hauling a pack full of bricks with him. After twenty or so steps, he had to stop to catch his breath, with Arthur supporting Mary's weight from the next step down. Another twenty and he was gasping and his legs were shaking like jelly.

"Let's swap," said Arthur. It was more difficult than they thought, juggling Mary from one to the other on the narrow steps, with Sarah watching on helplessly. It was hard enough for her getting up the steps herself with her pack and Mary's stick, with nothing to hold onto—there was little else she could contribute. Eventually they managed to swap roles and Arthur headed up the steps, this time more slowly, with Tom supporting her weight from behind.

At about the point where they thought they could go no further (Sarah had counted eighty-seven steps), Mary looked up, over

Arthur's shoulder and saw a rocky platform approaching above them.

"Look, we're almost there!" she exclaimed. With a final burst of energy, they covered the last steps and collapsed, gasping, on the flat rock. When they eventually managed to haul themselves upright to look around them, the vista was incredible. Miraculously, the dark clouds had skirted around the mountain, and they could see banks of rain in the distance, stretching across their view to the right, in the direction they'd come from—cutting a broad path across the track from west to east, and in the region of the road. The land in front of them undulated, with patches of trees interspersed with rocks in the foreground, becoming more densely green to the west. Looking to their left, to the south, it looked mostly rocky.

"What's that?" asked Sarah.

"What?"

"See – to the left, over those rocks – a pinky-red colour."

They looked intently where she was pointing and could see a strange colour stretching across the horizon, blanking out the landscape beyond. It seemed to shift and almost shimmer in the light; a moving, fluid mixture of red and silver.

"How weird," said Tom. "It reminds me a bit of the dome over the treehouse, but it seems to go straight up, as high as we can see."

In ominous contrast, behind them, carved into the side of the mountain, was a portal and a tunnel leading darkly into the volcano. They looked at it in silence.

"Hey, where's Hermione?" Sarah looked around—she'd completely lost track of when she'd last seen her. She'd been there when Mary hurt herself, but she hadn't noticed when she wandered off after that—they'd all been absorbed, trying to hold their energy together as they walked.

"Hermione," she called out, then realised how silly that was when they could share thoughts. She sat quietly and focused her attention inwards, then sent a thought wave of love to Hermione, with a question at the end of it—*Where are you?* A moment later she received a soft reassuring murmur somewhere in her head. *Almost there, I've just been checking the field of energy you can see in the south.*

They waited on the platform, eating sandwiches and sipping on their water, regaining their energy. Mary lay on her back on the rock, her foot propped up on her pack. The others gazed out at the changing skyline. The dark clouds and rain were moving further away, to the north, and although they couldn't see the sun they could feel that it was starting to retreat towards the horizon, and it would soon be heading towards twilight.

After about fifteen minutes, Hermione appeared at the base of the steps. She bounded up effortlessly, flopped on the rocks beside them and started to groom her glossy fur.

"So, Hermione, what did you find?" Tom asked.

"Well, I think that the force field is the barrier between North and South Feasgar. It stretches further than I could sense, but it's weak. The shimmer you can see is from the way the energy source is trying to hold the structure together. I can only imagine that the strangers who have appeared have somehow used that weakness to find a way through. I think the mountain has some role in holding the barrier, and I'm guessing that's where you all come in—to try to protect it so the barrier isn't breached entirely."

"You all? What about you, Hermione?" Sarah had picked

up on her language.

"Under the mountain is no place for a cat. Even though I can see in the dark, you're going to have to cross water, if your dream is literal, and I can't follow you there. I can be of better use out here to keep an eye out and warn you if there's any danger approaching from outside."

Sarah stroked her sleek fur, all the while feeling sick inside.

"You'll be okay, Sarah, you were brought to North Feasgar for a purpose; a purpose that's been prophesised for many years. You and Tom will do it together."

"What about us?" Mary and Arthur queried when Sarah translated.

"I'm not sure. It's really important you're here, but I don't know what role you'll play. Go with good heart and courage and see what unfolds. Now, it's time for you to go."

She rubbed herself against Mary and Arthur, and let Sarah and Tom pick her up. Sarah rubbed her face in the soft place at the base of her ear, and Tom gave her a chin rub. She then jumped down and scampered down the steps, disappearing from sight at the bottom into some scrubby bushes. They looked at each other, Sarah wiping a tear from her eye, and sighed.

"Let's go then."

They helped Mary to her feet, Sarah and Tom shouldered the packs again and they stepped into the mouth of the tunnel. Immediately the world seemed to hush. No wind, no birds, only the sound of their breathing and the soft footfalls of their feet on the rock. It had a clean smell, but somehow it felt ancient. They took out their candles and lanterns and lit them in the half-light coming in from behind them. The candles flickered, but their flames held once they were placed in the lanterns.

Looking around Tom noticed several tall sticks propped against the wall near the entrance.

"Look, I think they're brands for burning." They had heavy material wound tightly onto the top of the sticks so they looked like giant candles, and smelt of an unfamiliar substance. They must have been left there to light the way into the mountain, which implied that people regularly came here. Touching a flame to their ends caused them to flare brightly, before settling into a steady glow, much stronger than their lanterns, so they blew the lanterns out, shoved them back in their packs, and Sarah and Tom took one brand each, while Arthur focused on helping Mary.

The tunnel entrance opened out into a small cavern. The air inside was cold and clear. The flickering light reflected off very old rock walls, just reaching a high, rounded ceiling. Tom wondered how it had been made but kept his questions to himself. He'd read a bit about volcanic caves and lava tubes, but it somehow felt wrong to even speak in the cool silence. They were aware of a feeling of overlapping awe and fear that made them want to whisper.

"Are we ready then?" said Arthur quietly.

The others just nodded their heads mutely. Mary adjusted her position a little, leaning on her stick, and with Arthur on her other side, they slowly moved towards the back of the cavern where a dark slit indicated their way forward. Sarah caught her breath sharply, audible in the quiet space, and Tom reached out and took her hand and squeezed it. Sarah gratefully returned the gesture, pulled her jacket more tightly around her body and moved a little closer to him as they silently followed.

Chapter VIII

The Descent

The passage they entered was wide enough for three people to walk together, so they had space to walk easily two by two, with Arthur and Mary again in the lead. Mary found a rhythm of sorts between the stick and support from Arthur that was manageable, although slow. The light from their brands reflected eerily off the walls, a little too close for Sarah's comfort. They looked as if they'd been widened by people, as they were relatively smooth and dry, unlike the rougher walls of the cavern they'd just left. The passage sloped down and it felt surreal—their slow, hushed, steady descent inside the mountain. They didn't talk, each slipping into their own inward reveries.

Sarah was thinking about being very far away from her family and her school, and how different it was to feel so connected to the people she was with. Here she was, walking with Tom, Mary and Arthur, having such an adventure, even though they had no idea what was going to happen, somehow it was okay, that not knowing. Without being consciously aware of it though, her mind drifted to being under the mountain, to how deep they were, and to a kind of felt image of the mass of rock above them. Her breath became more rapid and her pulse started to race, as she recalled her dream of scrabbling through the narrow passage alone, on hands and knees, with something terrible behind her. Her hands were clammy and her breath started coming in short gasps as panic overtook her. The rock walls were closing in on her, there was no way out, and she couldn't breathe!

"Sarah!" Tom said. "Are you okay?"

She couldn't answer. Everything in her just wanted to run. She needed air—desperately!

"What's up?" asked Arthur from ahead.

"Sarah's claustrophobic," Tom replied.

Arthur came back to them and took both of Sarah's hands in his. He spoke calmly and clearly to her. "Sarah, take a deep breath." She did what he said, but there wasn't enough air. "Keep going. Another one. No, not with the top of your chest—a deep, belly one. Yes, that's right. Keep going. Notice that there's plenty of air; it's cool and clean, it's not stuffy, so there's a good supply of air. There must be lots of openings and caverns in the mountain. Think of it more like a holey matrix rather than solid."

Her breathing began to slow and she found herself starting to be able to think again rather than being trapped in blind panic. Arthur's hands were strong and reassuring. "But my dream—"

"From what I know of dreams, they're not literal." Arthur said, keeping his voice very even and reassuring.

Sarah took a really deep breath and let something go inside her...

After a while she could speak again. "I've been reading about dreams—I think they come from our unconscious and speak to us in a different way, like a sort of a metaphor. Sometimes they can be prescient, but even then, they're not rational—we have to work out what they mean."

"So, what *do* you pick up from them if you look at all of them together?" Arthur asked.

"Well, I have to go on a journey underground and it will be difficult—that's pretty real already, but I guess the scariness of it may be from my own fears rather than what I'm going to find. I know I'm doing something important, with Tom, and I think I might meet a woman, a special woman there." She'd moved out of her panic and could think properly again. "Thanks Arthur, I think I can keep going now," she said, and they resumed the rhythm of their descent.

Tom, listening to their conversation, was awed by Arthur and the way he calmly dealt with anything. He was incredibly grateful to have found a secure place with him and Mary. Things felt completely different for him now. He only had a vague memory, more an impression, of his dad, but it was a warm one. And his dad's parents, his grandparents were really good people. Imagine if he'd never had them in his life. How awful would that be, not to have any solid, loving connection to anyone?

A memory of his stepfather, Gerald, came unwanted into his mind. He was about eight, and he must have done something wrong—or at least Gerald must have decided he'd done something he didn't like! He had a partial memory of coming home from school feeling really good about his teacher liking a model he'd built for the science fair. He couldn't remember what happened next—maybe he'd said something Gerald didn't like? The next minute he was being yelled at for being too big for his boots and Gerald had smashed the model right through the middle with his fist. The next bit was blurry—he'd probably tried to block it out. He remembered being taken outside and made to sit and watch while Gerald broke a branch off a tree and slowly pared all the side branches off it. His coldness and deliberation were actually worse than his usual hot rage. As Gerald walked towards him, saying he'd take him down a peg or two, he'd been so scared he'd wet himself. He couldn't remember anything more, but he could imagine being ridiculed for being a baby as well!

He could feel himself tensing and becoming emotional remembering it. Sarah must have picked up something, because she squeezed his hand and he managed to bring himself back to the passage and force himself to relax. Maybe there was a lot more remembering yet to do. But not here—they needed to keep focused together. His mind suddenly made a connection to Jonnie though—from what Kayla had said, they'd had a terrible life. If Jonnie hadn't had any love from adults, how would he ever be able to accept the kind qualities offered by Mary and Arthur? He wouldn't be able to trust them. He thought of how vulnerable he used to feel, and imagined Jonnie covering those kinds of feelings with bravado. He suddenly felt some of his antagonism towards him evaporating, along with an almost overwhelming surge of gratitude for his grandparents, Leah and the special people on this journey with him. His eyes teared and he spontaneously reached out and gave Sarah's shoulder a hug. For a moment she leaned in towards him, then they continued their steady walk.

A short time later, the steady glow of their brands showed them a fork in the passage. The main passage appeared to go to the right – it looked similar to the one they were in now – well-worn and reasonably wide. When Tom held his brand in the opening of the other one, it was only just wide enough for two, with a lower ceiling and a rough floor and sides. Arthur and Mary headed towards the one on the right.

"Stop!" exclaimed Sarah. "Remember my dream with the woman in it—she said whenever we came to a fork in the path, to take the left one."

They looked at her dubiously—the left path looked much more difficult. There was a long pause, followed by a sigh from Mary and a shrug from Arthur.

"Oh well, let's go then," he said eventually.

They entered the passage. The ground was uneven and they had to really watch where they put their feet. The passage walls were also irregular and they had to be vigilant for pieces of rock jutting into their path. Tom ran his hand over the wall, marvelling at the porous texture of it. The slope was more pronounced, so Arthur had to hold Mary firmly as she struggled placing her stick on the bumpy ground. They walked in silence, completely over any anticipation they might have had. Sarah wasn't feeling good, but she wasn't in the horrible panicky state she'd been in earlier. Arthur was right, there was plenty of air, but she was really struggling to keep at bay an intrusive background thought that maybe something would block her path back, that maybe she wouldn't ever get out—the weight of the rock above her pressed down and she had to keep her thoughts focused on steady breathing and putting one foot in front of the other. Having Tom beside her made a huge difference and she realised how much she'd come to rely on him in such a short time. It seemed inconceivable that they'd only spent about ten days in each other's company over the period of a couple of years, and yet they'd been through so much together that a really deep connection had been made. Whatever would she do in the future? The pull to stay in North Feasgar was huge, but she still had her family to think about.

Arthur and Mary had slowed up ahead, as they'd come to another fork in the passage. This time there wasn't much difference in their choice, so it seemed easy to choose the left. *And at least*, Sarah thought, *going back up they wouldn't get lost if they could always choose right.* This passage though, soon narrowed again and wouldn't quite accommodate Arthur, Mary and her stick. Mary encouraged Sarah and Tom to move on ahead, but they all agreed that they were in it together, and had no intention of splitting up. Besides, Sarah thought she'd be terrified without Arthur's solid and calm presence. So reluctantly, Mary continued, with Arthur immediately in front, one hand on his shoulder, the other arm leaning on the stick, with Tom and Sarah closely bringing up the rear. Their little team made slow progress until Tom missed his footing and put out a hand to the rough wall to stop himself piling onto Mary.

"Ouch," he exclaimed loudly.

"You all right back there?" asked Arthur.

"Yep, just grazed my hand. This rock is rough—it's like a giant Brillo pad, and I caught the same palm I grated when I fell earlier." It really stung, and he blotted the small red beads of blood popping up out of his skin on his jacket.

Not long after, Mary said quietly to Arthur, "I don't think I can go any further. I'm all in." Her voice sounded strained and exhausted. She'd been almost silent since they entered the mountain, trying to hold all her energy close to her so she could just keep going. Now she was suddenly overwhelmed and completely depleted.

"Mary, love, you don't have a choice. We can stop for a moment to get a breath, but you'd never make it back up at the moment, so we need to keep going to the next flat place where you can rest properly."

There was a long silence. Arthur had turned to her and was holding her in his arms, trying to will her some of his strength. She sighed and agreed to keep going.

About ten minutes later, Tom asked them to stop.

"Shh—" he said. "I think I can hear something. Something steady in the background." The others looked at each other, puzzled. They couldn't hear anything, so they moved on again. Then Sarah registered it.

"Oh, I can hear something too, Tom's right."

Mary and Arthur still had no notion of what they were talking about, though Arthur thought to himself that that wasn't surprising, given the way he and Mary had spent years working with machinery. Their hearing would have deteriorated with age too, not like these youngsters.

"I can hear it more clearly now," Tom added. "It's mostly constant, with an occasional surge—I think it could be flowing water."

At last, something different to break up the interminable descent. It gave them a new spurt of energy, and they moved as quickly as Mary could manage. Another ten minutes and they stumbled through the passage opening to find themselves in another vaulted cavern. This one was more dramatic, with the peak of the ceiling stretching up way higher than their lights could reveal.

They dropped their packs and flopped down on the floor of the cavern, exhausted more from emotional tension than being physically tired, and tried to get their bearings in the flickering light from the brands. The space was large and was bisected left to right by a deep cleft through which a river was flowing.

"Tom, Sarah, I'm going to get Mary comfortable—why don't you two look around before we have a break and some food. Be careful of the river—there'd be no fishing you out of there!" warned Arthur. He turned to Mary and helped her to manoeuvre into a sitting position supported by the rocky wall, with her foot elevated on their pack.

"I'm really tired," Mary said. "My foot's aching terribly, although I don't think it's got any worse, despite being upright for so long." Once Tom and Sarah had moved out of immediate hearing to explore, she added, "But I don't think I can go any further for a while, and the idea of getting across that river seems completely impossible the way I'm feeling at the moment."

"Yes, I agree. I've been thinking about that. The problem is that Sarah and Tom don't want to leave us, even though they need to continue alone. Do we just not tell them until we've got them across the river and there's no going back?"

"Well... maybe... But then again, trust is such an important thing, especially for Tom. I think we have to sit them both down and tell them that we can't go any further but that we'll be here to keep a watch out and to help them return. I know it's a huge thing to ask of them to go on into the unknown alone, but it was always going to be about the two of them. I'm just not sure that they've really absorbed that."

Tom and Sarah had meanwhile walked over to the river. The channel through the rock was much narrower than the river's path on the outside of the mountain, so it must be very deep to compensate. As they looked down on it, it seemed dark and fast-flowing, almost like a living entity, a serpent, sliding its way through the mountain. Sarah shivered. It chilled them both to the bone, even thinking about what would happen if they fell in.

They could see remnants on each side where a bridge must have spanned it at some point. There were still posts on the other side, but on their side, it looked as if they'd been smashed down. They could just see where the bases were still anchored to the hard rock. It was just as well they hadn't planned on an easy crossing! On the far side they could make out an opening out of the cavern like the one they'd just come through. The whole cavern was like an irregular oval in shape, with rocks scattered around, probably from a rock fall long ago. Other than that, never-ending rock was all they could see. Sarah, on and off, still had to battle her fear of being closed in, so she kept her mind on problem-solving so that it wouldn't take over. She was getting good at distraction!

"So how do you think we'll get across Tom? I'm guessing the rope will be secured at this end and thrown over until the hook you made gets a good hold on the other side. Can we risk the posts do you think, or would a rock be better?"

"You don't seem too worried about getting across!" noted Tom.

"Well, compared to being underground, it's something I can

cope with—I've always been good at doing stuff in the gym, so long as it's not high," Sarah replied.

"I've never been a jungle gym kind of a kid, so I'm not looking forward to the idea of pulling myself hand over hand across rapidly flowing water!" Tom responded.

"But I'm thinking it's only about twenty hand-holds."

"Well that's about eighteen too many, especially with my grazed hand!"

Just then Sarah picked up something in her mind—Hermione! She put a hand on Tom's arm to quieten him. Once they both went still, he could pick up her thoughts too.

"Tom, Sarah, you have visitors. Willard, Jonnie and Kayla have arrived. They look like they're camping out for the night at the base of the steps to the tunnel. Jonnie has been up to check it out, but it's dark now and they've obviously decided to wait until morning. They're not prepared and will have a cold and hungry night."

"Thanks Hermione. We've got to the river and I think we're going to keep going after we've had some food. It's wonderful to know you're there—I've been finding it hard-going underground."

"If you're at the river, there's not far to go now. Take heart. I sense a good presence there and if the rumours are true, you'll be meeting someone really special."

"What rumours?" they both asked at the same time.

"Some of the villagers from Greyvyn hold a secret very close, but they are known to take supplies to the mountain every week. They are so loyal to whoever it is they support that even the villagers around them don't know exactly where they go or who they take the supplies to. But there is an unspoken agreement between them that the whole village supports something vital to North Feasgar, so important that they are not to ask, not to talk about it, just be available if ever they're needed. And they know to report it if anyone from outside the village starts snooping around or asking questions.

"So how do you know?" Tom queried.

"Who notices a cat?" she replied. "Before you knew me, would you ever have thought I could understand you, or talk to you?"

"Well you've got a point there!"

"I agree that you need to keep going tonight. It won't take long for the others to catch up with you in the morning. Hopefully the river will hold them up. Good luck." With that, her contact with them disappeared.

Sarah and Tom made their way back to Mary and Arthur, and noticed that they abruptly stopped talking as they approached, looking at each other.

"What's up?" asked Tom. "You're looking shifty."

"Sit down and have some food," said Arthur, "We need to talk to you—Mary and I can't go on the next stage with you. Mary isn't feeling up to it and I'm not going to leave her alone."

"But..." started Sarah.

"No. That's just how it has to be. I realise it's a huge thing to ask you, but with us here to watch your back, are you willing to go on together without us?"

"Willard, Kayla and Jonnie are camping out for the night at the tunnel entrance. What will you do when they get here? Will you be okay on your own?" asked Tom.

"What? Oh...Hermione!" Mary exclaimed. "Good for her. It's good to know she's out there. We'll be okay since we're forewarned. There are plenty of rocks we can hide behind if we have to, and I'd like to see them trying to cross the river if they haven't brought ropes! Don't worry about us. We're more concerned about you two being okay to continue."

"Hermione says she doesn't think it's much further, if her sensing is correct," said Sarah. "But she thinks we need to keep going now so we have as much of a lead on the others as we can. Can we go now? I don't want to think about it any more or I might chicken out."

"Fair enough. Let's talk through what we're going to do."

When they felt confident about how they planned to get across the river, Arthur took his rope with their handmade hook attached, and the three of them went over to the river. Arthur carefully scrutinised the other side and pointed to a rock just to the side, and a bit behind, one of the remaining posts.

"How about that one? See the taller one? It has quite deep crevices that I should be able to get the hook to hold onto. I don't think the posts will work—they're too smooth."

He stood back a couple of steps from the side of the river and threw the hook. The coiled rope snaked out over the river and the hook clanged on the flat rock on the other side. It fell short of the rock he was aiming for, so he dragged the rope back and recoiled it. He tried again, and this time it hit the rock but didn't manage to keep hold of it. Two more tries and it finally snagged and held onto the rock. Arthur pulled the rope hard and the hook seemed to sink more deeply into the crevice it had found on the other side.

"Well thank goodness for that! I was starting to wonder how long it would take."

Arthur unravelled more of the rope and took it back to a rock that he could wrap it around and use as an anchor. Pulling it taut, he wrapped it three times around the rock, pulling down on the rope to wedge it under a ledge to stop it working its way up, handing the end to Tom to hold as he pulled another length of rope out of his pack.

"Right, so who's going first?" he asked, automatically looking towards Tom.

"I will," said Sarah. Arthur looked surprised. "I'm lighter, so I'm better to test the rope, and from what Tom says, I'm more confident with using them."

"Okay…" Arthur said, looking at Tom, who gave him a nod of agreement. "I'm going to knot this second rope around your waist so that if you fall, I can pull you out of the water." Sarah ran over to Mary and gave her a hug, then went back to Arthur, who wound the end of the second rope around her waist and tied it firmly with a bowline knot. The other end he looped around the rock beneath the first one, before taking the first rope back from Tom and anchoring himself firmly against the rock. She threw her arms around his shoulders, giving him a hug, then Tom, before taking a deep breath and walking to the edge of the river. At least it wasn't too far down; she wouldn't need to worry about vertigo. She wiped her sweaty hands on her top and moved to the rope. A sudden twist in her gut stopped her, and she leaned forward, hands on her knees, trying to breathe through a spasm of panic. Hermione infused herself into her thinking.

"Sarah, stand up tall. Now take a deep breath, right down in your diaphragm. Slowly. Now breathe out. In again," she paused, "and out. Good, now find your centre, gather all your energy into feeling balanced. Be brave."

Sarah took another breath and reached up to the rope. Without any more thinking she launched herself out over the river. She moved quickly across to the centre of the river. Ten handholds, eleven, twelve... Tom and Arthur, watching anxiously, saw her hesitate and held their breaths, but she must have just been gathering herself together, because after a few seconds, she continued, hand over hand. Twenty handholds got her to the edge, then one more and she dropped lightly to the ground on the other side. Tom realised he'd completely stopped breathing and took a large gulp of air, raising his hands over his head as a salute to her.

"Yay, I did it!" she yelled back, feeling a mix of excitement and relief.

Arthur slackened his hold on the ropes, giving the main rope to Tom to make sure it stayed taut.

"Well done, Sarah. Now untie the rope around your waist and let it go—I'll pull it back in for Tom."

When he'd retrieved the rope, he turned to see that Tom had loosely knotted the main rope to the second one and had gone over to say goodbye to Mary. As he approached to give her a hug, she held out a strip of cloth to him, repurposed from the bottom of Arthur's shirt. At this rate, after both his and Mary's injuries, Arthur wouldn't have a wearable spare shirt!

"Hold out your sore hand Tom. If we wrap this around it, you'll be able to get a better grip on the rope." She wound it around his palm and the base of his fingers, making sure he could still flex his hand, and tied it off against the beginning of the bandage on the outside of his hand.

"Thank you, Mary. Take care—we'll be back soon!" He walked off swiftly, feeling emotional. He gave Arthur a hug, after which Arthur put a hand on each of his shoulders and said something quietly to him.

"Sorry, I didn't get that," he said.

"Tom, remember, we both love you," repeated Arthur.

Tom gulped and held back his tears. That was the first time anyone had ever said that to him. Even his grandparents hadn't... Fighting for control over the lump he could feel in his throat, he moved quickly over to the rope and, grasping it firmly, let his feet lift off the ground. The first few hand changes were fine, but he hadn't even reached halfway before he started to feel tired and panicky. By the time he was suspended over the middle of the river he was gasping, thinking he'd never make it. Another two handholds, then he stalled, holding the rope with his bandaged hand, his feet dangling heavily and his other hand flapping in the air.

"Tom, bring up your other hand. Don't let go. You can do it," encouraged Sarah. He managed to bring his other hand back up to hold onto the rope, but he'd lost momentum and didn't think he could move any further.

"Tom, come on, move!" Sarah yelled. He managed to get himself into a lurching movement—right, left; right, left. Just a couple more to go—he was near the far edge, but he couldn't do it. His arms felt like jelly, his legs jerked, trying to carry him forwards, but his hands were so tired!

"Tom, just one more, then if you push yourself towards me I can grab your legs and pull you over."

He took a deep breath, then managed to move one more hand. He pushed his legs towards the edge and felt Sarah grab them, and using the last of his strength he forced his arms forwards, propelling his body over in her direction, crashing into her, landing right on top of her at the edge of the river.

"Oumph…" all the air was forced out of Sarah's lungs as she landed hard on the rock, on her back. She felt winded and disoriented. Tom pulled himself off and rolled into a sitting position. Putting out a hand to her, he helped her up.

"I'm so sorry! Thanks for being my mattress! Are you okay?"

"Ow, my bum is sore! Feels like I landed on my tailbone first before falling flat on my back—But you made it!"

"How about your head?"

"No, I think it's okay," she said, putting her hand to the back of her head and feeling across the back of it gingerly with her fingers.

"Hey, you two, are you okay?" Mary was standing up, looking over at them anxiously.

"Yes," they both called back.

"You had me worried for a while there, Tom," called Arthur, "I thought I was going to have to haul you back in with the rope!"

"So did I!" said Tom, "It was pretty scary, so I was glad you had my back!"

"Can you untie the rope around your waist and tie it low around the rock?" asked Arthur.

When it was retied, Arthur fed his end of the rope through the straps of their pack and, holding it high above his head and as taut as he could, he let the pack go. It slid quite easily down the rope, making its way across the river. It caught briefly part way across, but a jiggle on the rope released it to continue its journey to Tom. Grabbing it, Tom untied the rope, took the pack off and retied the rope around the rock so it would be ready for their return trip, while Arthur did the same on the other side, just in case something happened and one of them had to make their way across to help. They had to take the risk that if Willard and the others found them, they'd have enough warning from Hermione to remove the rope before they got there.

Tom and Sarah looked at each other. They'd made it! They felt a huge surge of relief, along with something less definable. It was something to do with hoping they'd reached the last stage of their journey, feeling emotional about leaving Mary and Arthur behind, and about all they'd managed to achieve so far. They turned to wave to them, then walked together, hand in hand, into the tunnel. As they entered it, a sense of quiet wrapped itself around them, guiding them towards their journey's end. They'd had to leave their brand behind when they crossed the river, but the lanterns from their pack lit the way, their flickering lights illuminating the path deeper into the mountain.

They walked together in silence, with just the sound of their footfalls and their breathing. Strangely, Sarah's underlying sense of panic had evaporated, replaced by a sense that this was meant to happen, a portentous feeling that had been activated way back by finding the tarot card. It settled on her, giving her a sense of calm, as if she was moving towards her destiny. Tom, beside her, had less of a knowing about where they were heading, or what they'd find, but felt enveloped by her calmness and certainty. His sense of knowing was that they'd be okay.

After about fifteen minutes of walking, they noticed a change—a lightening in the passage ahead. As they continued, the light grew stronger, and suddenly they were out of the tunnel and in another cavern. Sarah gasped in awe at what was revealed in front of them. The cavern wasn't as large as the previous ones, but it had a soaring, vaulted ceiling, and its walls were lit with masses of candles, their soft glow reflecting off tapestries and a floor richly overlaid with carpets. They stood there, hand in hand, mouths open in wonder as they ran their eyes over the setting before them. Then Sarah saw her, with a strong sense of recognition... A slim woman, with pale skin and glorious, long, white hair that tumbled down almost to her waist. She carried an air of wisdom and serenity as she gazed at the two of them, arrested in movement near what looked, from a distance, like a stone table.

"You've come!" the woman said, her voice resonant with expectation and joy. "I've been waiting for you."

As they moved towards her, they noted the sparse but comfortable furnishings. The beauty of the space was almost overwhelming, following on from all the fear and uncertainty of the past twenty-four hours.

"You must be exhausted," the woman continued. "Come and sit down over here," she indicated to some fat, woven cushions on the floor, "and I'll bring you something to drink." She moved to a recess in a rock wall and re-emerged a moment later with an earthenware carafe and mugs, which she placed on a low table near them. Once they were seated close to her, Tom noticed that she looked older than he'd originally thought, or maybe just tired—she had an air of weariness and fragility about her. They sipped the liquid she poured into the mugs. It had a slight scent that reminded Sarah of fresh flowers and open spaces, and it tasted like a delicious light nectar. It was instantly refreshing—it felt quite magical. She caught Tom's eye and could tell he was experiencing it the same way.

They realised they still hadn't spoken since they'd entered the cavern. Its unexpectedness had completely silenced them.

"It's like a Persian cave," whispered Sarah, just as Tom cleared his throat to try to say something. But the woman began to speak.

"My name is Galawand. I imagine you don't really know why you're here—But I've met you," she turned her gaze towards Sarah, "in a dream." Sarah found herself flushing. "Why don't you tell me about yourselves and then I'll explain everything to you," the woman continued.

"I'm Sarah."

"And I'm Tom," he chipped in.

"We both come from another world," Sarah continued. "I come from a country called England, and Tom comes from the other side of our world, from a country called New Zealand. We believe that we came here through some sort of a rift a couple of years ago. When we went to the labyrinth," at this Galawand was nodding, "we saw that I had to return home and that Tom was to stay with our friends, Mary and Arthur. We also knew that we'd all be involved sometime in something really important for the future of North Feasgar. I started dreaming about coming back a couple of months ago, but I'd just got back when I had the dream about you, so we've hurried to get here."

"And where are your friends now?"

"They've waited on the other side of the river. Mary hurt herself and they thought it was better if we came on our own while they watch out for any trouble," Tom said.

"Trouble? Does anyone know that you're here?"

"Not directly. That is, we haven't told anyone, but we think we may have been followed. Our cat, Hermione tells us that they're camping outside the tunnel, so they'll probably try to find us tomorrow."

Galawand didn't appear to be even remotely phased by the mention of a cat who could communicate…

"Well, they may not find their way in this direction, and I doubt they'll be able to cross the river, but it does mean that there is no time to be lost. How did you cross the river?"

"We brought ropes and Arthur helped us."

"That was good planning. Did you see any other way across when you got there?"

"No? What do you mean?"

Galawand smiled. "Good. That means my magic is still holding, even though I'm weak—Now, if you're ready, I'll tell you my story."

***

Galawand's story revealed some of what they already knew about how Feasgar had been split to contain the dark magic threatening their country. The dark mages had been banished to the south, while those in the north had had to give up their powers in order to maintain a barrier between them, to keep the people of their land living in safety. This meant that magic was no longer available in North Feasgar. She had been highly practised in magic and had been part of the uprising that sought to prevent magic being used for power, control and evil purposes. She and her peers and apprentices had had to make the decision to sacrifice their powers, their art, for the greater good of the country.

When it came to creating the barrier, they knew it would drain all their powers to create it, and would need the sacrifice of one of them to maintain it for a lifetime. Galawand had volunteered, even while knowing it would confine her to a life lived in solitude. She alone had kept her magical powers, which were almost all used to maintain the barrier, leaving little else, especially now the dark magicians from the south were finding ways to weaken it, and weaken her. She was tired and could no longer hold the barrier safely on her own. That's where they came in.

"What do you mean? What can we do? We're not magic!" demanded Tom, feeling anxious. Whatever had they got themselves into?

"Some of my friends who gave up their magic to the barrier have maintained the Sight. They live quietly in the village of Greyvyn and bring me food and supplies. No one else knows who they are. From the outside, they're just ordinary villagers going about their lives. They've always seen that when it was most needed, help would come from two young people from another realm. While that rumour has been propagated through the good people of North Feasgar to give them some hope, the exact knowledge of what we do to protect them and where the power centre that maintains the barrier is located, has been held secret to prevent anyone from trying to destroy it."

"And what is it that we're supposed to be able to do?" Sarah asked, with a wobble of nervousness in her voice.

"My friends and I know that I cannot continue much longer alone. Each day my strength wanes, and with it, the barrier is weakening. You are here to help me, to reboot the energy of the barrier. No one from North Feasgar can do it. Too much had to be given up to create our safe place. We need fresh energy and the power of intuition and vitality that you bring from your world."

"Sarah's the intuitive one, not me!" exclaimed Tom.

"You do yourself a disservice. You've learned not to trust yourself or others. Part of your journey here is to reclaim your sense of who you really are."

They were quiet for a time, with Tom thinking about what she'd said, feeing quite overwhelmed. Galawand eventually continued: "My friends in the village have aged more quickly than me—many years have passed since we made the barrier. They have each had to pass on their knowledge and remaining skills to one of their children to ensure the lineage of what we've created is remembered and to support me in my role. They have chosen carefully, as it takes a person of utmost integrity to hold our secret and live humbly in service to the country. They tell me that the strangers who are now in their midst have the power to either appear or not be seen by the locals, as they choose. So far, they've been keeping close to Hunterdale, but those who choose to reveal themselves have been manipulating people to spy for them."

"That'll be Willard, and probably Jonnie," exclaimed Tom. "I've met up with a couple of them at school, watching me. How come I can see them but no one else can?"

"Because you're not from here. You haven't had your natural powers suppressed by the effect of the barrier. That's why you stand out, and why they're watching you. The good thing is that even though they've got through the barrier somehow, their magic is muted here too. They need to get other people to gather information for them—I imagine they can't function far away from wherever they've set up their base, and which is where they'll have an energy force."

"I know where that is!" Tom suddenly realised. "They're at Morwyn's place, between Riverstone and Hunterdale."

"Morwyn? She's part of this?" Galawand asked.

"No, she's dead, but they're using her place."

"How very interesting—She was a clever young thing, with great potential. But in the end, she didn't want to give up her magic to save North Feasgar. I wondered what might happen to her—she was one of the few who voted against our action."

"Well, she became nasty and tried to harm Tom and me when we first got here, and we think she'd hurt or killed some other kids before us," said Sarah.

"I'm thinking there's a lot more to this story, but for now we have important things to attend to in case we're interrupted tomorrow. Come with me."

She got to her feet, surprisingly agile, despite what she'd said about being weary. They followed her over to the stone table in the middle of the room.

They looked down on a ring of stones, illuminated by a rich, red glow. A narrow band with a silver, pearly lustre overlaid the red, creating a ring that bound the stones together. It flickered and rippled, seeming to be almost alive.

"This is the centre. It represents and holds the barrier that protects North Feasgar."

"It's the same colour we could see from outside the mountain," said Tom, "only it was a bit more silver."

"That's because it was more energised than now. The red is the colour of my magic and the silver is the energy that wraps around it and holds it together. As my energy wanes, the red becomes more apparent."

"That's beautiful," breathed Sarah, overcome by the enormity of what it represented. "What can we do?"

Before they began, Galawand talked them through a short meditation, getting them to breathe deeply into their diaphragms and focus on a slow rhythm of breath, in and out, and a feeling of being centred in their bodies. She then put the palm of her left hand flat on the stone in the centre of the circle, and instructed them to spread themselves around the table and for Tom to place his left hand, palm down on hers, then Sarah's on Tom's.

"Keep breathing deeply—in...and out..." Their rhythm now in time with each other, they began to notice a tingling in the soles of their feet. It slowly moved up through their bodies, a delicious feeling, up through their abdomens, centring for a time around the regions of their hearts, then up through their upper chests, their throats, to their foreheads and up through the top of their heads. It was uplifting—they felt open, joined and exhilarated, and at the same time somehow vulnerable. They'd never experienced anything like it before. The feeling throbbed and pulsed between them. After what must have been about a minute, but at the same time felt like forever, Galawand began to ease her hand out from beneath theirs and they came back to their normal presence in the room.

"That's enough for your first time. Look at what we've achieved."

They looked down to see the red around and between the stones glowing much more richly, and the silver now a thicker rope, trembling and pulsing as an overlay that looked as if it was protecting the red, moulding itself strongly over the top half of the stones.

"That's wonderful, thank you. We've accomplished so much in one night. How are you feeling?"

They suddenly realised how worn out they felt. The edges

of exhaustion were biting strongly at them, and Galawand led them away from the table and back to the cushions.

"I'm sorry I don't have beds for you, but the cushions pushed together should be comfortable."

She made them have another drink of her nectar, and within minutes of lying down they were deeply asleep, the full extent of their overwhelming day washed up on the cushions with them, an unconscious sleep too deep even for dreaming.

Galawand looked down on them, her face soft as she saw the fair-haired girl and the dark-haired boy, just as the seers had foretold. She turned and walked slowly to her sleeping pallet.

Chapter IX

The Power of Four

As dawn broke, Kayla became aware of being cramped and cold, curled in as small a ball as she could manage in a shallow hollow in the ground, with just a bit of scrubby plant cover to break the cool breeze. She'd started off curled up against Jonnie, but he'd moved away at some point during the night. She didn't know how she could have slept at all, but she'd been completely exhausted, emotionally and physically, by the end of the previous day, after trudging around the mountain until they'd reached the base of a set of steps that seemed to lead higher up the mountain. Sitting up, she looked around, to see Jonnie rousing himself nearby, and Willard's heavier form near another clump of bushes, lying on his back, snoring. *What an ugly picture*, she thought, looking at his slack mouth and unkempt beard and hair. A shiver went through her. He was truly disgusting in every sense, and she'd make sure she was never alone with him again.

She didn't know what she was doing here with them, or what she was going to do, but for now she didn't feel like she had much choice but to go along with them, while keeping her eyes open for what her gut told her to do. Jonnie may be all she had on her side in the world, but she wasn't going to let him make her be part of something she didn't want, something that served Willard's needs rather than hers. She wondered what she'd do if that meant she had to choose between Jonnie and her sense of what was right. She shivered. Something was telling her that that decision was closer now. She'd have to be strong.

"Jonnie," she whispered. He rolled towards her, opening his eyes. "What are we doing here? Are we really going to follow Tom and Sarah into the mountain?" He just nodded. "And then what? What's that supposed to achieve?"

"Dunno, but Willard wants to check out what they're up to."

"And what business is that of ours?" she demanded.

"He says they're up to no good."

"Oh sure, like I'd believe him over the Birches!"

"Well, you don't have to come. But I'm going with him—Willard says he needs me in case there's trouble."

Kayla shook her head in disbelief. How could he be so gullible—surely he didn't believe the Birches, and Tom and Sarah, were involved in something bad? She was sure it was more that he was mesmerised somehow by Willard wanting him. All that attention he'd never had from a man as a kid. He must see that Willard wasn't a good person. Or was that what he was drawn to? As she pulled herself into a sitting position, wrapping her arms around her knees, she caught a movement out of the corner of her eye. She turned her head, but there was nothing there. She could have sworn she'd glimpsed something like a cat. Like Hermione? Surely not! She didn't say anything—she knew Jonnie hated cats for some reason and wouldn't put it past Willard to be really cruel to an animal. They'd never had pets, but why would Jonnie hate cats so much? Maybe he was instinctively afraid of them?

Her mind wandered, thinking about Hermione. Maybe it was something about her being so free and independent, something that couldn't be controlled. Did Jonnie have to be in control? She guessed so—he'd always bossed her and her mum around, even though part of him was afraid of their mother's behaviour. That's what bullies did—hid their fear by trying to control or put other people down. She didn't want to think about him like that. He'd been the only person she'd ever cared about. What if he was so influenced by Willard that he became someone she didn't like? Then she'd be all alone.

Willard made a snorting noise, loud enough that he woke himself up. He lifted his head and looked around, dragging himself up from the ground, scratching his head and spitting into the bushes. *Charming*, Kayla thought. Once on his feet he grunted at them and started towards the steps.

"Come on, got to get going."

"So, who got up on the wrong side of bed then?" Kayla whispered to Jonnie. "No, wait, there was no bed; just the hard, cold ground, and no food or drink for the last ages!"

"Shut it Kayla," Jonnie warned.

"Did one of you say something?" Willard snarled without looking around.

"No, we're just getting ourselves together," Jonnie replied, hurrying to catch him up. At the bottom of the steps Willard paused to take a flask out of his back pocket.

Unscrewing the top, he took a deep swig and replaced it, without offering them any. Kayla assumed it was alcohol—what a good start to the day!

The two of them went up the steps ahead of her. Kayla noticed how Jonnie had unconsciously adopted a bit of Willard's swagger, or at least the set of how he held himself. Underneath though, she sensed something about him tight as a coiled spring. She wondered whether he was feeling anxious about going into the mountain, but wouldn't let himself show it to Willard. She wasn't particularly worried for herself—since she was little she'd gone into her bedroom, locked the door and pulled the curtains, curling up in the dark on the bed, fantasising she was somewhere out of harm's way, somewhere like a cave, where she could retreat and everyone would leave her alone. Jonnie though—she had the idea that whatever was coiled up inside him, something angry, was so set on breaking itself out into the world that he'd find it really hard to be confined. Maybe she was getting all mixed up between her world and her imagination though—maybe she couldn't really sense these things. Maybe she was a bit crazy!

"Kayla, hurry up!" Jonnie's voice broke her out of her thoughts. She looked up to see him at the top of the steps looking down on her. "Willard's found some stick things that we can light so we can see where we're going. I'd been worried we'd just have my cigarette lighter."

"If that even works. Don't forget it's been underwater," she replied.

"Plenty of time for it to have dried out," he said, as he pulled the lighter out of his pocket and snapped it with his thumb. It clicked, but nothing happened. He snapped it a few more times until it took, but it guttered and died out. Then, beginning to get impatient, he finally got it to light. "Yay, look, it works. Told you!" he said triumphantly. For a moment she could see the real Jonnie, her brother, not the person he was pretending to be since he'd been in North Feasgar.

She hurried up the remaining steps to join him just as Willard emerged from the tunnel opening with two long stakes of wood with something tied around the ends. When Jonnie lit them, they resembled very large candles. Carrying them, he turned with Willard and walked inside. She followed a few steps behind and was amazed when she saw how it opened out unexpectedly into a cavern. She looked around, but already Willard and Jonnie were moving to the other side, wanting to get going.

"Hurry up," Willard barked.

"Why don't you two take one of the lights and leave me the other in case you move on ahead of me," she suggested. Jonnie reluctantly gave his up to her, then continued into the passage on the far side of the cavern in step with Willard.

It wasn't long before they came to a fork in the passage. Willard moved down the path to the right, with Jonnie beside him, but when Kayla got there, she felt her feet dragging. Something was telling her this wasn't the right way for her to go. She walked on a little further, but it was as if she was walking against some deep resistance, with leaden feet, her footsteps moving slower and slower. She fell further behind the other two…

"Hurry up Kayla!" yelled Jonnie from up ahead. They didn't slow down. "We can't wait for you!"

"Hey, you know what, I don't like it down here—I'm going to find my way back to wait for you at the tunnel entrance," she called into the dark ahead—their light had already disappeared around a corner in the tunnel. She got some sort of muffled reply that she couldn't make out, and turned to make her way back to the fork. As she took the left passage, the air went quiet. She had a strong feeling that she was being summoned by something and was now on the right track. How weird. She wasn't even scared—well, not much!

***

Tom and Sarah woke after an unbroken sleep to find they'd slid together during the night and were lying back-to-back, half on, half off the cushions. Galawand had placed blankets over them in their sleep. They self-consciously moved apart and looked around them to see Galawand moving about the cavern, tending to the multitude of candles. She relit the few that had gone out during the night and replaced the ones that had burnt down.

"Do you need a hand?" Sarah called out.

"Oh, good morning. You've had a good sleep. If you look over in the alcove next to the mandala hanging, you'll find a basin of water where you can have a wash. Fill it from the container beside it. I'm afraid you'll have to make do with it being cold—I only bother to heat it up in the winter. You'll find cloths to dry yourself with in the box the basin is sitting on."

They took turns getting themselves freshened up and by the time they finished, Galawand had lit a fire in a small firepit, and had placed a flat metal plate over it to warm up.

"Where does the smoke go?" Tom asked.

"It seems to be drawn up through a crevice near the top of the cavern. I worried about smoke at first, but there must be a good updraft because it always burns cleanly." She was preparing something that looked like a batter, and tipped a small quantity onto the hot plate, swirling it with a small stick attached to a handle until it formed a thin circle.

"Pancakes!" exclaimed Sarah, her stomach growling in anticipation. She helped Galawand to cut up some fruit while Tom mastered the cooking of the pancakes.

Tom was quiet as he occupied himself. It was helpful to have something to do, because there was something he wanted to say to Sarah when he had the chance. When Galawand went to find some utensils, he finally blurted it out.

"Sarah, do you really have to go back?" He knew she had family to go back to, but he'd really missed her when she left last time. He hadn't been sure he'd ever see her again, despite what Hermione said. Since she'd been back he'd felt a weird mixture of happy, confused and awkward, but the one thing he now realised was that he didn't want her to leave again.

Sarah didn't know what to say. The conflict between staying and going was really strong in her. She knew she had to go back, even it if was just to find a way to say good bye to her family – she couldn't leave her grandad feeling responsible for her – but what if something stopped her from returning? She felt panicky even thinking about it. She knew too that there was a lot lying behind Tom's question. It had been hard for him to ask, because this time there was something new and still fragile growing between them that wasn't there last time. She felt flushed and self-conscious, wanting to run away and avoid his gaze and his question, but she forced herself to stay present.

"I honestly don't know Tom. All I can say is that if I go with my intuition, I know that I have some stuff I have to finish in England and that I'll come back. But I have no idea when. And, I'll really miss you. Coming back and seeing you again has been really important." She was amazed at how steady she sounded when the embarrassed part of her on the inside was flinching and trying to escape. Tom swallowed. He wanted to open up and tell her how much he liked her, but he couldn't do it. He busied himself instead taking the finished pile of pancakes over to the box Galawand used as a table, and got his breathing back to normal. This emotional stuff was so hard. How did a guy tell a girl how much he liked her? It looked like it was so easy for other people.

They sat down to the best meal they could remember—something about their circumstances, or maybe the magical quality of the cavern, meant that the fruit tasted sweet and sharp and fresh, while the pancakes melted in their mouths. It was simply delicious. As they sat together afterwards, sipping on a hot mug of tea, Sarah realised what had been playing on her mind.

"Galawand, I've been thinking about my dream, the one that you and Tom and I were in. The one that drew me down here to you..."

"Yes, the one we shared, that showed me that you would come."

"So, who's the fourth person? There was another girl in the dream."

"I've wondered about that. Dreams aren't rational. They come from our unconscious and they're often really hard to decipher because we can't use our conscious thinking to work them out. And time doesn't work the same way in a dream either. So maybe this person will be here sometime in the future to help us, or maybe she's about something inside you, not in the outside world. We just have to hold it lightly and see what happens... The prophecy says that when the correct two elements come together there arises the possibility of something emerging between them, something greater than them, represented by three."

"Oh," said Sarah softly as it dawned on her, "the Anam Cara!"

"Yes, the Anam Cara," Galawand drew out each syllable slowly, giving the words a feeling of enormous significance. "And from the three, there is the possibility of wholeness, represented by four. But I don't know how that idea of four is going to manifest, where it will come from, or when..."

"Is the ring of stones the ring in the dream maybe?" suggested Tom.

"Yes, it could be – the ring, the colours and the way we're all one within the ring – all the elements of that piece of the dream are present."

They were quiet for a while, thinking about the dream and what might unfold.

"Tell me about Morwyn before we try energising the circle again." Galawand broke the silence, "I sensed there was a story behind your reaction to her yesterday."

"When we came here, she kidnapped me and made Sarah go to find the nectar from Greyvyn to bring to her," blurted Tom, still so easily upset by all that had happened.

"Ahh... the nectar. Did you take it to her, Sarah?"

"No. I managed to find it, but we tricked her. Tom got away, but she fell from her tree house and died. It was pretty awful, but then, so was she!"

"So, what happened to the nectar?"

"Our friend Ryder, a hawk, took it to the mountains and hid it where no one else knows where it is, so nobody can make us get it for them."

"Well that was very wise of you."

"I was thinking about it this morning when I woke up," said Sarah. "Wouldn't it be put to good use if you used it to keep up your strength for the barrier?"

"I don't know how much you know about it, but you have to be very, very careful with it. It's seductive. Once you take it, you want more. It makes people do evil things to get it, as Morwyn did to the two of you. But one day you might need it. You might need to use it for a higher purpose, like for the good of North Feasgar, not for individual vanity, which is what Morwyn wanted it for."

"If we can't use the nectar to help you, what else can we do? I'm worried that we have to go back soon. Mary and Arthur will be waiting for us, and we don't want to draw Willard to you, or to them. He locked them both up to make them build a flying machine to get him up the mountain. Sarah rescued them!"

"Goodness, you've had some adventures! I'm hoping that with one more time like last night, a little longer this time, the white layer of the circle should stabilise enough to protect my magic better. That means I won't have to use so much power each time and I can recover my energy... And you'll be back, I can sense it, even if you have to go back to your world for a while Sarah. You have things to do yet, together."

As her words sunk in, Sarah was overcome with a profound sense of awe at this place, at Galawand, and at her knowing.

This is what she wanted for her future—a life that was more than just going to school or work, going home, buying things and having arguments—all the things that had been her life suddenly didn't feel enough. It was about purpose, but also having a magical quality and a connection to other people who were more like her.

"Tom, Sarah?" a quiet voice cut tentatively through the silence of the cavern. They turned towards the direction of the passage, looking puzzled. A small figure stood near the exit from the passage, half in shadow. Tom and Sarah looked at each other, then at Galawand, whose face looked more quizzical than concerned. The felt sense of this person wasn't a threat.

"Kayla?" Tom started getting to his feet. She stepped out of the shadow and hesitantly approached them.

***

Once she was on her own, Kayla had found her way relatively easily down the narrower passages from where she'd left Jonnie and Willard, only pausing briefly at the next fork, trusting her instincts to take the left turn again. For the first time in her life it felt like she was doing the right thing. She could feel a bit of fear gnawing away in the bottom of her stomach, but that wasn't about being under the mountain, on her own, it was worry about how she and Jonnie would find a place for themselves here—she knew now with certainty that there was no way she was going back to her old life in Auckland. Probably though, the bigger thing was that she somehow knew that she'd have to leave Jonnie and risk being alone. He seemed to need to act out things about his past in the outside world in a way she didn't want to be part of. All her own problems were internalised—she knew she took them out on her body, with all her anxiety stopping her from eating and maybe getting attention that way. *Hah,* she thought, *so we've literally just taken different paths inside the mountain. How funny is that!* At that, her stomach growled and she realised she was starving. She couldn't even remember when she'd last eaten.

The passage eventually opened out into another cavern that had a river running through it. Its sound gave her the idea that it flowed fast and deep—she could hear it, but there weren't any of the splashy sounds that you'd get from a shallow river. It took her a while to sense that she wasn't alone in the cavern. Something made her look to one side, towards a cluster of rocks. The hairs on the back of her neck went up, not in fear, but with the recognition that had always hovered near her mind, but too far away to be grasped—that if she trusted her intuition, she just *knew* things. She knew there were people there with her, and she knew their presence wasn't scary.

She moved over towards the rocks, holding her brand close to her body so that whoever was there could see her clearly and would know she didn't mean any harm. She heard the sound of someone getting to their feet and a dark, bulky form emerged from behind a rock.

"Kayla? It's me, Arthur. Are you alone?"

"Yes, Jonnie and Willard took a different path."

A small flame flickered, then lit another brand like hers, illuminating the rocky area where he and Mary had been sitting. Mary too, had struggled to her feet and they both made their way over to her, Mary leaning on Arthur's arm. Kayla realised how relieved she felt by their presence, much more solid and reliable than Jonnie's right now, and she wondered how she'd ever persuaded herself to go with him.

"Why are you here Kayla?" asked Mary, in a kindly, yet firm tone, obviously wanting to make sure of her.

"Willard and Jonnie are looking for something. They followed you, thinking you'd lead them to it, but it felt wrong to go the way they did through the passages. Something told me to leave them and come in this direction. While I've been walking on my own, I've realised a lot of things, and I don't want anything to do with what they're doing, even if Jonnie is my brother." It all came out in a bit of a gush and she found herself feeling teary and emotional.

Mary and Arthur looked at each other. She saw Mary give Arthur a nod, after which he brought Mary closer and led them both to sit down on a raised area of rock.

"Do you know what they're looking for?" Arthur asked.

"No. They wouldn't talk to me about it. Willard doesn't like me..." There was a pause. "It has something to do with Sarah and Tom though. Where are they anyway?"

"They've crossed the river. We don't know what they've found yet—they went over in the evening yesterday and we're hoping we'll hear from them soon."

"Will you help me to cross too? I'm not going to harm them in any way—I just feel as if I have to find them."

They agreed to help and showed her the ropes.

"I don't know how far behind Jonnie and Willard are, but I could unhook the rope from the other side so you can pull it back and hide it—they won't be able to get across the river on their own. When we want to come back, you can throw it over to us again." They tied her to the second rope and she surprised them both with her courage. She was nimble and hardly paused as she crossed, even though they both held their breath seeing how fragile she looked as she swung out over the water. If she dropped on the rocks on the other side, she would surely break! But she made it safely, unhooked the rope from the rock, untied the second from around her waist, and Arthur pulled them both back, as she disappeared into the passage on the far side with a wave.

***

Tom walked over to Kayla and took her hand, leading her back towards where Sarah and Galawand were sitting. Sarah suddenly felt a twist in her stomach. She tried to work out how she was feeling—she didn't want to get emotional the way she had the last time she'd seen Kayla. It was about feeling like she didn't have a place, was being rejected, that she wasn't wanted. She could feel tears welling up in her as she realised she also felt jealous, and she swallowed hard to try to keep her face looking calm. At the same time, she could see that Kayla looked startled, all big eyes and pale face, like a waif trying to find a way in from the cold. She looked really bewildered and vulnerable as she looked around at her surroundings; and Tom was kind—much kinder than her obviously! Suddenly feeling ashamed of her thoughts, she looked at Galawand, who was watching her with curiosity. Was she so easy to read then? Sarah gave her a wry look, shrugged and went over to Kayla.

"Hi Kayla, how on earth did you find us?"

"What is this place?" Kayla asked, looking around her, awed.

"Welcome to Galawand's home—it's amazing, isn't it?"

Galawand went forward then to meet her, and Sarah was struck again by how majestic she looked, as she moved gracefully towards them, her long white hair flowing about her, her poise, and her quiet sense of authority. She was no ordinary woman—she gave off a kind of a glow, an aura of mystique and wisdom. She could see Kayla's eyes fix on her, as if mesmerised. Galawand stretched her hands out to her, holding them as if she was calming a startled creature.

"Oh my, but you're so cold. Come with us and sit down. Tom, why don't you make some more pancakes, while Sarah gets you a hot drink."

Kayla had started to shake. Yes, she was cold, and hungry, but it was also all the strangeness and tension of the last few days suddenly overwhelming her. They draped blankets around her shoulders and soon her hands were wrapped around a mug of tea, her stomach grumbling at the delicious smells coming from the cooking fire. The food, when it came, was simple but so tasty that she didn't stop to think about it—she devoured it in a way she couldn't recall ever doing before, and she was left with a pleasant, satisfied feeling, a sense of being curled up in a safe place.

As she warmed up, her body started to relax, and Galawand prompted her to tell them how she'd found them. She told them a shortened story of what had happened to her since she and Jonnie had left Riverstone with Tom's bike. When she got to the bit about Willard in the basement of his house, Sarah gasped and reached out to her, remembering what it had been like being in his house herself, and finding Mary and Arthur locked up in the basement.

"He's a terrible man. I'm so glad you got away from him. You must have been really scared!"

Kayla continued her story about how they'd found their way to the mountain and how she'd known she had to go a separate way to them once they were inside. As she drew to a close, she saw them look questioningly at each other.

"Oh! You don't know whether to trust me, do you? All I can say is that I don't want to be who I'd be if I stayed with them, and that something *made* me come here. I can't really describe it, but I was drawn to you."

It was Sarah who responded first. She could hear in Kayla's certainty that she meant what she said, even though she surprised herself at how quickly she'd moved away from suspicion and jealousy. She was learning more and more to trust her intuition when things *felt* right.

"Galawand, I think Kayla might be our fourth person. We need her, and we need to trust her." She flashed Kayla a smile, a bit apologetic, and saw Tom and Galawand relax. She realised then that they'd already made up their minds about Kayla, and had been waiting for her reaction.

"We're agreed then. Tom, Sarah, why don't you tell Kayla what we're all doing here while I get ready for our next attempt at energising the circle."

Kayla sat in rapt attention as they talked to her about the barrier, why it was there and how they were needed to help Galawand to maintain it. She became increasingly worried as they spoke; not about what they needed to do, but because of the way Jonnie had been pulled into something he knew nothing about and the damage he could do without even meaning to. She felt torn between wanting to get as far from him as she could, but at the same time wanting to talk sense into him. He wasn't a bad person, he'd just got side-tracked in trying to cope with not having decent parents to help him to learn who he could be.

She recalled all the times he'd been there for her when she was little, to make sure she had someone. Walking her to and from school, making sure she was warm and fed, taking her to his room and distracting her when their mum was on a bender, or brought men home. He'd had to grow up so fast—it just wasn't fair! It was no wonder he was trying to find out who he was now. She felt herself wavering again, but deep down she knew she had to walk away from him. She felt overcome with sadness and could feel tears coming to her eyes.

"Kayla, are you okay?" Tom asked. They'd noticed her becoming quieter and more withdrawn as they talked. She nodded mutely and wiped the back of her sleeve across her eyes.

"Come child, have a drink of this," Galawand handed each of them some of the liquid they'd had the evening before.

"You'll feel better doing something, so come with us to the stone circle and we'll show you what to do. Remember, if you trust your deep sense of what's right, whatever happens, you'll be all right."

They got to their feet, following her to the centre of the cavern. As they had last time, they followed her instructions to centre themselves and join their left hands together in the middle of the circle.

This time, with four of them, the effect was even greater. Their experience was so deep it was as if they were connecting to something timeless, so much greater than them. They felt the air around them tremble slightly, taking on a different quality of stillness. They stayed like that for what was probably only a few minutes, but felt like it stretched into forever, until Galawand could sense that Kayla was tiring.

"Oh, my goodness," said Galawand, "I haven't felt that in a very long time. The power of four—not any four; the four of us. Thank you, my friends."

The red circle was now entirely encapsulated in a pearl lustre, that they could sense was strong and sure.

"How long will that last for Galawand?" Sarah asked.

"Quite some time I hope, but I'll have further need of you yet." Sarah's face drained and she looked down at her feet.

"But I don't know how long I'll be here for. I think I have to go back to my world."

"Don't worry child, you'll be back when you're needed—you have too much still to do. Our troubles aren't over yet, but this will hold them off for a while."

"I'll stay."

They looked around at Kayla. "I'll stay," she repeated.

"What do you mean?" said Sarah.

"I want to stay with Galawand. I can help her."

"But this life is not good for someone so young," said Galawand gently.

"I don't fit in the outside world. I've never felt so strong, and needed, as I've felt here with you. It's like finding part of myself," Kayla asserted.

Sarah and Tom looked at her, with Sarah suddenly feeling so ashamed of how she'd judged her when they were at

Riverstone. She went over to her and gave her a hug. "I'm so sorry I wasn't kind to you before—I was jealous of you."

"Jealous? What do I have to be jealous of?" Kayla demanded incredulously.

"I thought Tom liked you more than me," Sarah said in a low voice, looking down. She wasn't prepared for Kayla's laughter.

"That's funny! Everyone except the two of you can see that you're made for each other!" she laughed.

Tom and Sarah both blushed, but Galawand broke the awkward moment by talking to Kayla about what her terms were if she was to stay.

"If you're going to stay with me, you need to promise me that every day you'll go out through the tunnel to get fresh air, sun and some exercise. And you must eat everything we prepare together. I won't make you eat what you don't want, but if we decide together, you will eat what we make, or you won't have enough strength to help me. If you agree, I'll teach you everything I know. I can't guarantee your safety while the magicians from the south are trying to break down the barrier, but we'll be stronger together."

While she was talking to Kayla, Sarah sat there feeling a vulnerable kind of feeling that made her want to run away. At the same time, she was so drawn to Tom—she noticed everything he did and said, and was incredibly self-conscious and embarrassed in his presence. She wanted to experience being close to someone, to Tom, in a way she hadn't before, even though it was scary. She looked up and saw him watching her and flushed bright red. What was wrong with her? She angrily got to her feet and started tidying their breakfast things away. When he got up to help her, his hand brushed against hers as they reached for the plates at the same time. She felt sick; she felt giddy—actually, she didn't really know how she felt other than something she'd never felt before. And now he was watching her again... Awkward!

Tom was feeling the tension too, so he dropped his gaze and turned back to Galawand and Kayla, clearing his throat to recover his equilibrium.

"I think we need to head back to Mary and Arthur. They'll be worried about us."

"I'll come to meet them, but then I'll need to retreat back here," Galawand said. "I can't risk Willard and Jonnie turning up and seeing me. They need to think you found nothing and just camped out on their side of the river if they find you."

Tom and Sarah picked up their belongings and lanterns, and reluctantly followed Galawand and Kayla across the cavern to the passage. They found their feet dragging, not wanting to leave the safety and beauty Galawand had created—it felt more like a refuge than a space that held the future of North Feasgar within it.

They entered the passage and in the safety of the low, flickering light of their lanterns, Tom took Sarah's hand and squeezed it. She felt so distracted that she nearly tripped over her feet, but then she leaned into him and he let go of her hand to put his arm around her shoulders. His heart was thudding and he was really grateful for the darkness as he wondered whether he'd dare to do anything more.

"Sarah," he said quietly. She turned towards him and he leaned over and awkwardly kissed her—his mouth landing on the corner of hers. She giggled in embarrassment and ahead Kayla turned back to look at them. They sprang apart, hoping they'd got away without being seen in the low light.

"Come on you two," said Kayla, not letting on that she'd glimpsed what was going on. She turned back to Galawand, smiling, and feeling stupidly happy that there were some good things happening in this strange world.

The walk back through the passage seemed so much shorter than when they'd travelled it the first time. No longer anxious about what they'd find and knowing they were heading back towards the outer world made a huge difference, and in no time, they stepped into the river cavern. They couldn't see anything of Mary or Arthur on the other side, but when they called to them, they emerged from behind some rocks, just dark shapes until Arthur lit a brand. Tom and Sarah felt so happy to see them, their solid presence familiar and welcoming. They called to each other across the river and they introduced them to Galawand, telling them that she was going to return to her cavern, as would Kayla once they'd had a chance to talk. Mary looked surprised.

"Isn't Kayla coming back with us then?"

"No. I'm going to stay with Galawand. She needs someone to help her and I don't have anywhere else to be. I *want* to help her."

Arthur walked over to the rock that had the rope tied around it.

"I'll send the hook and rope back over to you. Stand back in case I don't throw it cleanly."

"Wait Arthur," Galawand said. "You don't need the rope. I still have a few tricks up my sleeve!" She walked a little downriver. Raising her hands into the air she chanted some words they couldn't make out. Sarah felt the air tingle—it kind of stretched, expanding and contracting, and when she looked up beyond Galawand she saw something emerging out of the air, as if an invisible cloak had been covering it and was suddenly pulled away. It looked like a framework, a bridge, which stretched over the river, maybe metal, maybe not. It shimmered, silver and clear. It rested on either side of the river banks, with a single step up on either side, and what looked like a silver mesh stretching across the river, supported between two curved hand rails.

"Galawand, that's amazing!" Tom exclaimed. "How did you do that?"

"Part of my payment for taking on the care of the barrier was that I could keep enough magic to keep the cavern and ring of stones safe. I was the only one to keep any powers, other than those who kept some of the Sight, which drew the anger of people like Morwyn. Several people wanted to take on the job for the wrong reasons, so the guardian had to be chosen very carefully."

"Can we cross it?"

"Yes, we'll all go over so I can meet Mary and Arthur properly, then I'll have to return.

Tom ran excitedly over to the bridge, followed by Sarah. Kayla and Galawand followed more slowly. When they got to the bridge and stepped onto the mesh, they were astounded by how solid and stable it seemed, even though it looked lightweight. It scarcely even rocked as they crossed the river, running straight into a warm embrace from Arthur. Mary made her way towards them slowly. Her ankle had improved remarkably with rest, but she was still favouring it, knowing that she'd need all the strength in it she could find for the trip back up and out of the mountain.

They sat down on the rocks on the other side of the river, catching up on all that had happened since the previous evening. When they outlined what Galawand's role was, Mary and Arthur exchanged glances. They felt quite awed at being in the presence of the person who was keeping them safe—they'd heard stories about the sacrifice made by a person or people, but no one knew who was involved or where they were located. It seemed like a huge burden to be resting on the shoulders of the small woman in front of them. When they heard that Kayla was going to remain behind with her, they questioned her carefully, to make sure that was what she really wanted. But she was determined—she knew she needed some time to retreat from the world and find out more about herself. A simple life felt right for now.

"I can be the one to keep Galawand in touch with the outside world, like with you, if I can come and go," she said.

"We could get Ryder to fly over the mountain each week—you could probably learn to understand his speech, but even if you don't, you could give him messages to take to Riverstone," said Tom.

"That would be really reassuring," Galawand agreed. "My friends from the village come once a week, but I've often worried about what would happen if they couldn't, or how I'd let them know if I had a problem. Now... I'm worried about Jonnie and Willard finding their way here. If they went down the other path, they will have got to the end of the passage some time ago. If they don't get hopelessly lost, they'll have found their way back to where Kayla turned off by now. I need to go back to the other side. Firstly though, come with me. I'm going to have to make the bridge invisible again and I need to make sure you know how to find it when I'm not here." She walked over to the remnants of the old bridge on the river bank. "If you start from this post," she pointed to the half post left in the ground, "take ten paces down river and you'll reach my bridge. Step it out now in case your strides are different to mine."

They paced it out and other than Kayla, found themselves right at the bridge. It took her eleven paces to get to the same place. Galawand told them to wait there and crossed the river.

"Right, Tom, walk slowly half way across the bridge and stop."

When he got there, she told him she was going to make it invisible, to hold the rails carefully and make his way to the other side. As she warned him to hold on, suddenly the bridge disappeared from beneath his feet. He was left suspended in the air, looking down sickeningly at the fast-flowing water below. His heart gave a disturbing thud and he could hear the blood rushing past his ears. He stayed frozen until his fear subsided— he was still supported; his clammy hands were still holding onto something more than air, and when he eventually shuffled his left foot forward, it still came into contact with the invisible mesh. He moved his right foot, then slid his hands further along the rails. Slowly at first, then with more confidence, he moved to the other bank.

"Don't forget the step," warned Galawand. "It's aligned with the rock edge, just one step down."

Feeling forward tentatively with his foot, he stepped down off the bridge onto solid ground, feeling elated. He spontaneously rushed over to Galawand and gave her a hug.

"Now, back again. Remember how many paces to find the first rail."

The trip back was easier, once his hand found the rail and his head could get around the first disconcerting step up onto the bridge—it was as if he was stepping out into space. Once he jumped off to join the others, Galawand made it visible again so she could go through the same process with Sarah and Kayla. Sarah had to really battle her nerves. Although it wasn't particularly high, she still had a moment of dizziness as she first put her foot into nothingness. She closed her eyes and trusted her senses, as each foot found a firm resting point on the bridge. To the others watching, it looked completely weird as they stepped off, seemingly walking on air.

"What if someone finds it Galawand?" Tom asked.

"In the extreme unlikeliness of anyone who isn't a friend being down here, I think it's highly improbable they'd walk along close enough to the side of the river to stumble upon it. If they did, they'd be likely to get such a fright they'd fall in..."

Tom and Sarah smiled at each other, both thinking of Willard, and wondering just how sorry they'd be if that happened to him!

It was time for Galawand to leave them.

"Don't be too long Kayla. There is much I have to teach you, and these good people need to retrace their steps out of the mountain before they have an altercation with Willard. It would be much simpler all round if they found this cavern empty and the river uncrossable." With a final wave, she disappeared into the passage.

The five of them sat for a while longer discussing how they would keep in touch via Ryder and how often they would visit in person.

"Kayla, when I go back to our world, is there anything you'd like me to do—to find out or keep in touch with? "Sarah asked.

"No. Jonnie is the only person I care about. I'm happy to leave all that behind, but thank you! How long will you be gone for?"

A cloud passed over Sarah's face. "I'm not sure. It's so hard—I have to leave good people behind whichever world I choose, but I think North Feasgar needs me more. I think my future is here." It wasn't missed by the others that she glanced self-consciously at Tom as she spoke.

"We'd better pack up then," said Arthur. "Tom, help me untie the ropes while the others repack our belongings." He'd just detached and packed his home-made hook, and Tom was coiling the ropes when Tom was alerted to a sound. It was the faint but unmistakeable sound of footfalls coming from the passage.

"Sshhh…" he whispered. "Listen—someone's coming!"

Chapter X

Confrontation

Kayla saw Jonnie, followed a few seconds later by Willard, stumble through the passage opening into the cavern. Instinctively she moved closer to Mary. Willard's shambling form looked unkempt and a bit 'blurry', reminding her of her mother. He must have been sampling liberally from his hip flask to help him on his journey. Jonnie looked around him, taking in first the Birches, Tom and Sarah, then his eyes fastened on hers.

"Kayla! You're here! I thought you'd gone back to the outside."

"Well I found my way down here instead," she replied.

"What are you all doing here?" Willard demanded.

"Well, Tom here," said Arthur in a level voice, "is interested in geology, so we decided to come on a trip inside a volcano so he could learn some more before he goes to university. We were just about to head back home."

"Likely story!" Willard said contemptuously. He was looking about the cavern, and not finding anything of significance, started to prowl over behind the rocks they were sitting on.

"What are you looking for, Willard?" Mary asked.

"None of your business," he growled. "Have you crossed the river?"

"No. We thought it might be fun to explore, but we weren't sure how to get there, unless you have a good idea," replied Arthur.

"I can see you've got ropes with you..."

"Yes, but no way of attaching them to the other side."

Willard didn't answer. He walked over to the river and stood with his hand on the remaining bridge post. Peering down, he spat into the water. Pulling out his hip flask he moved it to his lips, then pulled it away, shaking it angrily. It was empty... Scowling, he put it back in his pocket and started walking downriver along the bank, looking at the far side. Tom and Sarah looked at each other, feeling increasingly anxious as he neared Galawand's bridge.

"Willard," Tom called out to distract him, "what are you looking for—maybe we can help."

He turned to them. "Have you seen anything on the other side?"

"I don't think anything's been happening down here for a very long time, Willard," Arthur said. "You can see how old the remnants of the bridge are. I imagine people explored down here in the past, but there's no sign of activity now."

"I think the passages have been made from old lava tubes," Tom added. "People have smoothed them out. Are you interested in geology too, Willard? I'd love to talk to you about it."

It was incredible how knowing that Willard was on the back foot, not knowing what was really going on, gave him so much courage. He'd never have stood up to a bully or made fun of one in the past. But he wasn't alone now! Sarah kicked him surreptitiously, in an attempt to stop herself from laughing. He sounded so innocent. Willard just glared at him, but began walking back towards them.

"Bear with small brain," she whispered to Tom, both of them trying not to laugh.

Jonnie had moved over to stand by Kayla.

"Jonnie, what are you both doing here? I mean really?" she asked.

"Willard was told to follow the other four. Something to do with the barrier outside. Willard thinks they have something to do with it, so we followed to find out what."

"But that's not true," she hated lying to him... "You can see we've reached a dead end and there's nothing here."

"But there's a passage on the other side, so there must be a way of getting over there. Willard won't stop until he's gone as far as he can, because some people are paying him. The path we followed before we turned back to come here finished in a dead end, so he thinks whatever we're looking for has to be here. Although we passed another fork too that we didn't explore—we were worried about getting lost."

"And you, Jonnie? What do you want to do?"

He looked at her with a strange expression on his face. Part regret, part apology, but he didn't have time to reply, as just then Willard called out to him.

"Get those ropes over there, Jonnie."

"Do you mean our ropes, Willard?" Arthur asked. "Are you asking us whether you can use them?"

He didn't reply, but went across and picked one up off the ground. He looked at its ends and then at the river.

"He's thinking," Tom whispered to Sarah. "You can see how difficult it is for him—I can see the cogs slowly turning!"

Sarah smirked.

"You, girl!" he growled, advancing on Kayla. "Tie this rope around your waist."

"No," she replied firmly, even though he scared her.

He looked at her in astonishment and the next minute his hand shot out and grabbed her tightly by the wrist. He started dragging her towards the river—it took the rest of them a while to react, but by the time he'd grabbed the end of the rope with the intention of tying it around her waist, Jonnie had grabbed her other arm.

"Leave her alone, Willard, she doesn't want to do it. I'll do it instead."

Willard glared at him. It felt to Kayla like a tug of war—she was being split in two between them. Then Willard abruptly let her go so that she collided heavily with Jonnie and he had to struggle to keep them both upright.

"Willard, if you're going to make Jonnie swim across to the other side, at least do it properly so he has some chance of succeeding," Arthur said. "Wrap the other end around that rock over there so you can leverage against it once you're holding Jonnie's weight. That's what we were going to do, until we decided the whole thing was a stupid idea!"

"Let's look at the bank on the other side, Jonnie, so you can see the best place to swim for, then I'll show you how to tie a proper knot that will hold the rope," said Tom, letting himself feel a bit sorry for Jonnie now that he'd stuck up for Kayla. They looked over the side and could see a slight rocky outcrop part way between the old bridge and Galawand's that he could probably get a decent hold of to pull himself up the other side.

"You'll need to start out upriver quite a bit because it's

flowing quickly," Tom paced up the bank trying to estimate how quickly the river would take Jonnie to the point they were aiming for on the other side. He figured it should be simple physics if he could estimate the water flow.

While they were looking at the river, Arthur moved over to Willard.

"Willard, it isn't right to put a kid in danger for a daft idea. Why don't you do it yourself if you really must explore the other side?"

"That's the second time you've said I'm stupid," he growled, his lips curled disdainfully.

"No. I've said your idea is stupid. Anyone can see that there is nothing down here, so why put Jonnie in danger just to prove that?"

Willard didn't respond, but Arthur could see anger simmering just below his shaggy surface. His jaw and fists were clenched. He wondered whether to back off or push him further to try to make him see sense.

"He'll do what I say," Willard eventually growled.

"You know, bullies make other people do what they're too scared to do themselves—Nothing to say to that? Bullies also pick on the most vulnerable people—why didn't you try to make me do it? Why did you pick on Kayla?"

A look of fury spasmed across Willard's face, creasing his eyes and his forehead. His mouth had become a tight line and his body taut like a coiled spring. He suddenly lunged at Arthur, aiming a fist at his jaw. Arthur ducked, causing Willard to stumble forward, unable to pull himself out of his drunken trajectory. He bellowed and swore, turning back to face Arthur again.

Sarah, Tom and Mary were watching from a short distance away, partly aghast, partly fascinated. Sarah couldn't help herself.

"No, correction, a bull, not a bear!" she snorted. "Ohh... here we go!"

Willard had charged at Arthur again and they were locked in an embrace, his arm tight around Arthur's neck. They circled until Arthur managed to hook his foot around Willard's, bringing him crashing to the rocky floor. Willard grunted, winded, but clambered to his feet again. As he threw a wild punch at Arthur, Tom, watching on, experienced memories of his stepfather Gerald rushing back to him like a kick in the gut. It was all he could do not to double over to protect himself, but instead he gasped and stood, paralysed, as he watched Willard taking another swing at Arthur. It was more than two years now since he'd even seen Gerard, and yet he still had a total body and emotional reaction to violence. He felt stupid and embarrassed, like he was a wuss. Mary's hand rested on his forearm. He looked at her and saw such understanding and compassion in her eyes that he wanted to cry. Was he always going to feel this vulnerable? At least he'd never turn into a bully like Willard. At least he'd never hit a child!

Mary's support had snapped him out of his paralysis though, and he looked up to see Willard regrouping and turning. This time his fury carried him towards Arthur like a battering ram. He pushed into him head on, propelling them both towards the river. Both Jonnie and Tom simultaneously jumped forward, realising what Willard was trying to do. They raced towards the fighting men. Willard's weight and momentum had carried them dangerously close to the edge.

It all happened so quickly...They were grappling and swaying. Tom saw Willard raise his fist ready to hit Arthur on the side of his head, in the direction that would send him into the water. He leapt forward and seized Arthur's jacket from the back and jerked it hard to pull Arthur towards him. Arthur was destabilised, bringing him crashing back onto Tom, while Willard's punch only connected with air. Willard started to topple forwards, and in panic he threw out his arms, connecting with Jonnie. Holding desperately onto him, he fell forward, and as if in slow motion pulled Jonnie with him into the river. There was a yell and a splash, and then nothing.

"Nooo!" yelled Kayla.

As Tom and Arthur helped each other to their feet, Sarah and Kayla raced to the side and looked into the fast-flowing river. All they could see, just for an instant, was a fair head bobbing on top of the water, but the next second it was gone as the river carried Jonnie around a bend and out of sight. Of Willard there was no sign.

***

It had been so fast. Jonnie was gone. And with him, the only connection to her previous life. Kayla didn't know how she felt. Time seemed to weirdly stretch and contract. She was aware that she was sitting on the ground and that she was cold. Cold down deep into her bones. She was numb, but then strangely empty, like someone had gone in deeply and scooped out her insides. It was like a void, so vast that she felt her heart racing in terror; that she might be lost, that she might be alone, or fall forever. She gasped out loud and felt someone put their arm around her, they felt her shivering and quietly asked for something to drape around her shoulders. This act of kindness had such an impact on her that her shaking body turned into tears. They started slowly, then it was as if she completely dissolved. Water came out her eyes and nose in great gulping gusts. She sobbed until her body felt bruised and pummelled. She realised that she wasn't just crying for Jonnie, she was crying for her whole miserable life. Her dysfunctional mother, her lack of father, for having to be responsible, for her love and her disappointment in Jonnie. She became aware of a strange keening sound and slowly realised it was coming from her. She gulped, swallowed and stopped. She could now hear the low murmuring of voices.

"—don't know. I expect it comes out on the south side of Mt Greyvyn. It'll depend how rough it becomes and whether he's had much experience in the water. I can't imagine Willard is at home in it, but I care less about what becomes of him!"

What was that? Did they think there was some hope for him? She lifted her head a little and wiped her snotty nose on the arm of her jumper. The talking stopped as they realised she was coming out of her stupor. She'd stopped shaking and realised Sarah and Tom were either side of her, supporting her, sitting uncomfortably on the rocky floor of the cavern. Mary and Arthur hovered anxiously nearby. When they noticed that she was looking at them, they reached over and helped her to stand up. The ground had been cold and hard, and her body ached like she'd been punched.

Mary wrapped her arms around her in a hug, rocking her gently, trying to give her some of her strength. "I'm sure you're feeling really awful," she said. "We'll do everything we can to find him. You've got all of us here for you."

"Do you think he might still be alive?" she asked shakily.

"We don't know, but there's definitely a chance. The only thing is that we don't know where the river comes out from the mountain to the south. It may be that the barrier is in the way and we don't know what that would mean. We need to ask Galawand," Arthur said.

"Arthur," Mary replied quietly, "I think the rest of you will need to take Kayla back to Galawand. My foot is much better, but I don't think I can trust it on the bridge, since I've never tried to cross it before. I'll stay here and finish putting all our belongings away ready for when you return."

"I'd feel better not leaving you alone. I think Sarah and Tom could take Kayla back without us. Is that okay?" he said, looking at them questioningly.

They agreed, and took Kayla with them over to the bank, pacing out the steps to Galawand's bridge. Mary and Arthur hugged her, and she weakly squeezed them back. She felt as if she was drugged, and had to be guided up the step onto the bridge. They walked slowly across the bridge in a chain, her hand on Tom's shoulder in front of her, and Sarah's on her shoulder from behind. Once safely on the other side, Tom and Sarah waved at Mary and Arthur. Kayla walked between them, one foot in front of the other, doing what they told her to do. She felt as if she was enveloped in a see-through cushion—everything outside her had a muffled quality. Voices seemed very far away. She was alone in her fuzzy bubble; alone as she'd always been alone—as she would always be alone! She'd heard Mary saying she was in shock. Well it wasn't such a painful place to be, just a deadened and separate one. As they led her back through the passage to Galawand, she found herself bizarrely focusing on details like the curve and texture of the rock walls, the way the light from their firebrand danced off crevices. Anything, other than how she was feeling...

When the passage narrowed, Tom went ahead, holding Kayla's hand. Sarah, watching from behind, felt a stab of jealousy again. Cross with herself, she called out to Tom and asked if she could walk in front to try to stop her from feeling claustrophobic. As she switched places, an old saying of her mother's came to mind: *What your eye can't see, your heart doesn't grieve over.* Wow, funny that would pop up now. She got what it meant, but wasn't it a bit like putting your head in the sand? Why had that been important to her mother? She'd never been good at talking about emotional things, but did she bury them in herself and pretend that things she didn't like, didn't exist? Her mind went back to the problems her parents were having a couple of years ago when she first came here. Why didn't they tell her about the miscarriage? Why didn't they talk about why everything was so tense? Did they think she couldn't feel it? She'd found out afterwards that her mum thought her dad might be having an affair because he started avoiding the house, but he said he just didn't know what to do any more. She bet her mum had never even talked to him about it directly.

She slipped into a memory of other things she'd been upset about when she was little. Like the time some of the kids in her class had decided it was fun to pick on her—what she wore, her shoes, how she spoke. They mimicked her in a whiney little voice and she'd felt so confused that she wondered if she really was odd and unlikeable. She'd tried to tell her mum, but she'd just brushed it off with, "Oh, that's just kids, ignore them!" She and Gran both seemed to be 'get on with it' people who just ignored anything that hurt. Or, what about when she was really little, maybe about five, when she was new at school. Her first teacher had been scary. She wanted to go to the bathroom and put up her hand, but the teacher ignored her. She was too scared to speak up or just walk out, and she'd peed in her pants. She was so ashamed, but what made it worse, was that she couldn't even tell her mum, so she'd tried to smuggle the spare knickers the teacher had given her from the lost property box back to school in the bottom of her bag and her mother had found them. She couldn't remember what story she'd made up. But why did she need to? If she ever had a kid, she'd make sure she could talk to her. *And*, if she was feeling bad, she'd give her a hug and try to help her to understand why some people can't help being mean, and that it wasn't anything about her! She really didn't want to be like her mum. The first thing was to at least acknowledge to herself how she was feeling right now about Tom and Kayla, even when part of her knew it was only about her own insecurity.

She was jerked back to the present when she saw light coming from the end of the passage. When they got to the cavern, Galawand was waiting, but clearly not expecting to see Tom and Sarah.

"What's happened?" she said, stepping towards them, worry creasing her forehead. Her expression became more severe as they told her. She led Kayla to the cushions and wrapped her in blankets, holding her hands while they filled in some of the details.

"I'm so sorry Kayla!" she exclaimed. "We have to hope he'll find his way out the other side of the mountain."

"Galawand," Tom asked, "where's the barrier? Is it right on the side of the mountain or a bit further south? Like, if Jonnie manages to stay afloat and gets out of the mountain, will he be able to pull himself out before the barrier? And what happens if he can't?"

"It's located at the base of the mountain, but I'm sorry, I just don't know the answer to your other questions. The water goes through the barrier, so I suppose in theory a person could. It was set up holding in mind the need to keep people out, not to keep people in. Now, I'm going to make Kayla something to drink—she's in shock and needs something to warm her up." She walked over to her fireplace and boiled some water, pouring it over the spiky grey leaves of a herb. While she was waiting for it to brew, she walked over to the alcove where her provisions were stored and reached up to a shelf, taking down a glass jar. Taking off its heavy stopper she extracted a pinch of its contents, which looked like a greenish-grey powder. Dropping it into the herbal tea, she gave it a quick stir.

"What's that Galawand?" Sarah asked, having walked over to see what she was doing.

"Just a special crushed herb that will take the edge off Kayla's shock. It will relax her and make her a little sleepy. When she wakes up, she'll feel a lot better."

"When I come back, would you teach me about using plants for healing?" Sarah asked, "Morwyn had a lot and when she died, I took some, and one of her books, and left them with

Mary and Arthur. I'd love to learn how to use them."

Galawand took both her hands in hers and held her gaze, looking deeply into her as if she was seeing right down into her soul.

"Yes," she said, smiling warmly and taking Sarah's hands in her own, "you'll do nicely. It would be my pleasure to pass my knowledge on to you."

Sarah experienced a jolt of something like joy. Suddenly she knew clearly what she wanted to do and how to get there, a sense of purpose. Now she just needed to make it happen. For a moment the anxiety about how she'd leave her family passed through her, but she pushed it aside for later, as she went with Galawand back to Kayla and Tom.

Galawand waited until Kayla was sipping her tea before she stood up. "It's time to go. I'll take care of Kayla. You need to go back to Mary and Arthur and make your way back to Riverstone. Remember our plans to keep in contact, and I'll see you again soon, Tom. Sarah," she looked at her kindly, "I'm sure I'll be seeing you again soon too, and I'm looking forward to teaching you what I know." She gave them both a hug and pushed them gently in the direction of the passage. "Away now, and safe journey." They walked to the passage, turning once before they entered it to wave to her. Kayla was already lying on the cushions looking almost asleep, so they blew her a kiss and stepped into the tunnel.

***

Tom and Sarah walked side by side in silence. It was almost as if time had stopped, with a heavy hush that carried the aftermath of their shock and worry for Kayla. So much had happened in the last few days, and the energy that had propelled them forwards had suddenly gone. Sarah sighed deeply and then felt Tom's hand take hers. They continued walking quietly for a while, but Sarah's mind had gone back to her biggest worry.

"Tom, whatever am I going to do now?"

"What do you mean? Stay or go?"

"Yes. I feel completely torn."

"Well, of course I want you to stay."

"Do you?" she asked. He squeezed her hand. "I'm just so uncertain. If I could go and say goodbye to my parents and grandparents properly, I'd feel better about leaving, but my parents and Gran will never believe me. Grandad would be fine because he'd know I wasn't dead or abducted or something, and he wants me to do and be what I need to be. I don't really know what the others want."

"At least they love you!"

"But do they really? My parents don't want to live with me. I think they just want me to stay young and do what they tell me to do. They don't want me to grow up and be different to them. Just saying that out loud is dreadful, it's like I'm being really mean, but it's true, I think… They love the idea of me if I stay a mini version of them."

"Seems to me love is complicated. My dad loved me, but he died. I used to think my mum did before Gerald, but not enough to protect me. My grandparents loved me and Leah, but not enough to rescue us!"

Sarah was suddenly overcome by a feeling of sadness for Tom. He was right—she'd had so much more than him. She turned to him in the passage and reached up to kiss him on the cheek, but he turned to her at the same time and their lips brushed together. Suddenly the brand clattered as it was propped up against the wall and Tom had his arms around her. She held onto him tightly and their lips met again, this time in a long, deep kiss that felt like it drew them to the very edge of a precipice. When they finally let go of each other, Sarah's legs were shaky and they both felt strangely elated and vulnerable.

"Wow!" exclaimed Tom. He didn't know how to voice how he felt.

There was a brief, awkward silence before Sarah said, "I'm sure I'm blushing all over. We don't even need to talk about it if you don't want to, but I want to say that that felt *so* right." Tears came to her eyes. She had never experienced anything like it. The only boy she'd ever kissed was Matthew Oliver when she was about eleven. She'd been curious and they had a quick, wet, and rather unpleasant kiss and fumble behind the gardener's shed at school. She'd soon found out she wasn't very good at saying no to someone who was persistent, so she'd learned the art of avoidance, until the problem went away by going to a girls' boarding school. This was nothing like what she'd been so afraid of, and she felt breathless and excited all at once.

Tom, too, felt blown away. He stood there in silence trying to find words to say to Sarah in the confusion of all the thoughts jumbling around inside him.

"I—I—don't want you to go!" was all he could manage. He was scared about feeling so good about her when she might go away and he might never see her again. At the same time, he felt good that he'd decided just to jump in anyway—it would have been even worse if she'd gone and he'd regretted forever not kissing her.

"I don't want to go either," she said, feeling hot and flushed all over again, and happily agreed when Tom suggested they might need more practise so they had experiences to store up for the months ahead. Eventually they pulled apart, feeling like nothing would ever be the same again.

"The only thing I feel bad about," Sarah said, "is that I feel so happy, when Kayla is feeling so terrible!"

"Yeah, I know." They stood there in silence for a while, both lost in their own thoughts.

"Come on," Tom said eventually, "I guess we'd better get back to Arthur and Mary so we can get out of here and try to find out if there's anything we can do."

Tom shouldered the pack and they picked up the brand from where it was leaning on the passage wall and made their way more sombrely to the cavern where their friends were waiting.

"Actually," Tom eventually blurted, "I do want to talk about it. I've never felt safe, my whole life. But I feel safe here with the Birches, and now with you. It's like I can trust you and I know if we were in trouble, you'd be right beside me. And I think it will grow to be more than that—that's the scary part. I'm going to have to try really hard not to do or say stupid stuff and pull away because I want you here so badly."

"I know. It's a bit different for me—I'm going to have to try really hard not to get jealous because you'll be here and I won't know what you're doing; or to freak out because I feel so torn between being here with you and seeing my family. So, I guess all we can do is keep being honest and talking to each other. I don't want us to bottle things up the way my parents do."

Chapter XI

A Difficult Decision

When Sarah and Tom emerged from the passage into the cavern, Arthur was pacing up and down on the other side of the river looking anxious.

"At last! Is everything okay? How's Kayla?"

"Galawand's looking after her," said Tom.

"And she's given her something to help her to relax and sleep," added Sarah, as they paced out the steps to the bridge. She led the way across the river and Mary and Arthur were both there to meet them when they jumped down on the other side. They had the packs ready to go.

"Let's get out of here," said Mary. "I think I've had about enough of being underground for now!"

Tom and Arthur pulled on the packs, while Mary and Sarah picked up the brands. Mary and Arthur led the way into the passage out of the cavern, walking quietly, Mary concentrating on stepping carefully so she didn't stress her ankle, setting the pace, the others contemplating the events of the last couple of days.

"Have you two heard anything from Hermione?" asked Mary over her shoulder.

"Not since we left here before. We thought maybe we were

too deep into the mountain. I'll try to reach her now." Sarah quietened her mind and reached out to Hermione. "Hermione, are you there? Hermione?"

"Sarah. Yes, I'm here. I've been waiting for you. You've been out of my range. What's happened? I'm picking up worry, sadness and excitement—that's a very confusing mixture."

Sarah told her about Jonnie and Willard and how Kayla was staying with Galawand. "That's very sad for Kayla—But that's not all. I can sense something between you and Tom—Now I can sense your blush, and Tom's. You mustn't feel guilty for being happy with Tom—it was always going to happen and you're allowed to be happy even when things aren't going well for others. You need to be together, and Kayla needs to experience the difficulties she's facing if she's to fulfil her destiny. Embracing the obstacles you're all facing is what will make the three of you have an important future here in North Feasgar."

Sarah squeezed Tom's hand, knowing that he would have picked up on most of their conversation.

"How do you know that Hermione?" Sarah asked.

Hermione took a long time to respond. "Call it instincts—I'll be waiting for you when you come out of the mountain. Everything's quiet here. I'll see you soon." With that she was gone and Sarah and Tom were left looking at each other with the question still hanging in the air between them.

The rest of their ascent to the tunnel opening was quiet, slow and quite sombre. They made multiple stops for Mary to rest and it seemed so much further than it had when they were going down into the mountain. When eventually they saw light ahead, their mood lifted and they emerged onto the stone platform on the mountainside to see that the end of the day was approaching and the sun was starting to go down. Sarah stood on the edge of the platform looking over to the barrier, now glowing pearlescent rather than red. She calculated that tonight would be the end of the fifth day since she arrived in North Feasgar, and she'd promised her Grandad that she'd return within a week. As she was silently processing this, Tom walked over to her and stood, his shoulder just touching hers.

"Isn't that view amazing?" he said.

"Mmm…" she replied.

"What's up?"

"I've just realised that I have to be back in two days, or my Grandad will call my parents. I promised I'd be back inside a week."

He put his arm around her shoulder. "Don't worry, we'll work out what to do…"

Arthur walked over to them. "We need to get going. We're running low on food and we really need to try to get back to the truck before nightfall. It would be best if we don't spend a night out in the open."

They left the brands inside the tunnel entrance, pulled on the packs and left the mountain face. After descending the steps, they followed the path back around the perimeter of the mountain. Within a few minutes of starting out Hermione silently appeared beside them, emerging from a stretch of scrubby bushes. Sarah scooped her up and rubbed her ears and chin. Hermione pushed her head into her hand and let herself be caressed by her and Tom for a moment, before breaking away and bounding off ahead along the track. It was rougher than they remembered and seemed to take forever to reach the stream where Mary had injured herself. They'd finished the last of their food and water while they were on the platform, so they were grateful to be able to quench their thirst from its water, flowing swiftly, clear and cold down the slope away from the mountain. As they slowly continued on, plodding, one foot in front of the other, Mary leaned heavily on Arthur, while Sarah and Tom carried the packs.

They were hungry and tired, emotionally and physically, by the time they approached the glade that hid the truck. They let out a collective sigh of relief as Arthur pulled back the branches to reveal it was still where they'd left it. Mary gratefully climbed straight into the passenger seat of the cabin as the others cleared the way so they could back it out. Hermione had been scouting around and soon alerted them to where Willard and Jonnie had left Morwyn's car. They checked it out, but without a key they couldn't do anything but leave it for now.

"Tom, we can come back tomorrow and have a go at seeing if we can start it," Arthur said.

They wearily went back to the truck and Tom and Sarah clambered onto the back. Hermione jumped in with them and curled up on Sarah's knee, purring loudly to show her pleasure at seeing them again, safe, and having achieved their purpose. Sarah and Tom leaned together on the tray of the truck, backs to the cab, as Arthur carefully reversed and set off for Riverstone.

They were so exhausted that they fell into a doze and it seemed like no time before Arthur drew up to Riverstone. Tumbling out of the truck, they silently made their way inside and collapsed on the chairs and couch in the living room. It was so good to be back! After a while Tom got up and went to the kitchen to make them a mug of tea, and Arthur yelled out that there was fruit cake in the cupboard. It tasted so good, but they could barely keep their eyes open and they quickly headed to their beds, each of them falling immediately into a deep sleep, Hermione curled up under Sarah's chin, nestled into the pillow.

***

Sarah emerged from sleep in the morning not feeling rested; instead a feeling of disquiet chased her into consciousness. She'd been dreaming, but didn't have so much a memory of the dream, but more a sense impression of agitation and unease that had something to do with her grandad. Feeling disturbed, she walked across the hallway to Tom's room and quietly opened the door. He was still asleep, lying half on his back, with one arm thrown above his head over the pillow. She lay down on top of the covers beside him and snuggled up against him. He sleepily opened his eyes and saw that a tear was sliding down from the corner of her eye and was tracking down her cheek. He put his arm around her shoulders.

"What's up? Has something happened?"

"I think I have to go back today—I really don't want to, but I had a dream and I think something's happening at home!" She was crying properly now and rubbed her arm across her eyes to catch her tears. They heard a soft knock on the door and Sarah got up to find Mary outside.

"Are you two okay?"

"Oh Mary, I think I have to go home now and I'm not ready to! What if I can't get back again?" She was panicking now, and Mary put her arm around her and pulled her close.

"Hush now. Why don't you have a wash and get dressed—

when you both come downstairs, we'll have a good talk about it over breakfast." She went to the door. Sarah followed her and went to her room. She pulled the clothes out of the cupboard that she'd worn when she came through the rift and picked up her phone from where it was sitting on the bookcase. Turning it over in her hand, it really was like it was from a different world that seemed so far away. With a jolt she suddenly realised that she'd have to go back through the water in the labyrinth pool to return home. What would happen to her phone?

By the time she joined the others downstairs she'd worked herself up into a whirlpool of anxiety.

"I think something's happening to my Grandad. Something feels wrong and I need to go back. What am I going to do? What if I can't come back again? I need to come back next time the way you guys did, with my body, through a rift. What if I can't find one in England?"

"Sarah, I don't think you'll need to find a rift—I think a rift will find you if you have something here you need to do," said Mary calmly. "If it makes you feel better, we'll tell you where we found ours. Come and sit over here and we'll draw you a map." She sketched out for her the town they'd come from in England, and the route they'd taken through the countryside to where they'd found the rift to North Feasgar. Arthur corrected her a few times, neither being entirely sure that they remembered it accurately so many years after they'd left.

"Of course, the countryside might not exist like this any more. It might have been taken over by other towns, or roads, but at least it's a possibility," Arthur said.

Sarah stared at the map for a long time.

"I'm trying to memorise it, because I can't take the paper with me through the pool."

"Why don't you take a photo on your phone?" suggested Tom.

"But how am I going to keep my phone dry?" she asked tearfully.

"Hold on a minute, I've got an idea," Mary said, getting up and heading for the kitchen. She re-emerged a few minutes later with something in her hands.

"Here we take fabric and melt bees wax onto it to make a kind of wrapping that keeps food fresh for a fair while, and it's quite waterproof too. If we wrap your phone in this, it will self-seal and we could then put it in a piece of oilskin. That would probably keep the water out for the short time you'll take to get back."

"Oh, I think I've seen that at home too; it's been introduced as an alternative to plastic, because they've finally realised plastic's so bad for the environment," Sarah said, turning it over in her hand. "That's so cool! Hopefully it will work." She turned on her phone, which still had about fifty percent of its battery life, took a photo of the map, then a photo of Tom and the Birches before turning it off again and wrapping it in the beeswax wrap. Arthur had meantime found a piece of oilskin and when it was encased in both layers she tucked it in her pocket.

"Why don't you two go and find Ryder and Hermione. You'll want to see them before you go," suggested Arthur.

"Hermione was asleep with me last night, but she probably went hunting—she wasn't there when I woke up." She and Tom went outside and called for both of them, Tom out loud and

Sarah in her mind. Hermione couldn't have been far away, because she bounded up to them within a few minutes. Sarah sat down on the bottom step with Hermione on her lap, stroking her, while they waited for Ryder. When at last they spotted him, first as a black-looking dot in the sky, then resolving into his majestic, dappled plumage, Hermione jumped off her knee so Sarah could get up and walk over to where Ryder had lightly drifted down to the ground.

"Ryder, Hermione, I have to leave sooner than I thought. I'll be back as soon as I can, but please look out for the Birches and Tom..." she brushed away more tears. "Ryder, don't forget to check on Kayla too, and make sure the elixir stays safe. Hermione, do you think you can send me another dream if something happens? I wish I could let you know somehow when I'm coming back."

"Why don't you try? If you let yourself sink into a half awake, half dream state, send me a thought message, like I do to you." Hermione wound herself around Sarah's legs so she would pick her up again. She gently rubbed her nose under Sarah's chin, then licked her.

"Eeuww—that's rough Hermione!"

Ryder came over close to Sarah so she could bend down and stroke his beautiful, soft feathers. She picked up his rough thought patterns.

"I've been checking out what's happening in Hunterdale. Willard's house is empty, but the forcefield is still working at the tree house. I didn't see any sign of anyone, but I presume the strangers are still there. There were none in the town."

"Thanks Ryder. I guess we weren't expecting that they'd suddenly disappear, but hopefully now the barrier is strong again they'll find it hard to keep in contact with the south, or to do much while they're here. Please keep an eye out for us. If Tom can't understand you, Hermione can let him know what's happening. I'm going to really miss both of you. Please keep safe while I'm away."

She gave him a last stroke before straightening up and going back into the mill house, followed by Hermione and Tom.

Mary had been watching them from the window and had noticed Tom starting to pull away into himself. By the time they returned she could sense his remoteness. She tried putting her arm around him to check out that he was okay, but he pulled himself away and she wasn't surprised when she saw him quietly make his way upstairs to his room. Sarah was talking to Arthur, so she went over to them and heard them making preparations for Sarah to leave.

"Sarah, I think you might need to spend a bit of time with Tom before you go."

"Oh—of course! Where is he?"

"He's gone to his room. You may want to think about what it's like for him to see you again, and then have you disappear after a few short days. I know you're anxious about your grandad, but for us it's all quite sudden and we have no idea when you'll be back. Also, remember that you need to approach the labyrinth in the right frame of mind, or you won't get to see the next part of your destiny on the pool's surface. If you leave here without making your peace with people important to you, or not feeling centred, I'm not sure that you'll be able to see what the pool has to reveal, which means you may not be able to return through it. Right now, you have some emotional work to do with Tom, and to get yourself into a calmer state before you leave."

Sarah immediately felt bad, like she'd just been told off, though she knew what Mary said was true – she'd hardly given anyone else any thought – she'd been so focused on her worry about her grandad and practical things like how she'd get back to North Feasgar later. She flushed with embarrassment, squeezed Mary's arm in acknowledgement of what she'd said, and made her way up the stairs to Tom's room.

He was standing, back to the door, looking out the window.

"Are you all right?" she asked. There was no response. She crossed the room to stand beside him. "Tom, are you okay?" she repeated.

"I'm fine," he said curtly. It felt to Sarah like a complete shrug off.

She tried again. "Can we go outside for a walk by the river?"

"I thought you were in a hurry to be off…"

"Oh Tom, I'm really sorry. I was so caught up in feeling bad myself and trying to drive my way through it by working things out, that I didn't let myself think about you or us. Please can we go for a walk? I need to get out of the house and have some space with you."

He turned reluctantly and followed her out of the room and downstairs, heading for the back door into the garden. He felt like he was being a sulky child following her outside and didn't like how he must be coming across, but was feeling swamped with fear. Fear of getting to like Sarah too much, and her leaving just like his dad did. He remembered that he'd talked to Sarah about this possibility just yesterday, but it was like he'd been taken over by emotion and he couldn't stop himself. He could only handle it by withdrawal. He felt really stupid.

When they got outside, Sarah took his hand and led him across to the river. It was still running high, even though it hadn't rained much since she'd arrived.

"Tom," she said, "please talk to me. I'm feeling really bad that I have to go back, but you need to trust me that I'll return."

"But what if you can't? I can't trust that things will work out for me even if you do your very best. Something will go wrong."

"That's not you talking. That's the little you who's dad died. You know good things have been happening for you ever since you got here. The Birches love you to bits and you're getting to do things you never would have at home. *And* you and I have lots still to do for North Feasgar." She'd wanted to say *and* she loved him too, but couldn't quite get the words out of her mouth. She wanted to kick herself but she'd never felt like this before and was feeling vulnerable and awkward.

"I know. I'm sorry, I'm just feeling sorry for myself."

Sarah turned to him and, with one hand either side of his face, kissed him gently. Tears came to his eyes and he pulled her to him, holding her tightly.

"Tom, will you come with me to the labyrinth?" she asked him eventually. "I can go on my own, but I'd much rather you went with me. I have the idea that if we both look on the pool together, we might see what is meant for the two of us in the future. That way we'll know…"

"Oh, right…" he paused for a long moment. "Yes, I'll come with you. Like, if you're coming back, I'll wait as long as it takes, but if you're not, I'd rather know now so I can get on with my life—and how I feel about you! And, I'd go with you anyway—it's not just about me!" He gave her another hug before they headed back along the river hand in hand to join the others at Riverstone.

***

The trip to the labyrinth seemed faster than they remembered. Hermione sat with them again on the back of the truck; Ryder flew overhead, wheeling in great arcs around them. The sky was overcast as it had been the whole time Sarah had been there, with grey clouds dancing across the sky, offering an occasional lighter grey sense of hope that sometime they'd break up and finer weather would arrive again. Tom couldn't remember the last time it had been sunny—maybe now that the barrier was strong again it would change. The weather all seemed linked somehow to the arrival of the strangers and the weakening of the barrier to the south. Dark times, dark weather!

They both remembered the changes in the landscape as they travelled closer towards the centre of the plain. As they started to descend from the outer rim towards the plateau they noticed the view of the labyrinth in a way they hadn't been able to appreciate last time, when they'd been so shaky after their encounter with Willard. As they descended, a shift in the cloud formations momentarily allowed a few rays of the sun to break through between the clouds. Tom had been looking forwards through the cab window and he seized Sarah's hand and pulled her up so they were both standing, facing forward over the truck, holding onto the cab. The rays streamed down, illuminating the labyrinth in the centre of the plateau. It stood out in sharp relief against the surrounding bare earth, looking completely magical for a fleeting moment before the cloud cover closed over again.

"Did you see that?" Tom breathed, along with a feeling of awe. "It was like something was showing us where to go." They'd been completely entranced, and that feeling stayed with them until their arrival outside the stone formation.

Sarah gave Mary and Arthur a hug, telling them she'd return as soon as she could and to look after Tom, Hermione and Ryder. *As if they wouldn't!* she told herself as the words came out of her mouth. So much easier to say the obvious than to tell them how she felt about them, so she made herself stop and thank them for everything they'd done for her and told them how much she would miss them. She picked Hermione up and buried her nose in her silky fur, not wanting to ever let her go. She started to cry until Hermione bopped her on the nose with her paw.

"Put me down—it's time to go. You don't want us waiting out here all afternoon for Tom to come back, do you?" In response, Sarah stroked her one last time on the back of her head and placed her on the ground. Taking Tom's hand, they walked together into the labyrinth entrance, turning once to wave good bye.

The same as last time, a hush seemed to descend on them the minute they turned the first corner. They stopped momentarily so they could both focus on feeling centred and together. They slowed their breathing and started to walk slowly and steadily along the turning path. Time seemed to almost stand still—it was so silent that they could only hear their footfalls on the hard ground. They forgot that Ryder would have been flying above to make sure they were okay; they forgot about Mary, Arthur and Hermione waiting patiently at the entrance; they forgot about everything that worried them; they forgot about everything other than their shared, steady progress.

After an indeterminate time, they finally reached the centre. The pool was up ahead, raised off the ground in a cluster of large stones. Tom clambered up onto the edge of the pool and pulled Sarah up beside him, where they stood gazing at each other.

"Please, I want to do this quickly, or I won't be able to," Sarah said. She leaned into him and kissed him long and slow on his lips. His arms tightened around her and time stopped again, until eventually they pulled apart and stood hand in hand facing the pool. The wind was lightly rippling the surface, but as they stared at it, it began to still and clear. In the emerging reflection they could see the two of them standing, as they were now, but in the dark on an elevated rocky platform, looking out over a cavern at a deep-red glow coming from somewhere far beneath them. Then the image shifted to show them outside, their clasped hands raised together and a white energy pulsing from them, pushing upwards, streaming towards something oscillating in the sky far above.

They both gasped and the image rippled and broke up.

"So, there's your answer, Tom. Yes, I'm coming back and we do have something important to do together. It looked terrifying, but we were okay."

He kissed her again and stood to the side so she could face the pool alone. As she gazed onto the steadying surface, it resolved into the image of her grandfather lying in a bed with her grandmother sitting in a chair nearby holding his hand. She was nowhere to be seen, but she could sense herself somewhere close by, moving towards him. She quickly moved to the stone lip at the edge of the pool, turned to smile one last time at Tom, and neatly dove into the water.

Chapter XII

An Ending Too Soon

Sarah slowly opened her eyes, focusing first on a rectangle of light that resolved into a window, then by turning her head to the left she saw a fuzzy shape slowly turn into a woman sitting slumped in a chair, asleep. Her mother... She forced herself awake and sat up, finding herself in a hospital bed tethered by a drip that was taped to her arm. *What?* This wasn't how it was supposed to be. And where was her grandad?

"Mum," she called out. "Mum!"

Her mother roused herself, looking around blurrily, then realising that Sarah was awake, got up quickly and went to the side of her bed.

"Mum, what's happening? Why am I here and where's Grandad? It wasn't meant to be like this."

"You're in hospital."

"Yes, I can see that. But why? Grandad and I had it all worked out."

"That's what he told your gran, but it all sounded so far-fetched that she got really angry with him and broke your plate."

"What? What do you mean? Why would she do something so stupid!" Sarah was yelling.

"Sshhh—keep calm."

"No, I won't keep calm. Why did she have to meddle?"

"She was worried about you and thought he was being irresponsible. She broke the plate so that when you woke up you wouldn't have any stupid ideas like that again."

"More like she broke it because he wasn't doing what she wanted and she got angry! Where are they anyway?"

"Oh Sarah, I'm so sorry, but your grandad was so upset by it all that he had a heart attack. He's all right, but very weak. Your gran called the ambulance and they took you as well, then she called me. I just got here today. Grandad said something about you waking up before tomorrow. How did he know that, do you think?"

"Because we talked about it before I left," she said, unable to keep a scathing note out of her voice. "Mum, I know you don't believe us, but what I talked to Grandad about was true. Now I need to see him. Could you please call a nurse to take this thing out of my arm?"

Her mother looked at her with a dubious look on her face. "Mum, call a nurse right now or I'll pull it out myself!"

While her mother went out the door and down the corridor in search of a nurse, Sarah got out of bed and pulled her clothes out of the locker beside the bed. As she pulled her jeans on, she marvelled that they weren't even wet. She patted the pocket of her jacket and found the reassuring bulk of her parcelled up phone still in it, then sat on the edge of her bed waiting for the nurse to come to take out the drip so she could put the rest of clothes on. Her heart was hammering with a mixture of anxiety and anger. Anxiety for her grandad and what she'd inadvertently put him through, and anger with her gran for not trusting them just for a week.

The nurse who came to see her was surprised by her swift recovery, but by the time she'd checked her out she agreed that there was no need to keep the drip in, though she didn't want her to be discharged until the following day so they could keep an eye on her.

"That's okay, I just want to go and see my Grandad," Sarah said. "I'll get you a wheelchair," the nurse said.

"No thanks, I'm quite able to walk." She jumped down from the bed and started pulling on her clothes quickly so her mum and the nurse wouldn't see that she was actually feeling quite wobbly. She sat for a minute and had a drink of water from a plastic cup on her bedside cabinet, before asking her mother to take her to her grandad's ward.

Once her legs got used to being mobile again, she rapidly felt better and it only took a few minutes for them to take the lift to the next floor and to his room. He was sitting up, looking tired, hooked up to way too many machines, but his face lit up in a huge smile as she walked in the door.

"Hello gorgeous! I told your gran you'd be awake before long. You're a day early, aren't you?"

She ran over to him and buried herself in his chest, while he wrapped his arms around her and stroked her hair.

"Oh Grandad, this wasn't supposed to happen! What if you'd died? I'm so pleased to see you sitting up and smiling!" she said in relief.

"Well your gran can't get rid of me quite so quickly, though she did her best to try," he said wryly. "She's just gone to buy me a magazine to read. Hopefully I can get some other goodies too, like my favourite grapes, while she's feeling guilty! Once she sees you, just the way I said, I wonder if she'll manage to see that she's made a big mistake?"

"Just wait until you see this Grandad," said Sarah excitedly taking out her phone package and pulling off the oilskin and waxed paper.

"Whatever do you have there? You didn't have that in your clothes when you left."

She retrieved her phone and turned it on. Quickly she went into her photos and showed him the quick snaps she'd taken of Tom and the Birches, and especially the mill house, looking recognisably like it did in the plate. Her grandad slowly looked through them, with a look of incredulity being quickly replaced by a huge smile.

"Well, Sarah, there's no understanding this, but it's absolutely impossible you could have taken these while you were supposedly asleep at our house, yet the dates prove that they were. It's amazing. And who's this handsome chap?" he asked, looking at Tom. Sarah flushed.

"That's Tom. I told you about him. It was really good to see him again, and the Birches."

"Yes, I can see that," he said, taking in her high colour and shining eyes. "Now I see that your mum had the sense to let you come in to see me on your own. I suggest that you keep these, but don't show them to anyone yet. How about letting me talk to them first and kind of broach the possibility that things they can't understand may still be possible?"

"Thanks Grandad. It can wait. You're the one I wanted to show them to. I need someone in this world to believe me. And—I might need to go back, so I need to make sure someone here knows so that they don't all worry about me."

He looked at her with a really worried expression on his face. "I'm really sorry to have to tell you, but your gran broke the plate in a rage, so I don't know how you'll be able to go back. I was so worried that you might not be able to return to us without it, even though you told me about the labyrinth."

"Yes, mum told me. But I'll find a way. I don't dare think about it too much right now or I'll start to panic, but I know a rift will find me somehow." She held his hand and looked into his kind eyes. Her own eyes started to fill with tears as he gently stroked her other hand.

"Sarah, always remember that I love you, and I'm so proud of you—" his voice trailed off as the machine that had been beeping regularly in the background started to change and emit a shrill bleep. And then time stood still as she saw her grandad close his eyes and the room fill with people; doctors and nurses, trying desperately to resuscitate him, while she watched on helplessly...

A Jungian Perspective for the Older Reader

Once again, I'm using the medium of a story to offer older readers a glimpse of the emotions, psychology and symbolism that often lie beneath the happenings of the external world. It may offer some understanding of what readers, or others you know, experience and find hard to understand and articulate.

In 'Through the Labyrinth' readers were introduced to the potential psychological meaning of some of the tasks our two main characters, Tom and Sarah, undertook before finding their way to the labyrinth at the end of the story. In particular, it addressed the need to discover what lies in our shadow, to find parts of ourselves that we have 'lost'. The coming together of the masculine and feminine parts of our psyches was illustrated through Sarah and Tom's growing friendship and trust. This second story, 'Return to Greyvyn', takes the idea of exploring shadow further, deepens Tom and Sarah's friendship and also introduces new characters to portray increasingly complex relationships in the story.

In many myths and stories, you may notice the theme of descent; of going into the dark, into the unknown, and the characters finding their way back to the light again. For example, in the myth of Psyche, her descent into the underworld is the fourth and final task set by Aphrodite, her jealous mother-in-law to be, in which she has to ask Persephone, the goddess of the underworld, for a cask of her beauty ointment to take back for Aphrodite.[2] This final task is the most difficult and is one that she wouldn't have succeeded in if she hadn't learned so much from her previous tasks (as seen in 'Through the Labyrinth').

In the Sumerian poem of Inanna and Ereshkigal, Inanna descends to the underworld, where her sister Ereshkigal is the queen. She passes through seven gates, at each one having to remove one item of clothing. She arrives to stand before Ereshkigal, naked and powerless. She is judged and found guilty, and is then struck dead and hung up for everyone to see. However, she is revived and rescued. In this way, Inanna, through her descent into darkness, sheds everything about herself, her persona, and confronts her shadow, which results in her death and rebirth.[3] Inanna's journey into the unconscious can be seen as renewal, and as movement towards wholeness.

The process of descent is sometimes named 'the dark night of the soul', a term that comes from the Christian tradition of St John of the Cross. Or in the Jungian context of analytical psychology, it is referred to by the alchemical term 'the nigredo', or the blackening. Jung referred to alchemy as a symbolic process, using it as a metaphor as a way of thinking about the unconscious, a bit like a way of tracking psychological growth and change.

The stage of nigredo, in a therapeutic process, or in a person's experience, is that time when we turn inward, when there is a darkening around us, a feeling of dropping down into something, often scary, often bringing with it a feeling of being very alone. It may take the form of a depression, and it may generate a lot of resistance, because it involves a confrontation with disturbing things inside ourselves. Maybe things we would rather not remember, things we don't want to be, or our parents don't want us to be, betrayals, lacks, internal messages that demean us and make us feel smaller.

In the notes at the end of 'Through the Labyrinth', in introducing readers to the idea of shadow, I commented that we ignore our shadow at our peril. If we ignore it, it may break through in anxieties, crises, or projection onto other people who we decide we 'hate' or drive us crazy. Robert Bly[4] reminds us that those things we relegate to our shadow become regressive and hostile, so when it comes to exploring our shadow and attempting to make meaning from it, it's natural that we'll feel afraid. However, it is essential for us to confront and own the dark things inside us if we want to become whole, to have the potential to become who we're meant to be; or using Jung's term, to individuate. If we don't, we'll have to face it again sometime, and in the meantime, it may have accumulated more destructive energy than when we were first given the opportunity!

'Return to Greyvyn' brings the black magic of South Feasgar (representing shadow) closer to a breakthrough into the north. In order to maintain the barrier that holds the south at bay, Tom and Sarah need to undergo a descent inside the mountain. The descent is signalled at the beginning of 'Return to Greyvyn' when Sarah comes across the tarot card 'The High Priestess'.

This card portrays Persephone, who ruled the underworld with her husband Hades. She had been abducted by him, and while in the underworld, she ate a pomegranate seed, and having tasted the fruit of the dead she was compelled to stay with him in captivity rather than return with Hermes, who had been sent to rescue her. As a compromise it was agreed that she would live part of each year (stories differ, some saying half, others one third) in the underworld with Hades, and the other half (or two thirds) with her mother, Demeter.

As another myth illustrating the feminine need for descent, journeying underground to meet Persephone symbolises our need to encounter our unconscious, the mysterious inner world that we're often afraid of, yet which is full of riches and undeveloped potentials.[1] As described by Juliet Sharman-Burke and Liz Greene in 'The Mythic Tarot Book', 'Persephone, the High Priestess, is an embodiment of that part of us which knows the secrets of the inner world... and appears through the fleeting fragments of dreams, or through those strange coincidences which make us begin to wonder whether there might be some hidden pattern at work in our lives'.[1 (p.31)] The passage referring to the High Priestess that Sarah reads in Chapter One, indicates the strengthening of, and growing capability for her to trust her intuition, followed by an encounter with her inner world. Her encounter with the High Priestess is represented by meeting Galawand, whom she finds inside the mountain.

Tom, of course, accompanies her. In 'Through the Labyrinth' I drew attention to Tom's responses to his experience of abandonment as being similar to the tasks explored in *Hansel and Gretel*. Having confronted the negative feminine (like the witch in *Hansel and Gretel*, represented by Morwyn in the story), Tom begins to learn to trust again. Mary and Arthur offer him the secure base he hasn't had in his own family, and he relaxes and grows in his sense of who he is under their care. Being with Sarah though, brings up again many of his old insecurities. He has to safely cross the water in the form of the River Dearth, as it runs underground beneath the mountain. This represents a transition—a rite of passage associated with the feminine, and for Tom is part of the healing process of his feeling function that allows him to grow in his sense of wholeness, and in his relationship with Sarah.

Attachment theory, pioneered by John Bowlby and expanded by Mary Ainsworth in the mid-20th century, explores the emotional relationships we form with our early caregivers. They found that early experiences with our caregivers strongly influence the development of the way we interact and behave in other relationships we have later in life. A 'secure' attachment will help us to thrive, enabling us to explore our surroundings, trusting that support will be available to us, and is likely to create an environment that prepares us for a healthy relationship as an adult. In contrast, an insecure attachment may take one of three forms, all of which invoke anxieties and fear. According to Jeremy Holmes, 'an insecurely attached person may have a mixture of feelings towards their attachment figure: intense love and dependency, fear of rejection, irritability and vigilance'.[5] (p.67) Sometimes a person with an insecure attachment will want to get close to another person, but at the same time be afraid of rejection, so will push them away. Alternatively, they may try to punish the desired person if they show any signs that they might leave.

Tom's childhood was scary and unpredictable, and meant that he couldn't learn to trust that the adults in his life would be available for him in a positive way. He felt abandoned and betrayed. The same impulse he learned as a child can still be seen repeated in his relationship with Sarah, in the way he doubts their connection, his fear of abandonment driving him to withdraw from her. It goes through his mind that if he avoids her, he can't get hurt!

At the end of 'Through the Labyrinth' I introduced readers to the idea of the anima and the animus, the feminine and masculine components of our psyche (not bound to gender) that we need to develop as part of our search for balance and wholeness, and for 'soul-making'. We may search for this part of ourselves in the external world, and when we find it, experience 'falling in love'. We may experience the need to be with another person to complete ourselves, which brings with it a huge intensity of feeling, including the possible generation of separation anxieties, fear of loss and the development of dependency on the other. The idea of the anam cara, or soul friend in the book series, alludes to the relationship between Tom and Sarah transcending these anxieties; a deepening that generates something that is going to be greater than the sum of their parts. This strengthened relationship is going to be needed to save North Feasgar.

Jonnie and Kayla appear in 'Return to Greyvyn' to add to the complexities of the story's relationships. Through them we can wonder about the effects of what it might be like to grow up with an alcoholic and unavailable mother, an absent father, and the dynamics of eating disorders that were briefly mentioned in 'Through the Labyrinth'. Jonnie, in particular, has suffered through lack of a positive father figure in his life. Guy Corneau, in 'Absent Fathers, Lost Sons', writes that, 'lack of attention from the father results in the son's inability to identify with his father as a means of establishing his own masculine identity'.[6] (p.13) This lack makes it very difficult for a son to advance into adulthood feeling competent as a male, happy and confident in his own skin. Lack of a father's reliable presence can often result in children, particularly boys, turning to 'risky' behaviours such as smoking or drug use, criminal activity, and lower educational attainment.[7] Jonnie had no positive masculine presence in a life dominated by the negative feminine (his alcoholic mother). He behaves in problematic ways to express his anger, to try to find out who he is, and to attempt to find what defines him by testing his boundaries. This propels him into Willard's realm, someone he mistakenly thinks is strong, and whose approval he seeks. Jonnie looks up to Willard, ignores his conscience and his feelings for Kayla, and devalues any kindly or well-meant actions from people around him. He sees the world as being out to get him.

Kayla has had to grow up too fast, in the face of her dysfunctional, alcoholic mother. She has learned that her needs won't be met; that her mother isn't there for her, instead having to become responsible herself from a young age. It has become her role to fix things, to make sure that the turmoil in their lives is smoothed over as much as possible. In a physical sense she learns to care for her mother and Jonnie, doing the practical things like shopping, cleaning and cooking, while maintaining a fragile grasp on her own emotional state. The message she tells herself is that if she doesn't keep going and keep carrying these responsibilities single-handedly, she won't survive.

The only way Kayla can alleviate the tension she continually experiences, with no sense of control over her mother's behaviour, or the consequences of it, is through exerting control over her own eating. She has developed rituals to help hold herself together. Repetitive patterns fulfil a role in helping people remain unaware of their terror or other emotions, in the face of addictive dynamics. This can lead them to become more and more obsessive as they spiral out of control and try to bury, rather than own, the self-destructive nature of their behaviour.[8] As Marion Woodman,[8] a Jungian analyst says, ritual is a small madness that keeps other madness averted.

Complexes relating to food are said to originate in encounters with the negative feminine.[8] Kayla has experienced her mother as the negative witch mother and translates her mother's poison into the way she sees the world metaphorically as undigestible, as being 'too much' and needing to be restricted. Woodman suggests that: 'So long as she is obedient to a mother – actual or internal – who unconsciously wishes to annihilate her, she is in a state of possession by the witch; she will have to differentiate herself out from that witch in order to live her own life. Only then will she be able to nourish herself, and thereby transform a demonic ritual into a sacred one'.[8] (p.37) Seen in this light, leaving her mother and staying with Galawand to learn the secret rituals that keep North Feasgar safe, is a transformative act for Kayla.

Meanwhile, Mary, Arthur, Hermione and Ryder keep watch over them all, maintaining their presence to support them, and to rescue them if needed. None of the four teenagers have experienced consistent support in this way before and they are all at different stages in learning to trust it. Jonnie can't trust or tolerate Mary and Arthur's kindness, and neither he nor Kayla are yet ready to understand the magical nature of the care offered by Hermione and Ryder.

The end of 'Return to Greyvyn' presents us with an unanticipated tragedy; one that in Jungian terms refers to the need for us to embrace the life-death-life cycle of renewal. It's here that we leave our story and await what happens next in 'The Rising of the South', the conclusion of the Anam Cara series. In this third book of the trilogy, our characters will realise they need to face the south more directly, in a confrontation that threatens the whole of the land of Feasgar. The dynamics present in 'Return to Greyvyn' will be deepened, as they learn that they can no longer maintain the split from the south (the shadow)—it has to be faced, explored and made conscious. The repair that is needed may be painful, and they will need to find their courage and trust themselves enough to stand up for what they value and let themselves be seen and heard.

References

1. Sharman-Burke, J., & Greene, L. (1992). *The mythic tarot book. A new approach to the tarot cards.* East Roseville, Australia: Simon & Schuster.

2. Johnson, R. (1989). *She: Understanding feminine psychology.* New York: Harper Collins Publishers.

3. Mark, J. (2011). *Inanna's descent: A Sumerian tale of injustice.* Accessed 21 January 2022 from the World History Encyclopaedia website: worldhistory.org/article/215/inannas-descent-a-sumerian-tale-of-injustice/

4. Bly, R. (1988). *A little book on the human shadow.* New York: Harper Collins.

5. Holmes, J. (1993). *John Bowlby and attachment theory.* London: Routledge.

6. Corneau, G. (1991). *Absent fathers, lost sons.* Boston: Shambhala.

7. McLanahan, S., Tach, L., & Schneider, D. (2013). The causal effects of father absence. *Annual Review of Sociology. 39*:399-427. Doi: 10.1146/annurev-soc-071312-145704

8. Woodman, M. (1982). *Addiction to perfection. The still*

unravished bride. Toronto: Inner City Books.